ALSO BY CRAIG ROBERTSON

BOOKS IN THE RYANVERSE:

THE FOREVER SERIES (2016)

THE FOREVER LIFE, Book 1
THE FOREVER ENEMY, Book 2
THE FOREVER FIGHT, Book 3
THE FOREVER QUEST, Book 4
THE FOREVER ALLIANCE, Book 5
THE FOREVER PEACE, Book 6

THE GALAXY ON FIRE SERIES (2017)

EMBERS, Book 1
FLAMES, Book 2
FIRESTORM, Book 3
FIRES OF HELL, Book 4
DRAGON FIRE, Book 5
ASHES, Book 6

RISE OF ANCIENT GODS SERIES (2018)

*RETURN OF THE ANCIENT GODS,*Book 1
RAGE OF THE ANCIENT GODS, Book 2
TORMENT OF THE ANCIENT GODS, Book 3
WRATH OF THE ANCIENT GODS, Book 4
FURY OF THE ANCIENT GODS, Book 5
FALL OF THE ANCIENT GODS, Book 6

TIME WARS LAST FOREVER SERIES:

RYAN TIME, Book 1 (Due in early Fall 2019)

STAND-ALONE NOVELS:

ROAD TRIPS IN SPACE SERIES (2019):

THE GALAXY ACCORDING TO GIDEON, Book 1
THE EARTH ACCORDING TO GIDEON, Book 2 (Due in late 2019)

OLDER NOVELS

THE CORPORATE VIRUS (2016)
TIME DIVING (2013)
THE INNERgLOW EFFECT (2010)
WRITE NOW! The Prisoner of NaNoWriMo (2009)
ANON TIME (2009)

The Galaxy According to Gideon

ROAD TRIPS IN SPACE SERIES, BOOK 1

by Craig Robertson

Get ready, galaxy, Gideon's coming. Here's a hint: cover you wallet.

Imagine-It Publishing
El Dorado Hills, CA

Copyright 2019 Craig Robertson

ISBN: 978-1-7331137-6-2 (Print)
978-1-7331137-5-5(E-Book)

Cover design by Alexandre
http://www.designbookcover.pt/en/

Editing by Michael R. Blanche

Formatting services by Polgarus Studio
http://www.polgarusstudio.com

Beta reading help by Charlie "The Bagpiper" Pitts

First Edition 2019

Imagine-It Publishing

To the one, the only, and the principle inspiration for this series, Doug Adams.
He was a good man.

ONE

Ramurpart was, by any standards, a dull and pointless planet. No other settled world combined its lackluster qualities of being completely without grace, charm, or beauty. The proposed solution, by the combined government of the world, to its seemingly insurmountable shortcomings was to make it the very talk of the galaxy. How do you convince an indifferent public that something is what it isn't? Yes, a good ad campaign. If you can't *be* inviting, pound it into the heads of all who will listen that you *are*. It's a tale as old as time.

Plan 1, of the Powers That Be on Ramurpart: Increase tourist visits. Spread a good word, as it were, and draw in masses of cash-laden visitors. The problem they immediately faced turned out to make that a real non-starter. There was absolutely nothing on the forlorn planet to spread a good word about. The government, in keeping with its record of dubious wisdom, decided that the way to make Ramurpart a bucket list destination was to transform the rocky planet into one composed entirely of plastic. Such technology was, by then, passé. Consequently, the task could be accomplished easily, quickly, and most importantly of all, cheaply.

A senior legislator, one Frib Delbet, to be specific, conceived the whole idea in a fit of uncharacteristic thought. He reasoned that a *plastic* world would be so new and so alluring that there would simply *have* to be a significant bump in tourism. As there was no tourist traffic on Ramurpart in the first place, everyone agreed his goals were doable enough. The other council members were, also, too disinterested generally to discuss, debate, or vote on any matter. Hence, by a one-to-nothing tally, it was decreed that Ramurpart's substance was to be transformed into plastic.

Rigel Rettlebutt was not the brightest star in the heavens, but neither was he a fool. He was, it should be noted, an immigrant, not the typical dim-witted local. Rigel realized at once that the planet's molten core and tight orbit around its parent star promised to end in disaster for the soon-to-be plastic world. So, he tied up a few matters of a personal nature, put a hold on his mail service, and secured passage on the next ship off-planet. He didn't even know where, in the vast galaxy, he was going, but he knew anywhere was preferable to the sea of boiling plastic Ramurpart was about to become soon, and very soon.

He boarded the transport ship, bringing along no more than the recommended volume of carry on items. His next task was to angle himself toward the stern to find his assigned seat. His head snapped back and forth. 17 CDE, 18 ABC, and 19 CDE passed before him like a tennis match. Finally, his eyes rested on his window seat, 20A. Rigel was a man of modest needs, but, he did so relish his window seats. He had ever since boyhood. Window seats were, in fact, the only warm, joyous memory he had of his otherwise painfully dull upbringing. What's more, he felt that sole positive recollection was more than enough.

But, as fate always seemed to insist, there was an issue. A rather large humanoid male occupied 20A, fumbling with the magazines and safety notifications housed on the back of seat 19A.

"Excuse me, sir," Rigel said as nasally as possible, "you seem to be in my seat."

Without turning his head, the occupant of 20A pointed to 20C and said, "No, that's your seat. Be a good egg and settle in quietly."

"I shall do *nothing* of the kind," Rigel responded hotly. It was a rare event in his life, to date, when he stood upon such a clearly superior and defensible moral turf. "Please move, or I shall summon the steward." Rigel raised his one carry on burdened hand to indicate the direction he would be summoning assistance from.

The occupant of 20A shook his head energetically and rose. "Give the steward a break, would you? I've had to scrub his memory three times already." He held up a small brain scrambling unit, which resembled a ballpoint pen. "When I arrived, he was married with three kids. Now he thinks he's a descendant of squids and lives in a castle full of butterflies. Don't you think he's had enough for one flight? Ease off, sport."

Rigel studied the man's face, then glanced toward a steward standing near the front of the craft. The attendant was presently engaged in a heated discussion with the curtains. The curtains seemed to be winning.

"Why did you scrub his brain three times?" asked Rigel.

"I had to. The dope kept coming over and asking me the same thing." He raised his palms to ear level. "Can't have that, now, can I?"

"What," pressed Rigel, "did he keep asking you?"

"For my *ticket*, of course. What, did you hatch this morning?"

"No, I did not hatch this morning. *I* am a paying customer, unlike yourself. *I* am entitled to what is rightfully mine. Please exit my seat and steal another."

"Sorry. No can do. My ... traveling companion expects to find me," he set a hand on 20A's headrest, "right here. They're in 20 B. To alter any thought in that spin-cycle brain is to court disaster."

"Then I will be happy to redirect him—"

"Her. I'm traveling with a *her*."

"*Her* to wherever you relocate. Now go."

Somewhere toward the front of the ship, a man screamed in mortal terror.

"Oops, there she goes again. I'll be right back."

The seat thief muscled past Rigel and sprinted forward.

Most excellent. Rigel stowed his larger carry-on in the overhead compartment and then, triumphantly sat down in the perfectly vacant seat, 20A. He set his satchel under the seat, and rested back with a self-contented glow.

That's when a fat, snorting Ramurpartian native lumbered up to aisle 20, swung his massive, yet ineffectual head side to side, then plopped into 20B with a squishy thud. Seats 20 A and C were tossed upward by his prodigious downward force. Before the row could come to rest, the new occupant of seat 20 B blew his nose into his jacket's elbow and slammed his head back against the poor headrest. He was sound asleep, instantly. He commenced to drool, and that liquid was, in turn, aerosolized by his thunderous snores.

The former, illicit, occupant of seat 20 A returned to the aisle and glared at both seated men with a disapproval that bordered on disgust. "This will *never* do," he said, as he reached across and shook the slumbering giant. "Hey, buddy. Rise and shine. Wakey-wakey. Time to go."

The Ramurpartian slowly returned to consciousness. His eyes grasped absently for the cause of his arousal. Finally they fell on the seat thief. "What?" he grunted.

"Sorry, you'll have to take another seat. This one's spoken for." He thumbed over a shoulder, suggesting the direction he could search an alternate seat in.

"This is *my* seat," he said. Then he shut his eyes and was asleep, again, before the lids met. It was very useful, in the stressful universe, to be a member of such a dull race.

The seat thief eased closer and slapped the occupant of 20 B's cheek repeatedly, more soundly than either decorum or wisdom suggested might be prudent.

The offended party lurched awake. "Leave me alone, or I'll summon the captain."

"I *am* the captain, beefcake. Now move." Again, with the thumb. "I'll have security toss you off this flight *sans* the boarding-ramp, if you don't move, *now*."

Befuddled, which was a totally natural state for residents of Ramurpart, he protested loudly. "You're not the captain. Where's your uniform? Hmm? Captains have uniforms."

"Uniform? Wow, and to think I mistook you for a savvy guy. Man, was I wrong. Pilots don't wear *uniforms*. We'd be too easy a target for abduction, assassination, and all forms of flight-disrupting mayhem. No, to protect *you*, the flying public, we try to blend in as best we can. It's just part of the commitment we're all prepared to make for *you*, the little guy."

"What about all those people sitting in the cockpit, the ones with hats and well-pressed uniforms? What do you call them?" This Ramurpartian was intellectually, clearly, a cut above.

"I call them paid actors, and heavily armed ones at that. They run around, pulling empty suitcases, to draw any evildoer's attention away from the *actual* flight crews. Now, come on. You're not making me late for takeoff. Move."

"I *will* not. What type of idiot do you take me for?"

"Asteroids of pure crap, I don't have time for this. Okay, but just this once. List for me what *types* of idiot there are, and then I'll render upon you my opinion as to what type, or types, you are. For example, you might be a *complete* idiot, a *driveling* idiot, or a *pathetic* idiot. You could be all three at the same time, you complete, driveling, pathetic idiot. You see? I need something to work with, here."

The steward broke off his heated exchange with the curtains and approached the disruption he noted in aisle 20. "Excuse m ... me —" he began to say. Then he looked at the seat thief, who was tapping himself on the chest and mouthing the word *captain*.

"Excuse m ... me, *Captain*. Is there a problemm ... m here?" the attendant asked, rather absently.

"No, none. This gentleman just needs your help finding him a new seat. Would you be so kind?"

Though his eyes were unable to focus, the steward rotated to locate the outline of the figure seated in 20 B. "Please cooperate fully, with the uniformed crew members, madam. Come with me."

"I will write a letter to someone concerning this outrage," said the local as he struggled to rise. Of course, everyone ignored his threat. The very thought. A *Ramurpartian* ... writing a *letter*. It was to laugh.

"There's a good man," said the plain-clothed captain, as he clapped the discombobulated steward on the shoulder. He then dropped lightly into 20 C.

Rigel had to ask. "You're not really the captain, are you? I mean, why would you sit back here if you were required to fly the ship?"

"Of course I'm not the captain. What is it with you today?" He began to whistle, softly, annoyingly. After a minute's concert, he said, without turning his head. "If I was you, I'd switch seats with me."

"If I *were* you."

"If you were me, what? By the way, you should be so lucky."

"No, the correct way of saying what you said was *were* not *was*."

"You're worse off than I thought. Can I get you a drink?" He reached into his pocket and produced a huge number of miniature liquor bottles. "Name your poison."

"No, thank you. I am quite selective about my drinking partners."

The fellow bit off a screw top, spat it to the floor, and polished off the contents in one splash. "Selective about drinking partners?" He bobbed his head in contemplation. "May not be such a bad policy." He slapped Rigel's shoulder. "You know what? I might just try it someday. Not today, of course. But, who knows, maybe next week, I'll give selectivity a shot." He held out a handful of bottles to Rigel.

Rigel studied the options and drew out an Irish whiskey container.

"*That's* the spirit" The man stuffed all but one of the liquors back into his pocket. That one he clinked against Rigel's. He tossed it down before Rigel even had his open.

A wipe of his chin later, he went on. "Ah, about that seat switch. Best to do it now, while you still can."

Rigel blinked his eyelids in irritation. "Why might I not be able to later?"

"Humf. Well, that's easier to see than explain. Once you see why … hey. You know what? You're right. No big deal. You stay *right* where you are," he tapped 20 AB's armrest, "and I'll be just fine here," he patted 20 BC's armrest.

Rigel grew suddenly suspicious. "Why did you say that? One moment, you're browbeating me into switching, and the next you just drop it like a leprous donut?"

"Hey," he said with a gurgle, as he downed another two shots. "Where are my manners?" He reached a hand across. "I'm Gideon, Gideon Prime. Pleasure to meet you."

Rigel introduced himself as they shook. "That's a rather unusual name. Are you from Questar?"

"No, Lothar. Everyone there has *prime* in their name. It's was all the rage, back in the day, I'm led to believe."

Rigel elected to drop the subject. He did make a mental note to find out *where* Lothar was. He couldn't recall hearing the name. "You referred to your travel companion. Where is she? We're scheduled to take off pretty soon. The sign," Rigel pointed to the back-lit seat harness sign, "says everyone's supposed to be secured in their seats." Then he giggled rather stupidly, and only partly because the Irish was finding its mark. "Or someone else's." With a large, silly grin on his face, he belched.

"Probably the bathroom." Gideon developed a sudden look of concern on his face, then smiled amiably once again. "I *hope* she went to the bathroom."

"Where else—" Rigel begin to ask, when a woman thudded against Gideon's shoulder, forcing him to spill an otherwise serviceable bottle of low-end vodka.

"There you are, you little doll," Gideon said as he stood and turned. He placed his hands on either of her shoulders, steadying her. This eclipsed her from Rigel's view. Gideon moved to his right and rotated her butt toward 20 B. All the while he kept hold of her shoulders, so she faced away from Rigel as she hit the seat.

What, Rigel wondered instantly, was that smell?

Gideon popped back into his seat and dusted his jacket off. "There. One big, *happy* family."

How very odd. Rigel raised a finger and leaned toward Gideon to ask what that remark meant. As he did the woman turned to face him. Rigel leapt backward so forcefully he struck the service call button with the top of his head. Rubbing the spot where a lump would form, he pointed to the woman and declared, "She's a *zombie*."

"Sorry, Rige. Was that a question or a statement?"

"S ... sh ... she's a *zombie*."

Gideon angled an ear hoping to catch more of Rigel's meaning. "Ah, still not sure. Doesn't matter, I guess. Yeah, she's a zombie." With a serious tone, he added, "That's not a problem for you, is it?"

Rigel finger was yet to move. "She's—"

"I know," interrupted Gideon, "we've been over that already. Can we talk about something else? Hey, how about a drink?" He pulled a handful of bottles out, again. "You're an Irish man, right?" he asked as he picked though the pile.

The brain-addled steward staggered to aisle 20. "May I he ... help you and those lovely goslings?"

"No," snapped Gideon, "Why do you ask?"

He pointed above them. "The call button. Someone hit the button."

"Oh, yeah, right. That was just a safety check," Gideon stood halfway and patted him on the arm. "You did fine. I'm promoting you to Grand Poobah of this *entire* flight. You're welcome. Now go away."

The steward stood looking even more confused.

"Scoot, Mr. Pooh*bah*. We're talking here," said Gideon, as he flashed a finger between Rigel and himself.

Rigel had never seen a zombie. He had also never smelled one. He wasn't sure which was worse, being *next* to one, or *smelling* one. Everyone knew zombies existed. They had for a long time. But, they were quite rare, and mostly found on planets far from this sector. He studied her face. It was the wrinkled yellow gray he'd seen in photographs, with blunted features. Still, he could tell she'd been beautiful ... before. She had dainty angles, almond-shaped eyes, and perfect teeth. My, Rigel reflected, her teeth were quite prominent, weren't they? Possibly even in a not-so-good sense.

He angled his head so he could speak around her to Gideon, leaning forward so as not to get any closer to the occupant of 20 B. "Does she talk?"

Gideon spit out the gin in his mouth. "Does she *talk*? Are you kidding? Buddy, she's a *woman*. Of course she talks. Ever try to get one of those to stop jibber-jabbering?" He elbowed her. "Say something to the nice man, honey. *Introduce* yourself." Gideon snickered quietly. "Maybe shake his hand." He snickered again, louder.

Her jaw started shaking, roughly in an up/down direction. It was like her mouth was a farm machine, straining to pick up speed to be able to function. "A ... Arr ... Arga ... ga ... *Arrgagar*," echoed from her mouth. Her right hand raised off her lap about a foot. "Argagar," she repeated.

Her breath was strikingly repugnant.

"Is she growling at me?" asked a very concerned Rigel.

"Growling? No, you goon. She introducing herself. *Argar*. That's her name."

"Who would name a child Argar?"

"No one. Her name's *Hephzibah*." He motioned over her face. "I guess her jaw and tongue have trouble pronouncing it correctly. Comes out as *Argar*. Hey, it's quicker to say that way, anyway, so I'm all for it." He then snatched up a magazine and began reading an article concerning the pros and cons of sending your clone on vacation in place of you. "I like the angle of no STDs for the original," he mumbled to himself.

"You're traveling with a *zombie*." Instinctively, Rigel pushed back up against the bulkhead.

"Aw. We're not back to that again, are we? Rige, baby, move on."

"Is that offer to switch seats still open?"

Gideon smiled like as gambler raking in a big pot. "Oh *now* you want to move. What? Is it the fact that, in spite of your best efforts, you might *accidentally* fall asleep. Are you imagining yourself waking up to Argar ripping into your neck, with you pinned against the bulkhead, with no escape possible?"

"That is a scenario that has occurred to me."

"But, if you were in good old, reliable 20 C, on the aisle, you'd have a fighting chance of escaping to freedom before your life's blood stained that patchwork sport coat of yours."

"Escape *would* be more likely."

"Well, forget it. She's not ... almost *certainly* not ... likely to not attack you. You're perfectly safe, sort of. Well, let's hope for the best. In the end, that's all we can ever do. Am I right?"

"I would rest easier in your seat, friend Gideon. *Please*, might we switch?"

"Shucks, since you put it that way, sure." Gideon backed into the aisle and Rigel gingerly stepped past Argar.

When they were all cozy in their seats and the alcohol was beginning to fully loosen his tongue, Rigel asked, "Why do you travel with Argar? It would seem to complicate matters for you."

Gideon thought carefully about his response before speaking. "I guess I felt responsible for the little sweetheart." He patted Argar atop the head.

"Is she family?"

"No. Just friends. *Business* friends, I guess you call it."

"Ah, she was a coworker?"

"No. Hey, what is this? Twenty question? Yes, she's bigger than a breadbox, too."

"What business are you in, that she was part of?"

"Maybe I misled you, a tad. I was a *customer* of hers."

"Hmm. What *service* did she provide, if you don't mind my asking?"

"In fact, I do. The service was of a highly *personal* nature."

"Your tax accountant?"

Exasperated, Gideon threw the magazine he'd been scanning to the floor. "She marketed sexual favors for cash. There. Are you satisfied?"

Rigel didn't see that coming. "She was a *prostitute?*"

"No. Please, show her some respect. Her business card states specifically that she is an *intimate services consultant.*"

"Stat*es*, not stat*ed?*"

"Yes, well, technically she's still a practicing consultant."

"Now I know you're joking. I can tell."

"No, seriously. But her business has really tanked significantly since … you know, since she changed."

"Tanked? Are you suggesting *anyone* would retain her services, *now?*"

"See, I knew you were a perceptive guy. Honestly, not too many. There was a drunk in a bar a few weeks back. He asked her to come to his room with him just before he passed out." He clicked his tongue. "Damn shame, it was. When he fell off his barstool, his cane hit the floor and snapped in two." Gideon snapped his fingers, by way of amplifying the mental picture he was crafting.

"That short a fall wouldn't split a man's cane."

"Sure did. Those long white ones aren't as sturdy as they look to you and me."

"He was *blind*?"

Gideon rocked his head in agreement. "Most likely. She never really had a chance to find out."

"Wait. How could you know all this. Are you her *pimp*?"

"Hey, I've killed men for lesser insults. No, I was just keeping an eye on her, like now."

"So you went to a bar with a zombie prostitute to be a good Samaritan?"

Gideon formed a crooked smile. "Yeah, I guess I did. Thanks. It was rather *charitable* of me, when you frame it like that."

"And now you're accompanying her ... wait. Where would a zombie need to travel to? This is getting more and more ridiculous by the second."

"Oh, now there, you're wrong. Dead wrong. No. It is *I* who needs to relocate. It's kind of a spur of the moment sort of thing, too. I brought her along because I'm not likely to return to Ramurpart in the foreseeable future."

"No one will."

"Pardon?"

"I said no one will be returning. You heard they're transforming the planet into plastic, right?"

"No more booze for you," Gideon said with a finger wag.

"Seriously." Rigel swung his arm around. "Ask anyone. It's true. By next week the entire planet will be plastic. A few weeks later, the whole thing's going to melt. No one's returning, unless they want to scuba dive in melted plastic."

"Do they know it's going to melt? I mean, it's sort of silly to proceed with that plan if they do."

"Apparently, I'm the only one who thought it through to that extent."

Gideon grinned widely. "Kudos to you, then. I like smart people. The universe needs more smart people."

Rigel tried to appear humble in his response. "Thank you."

"Say," asked Gideon, "since I sort of sneaked aboard this ship, I didn't check. Where's the ship headed?"

The roar of the engines hurling them into orbit forced him to repeat his question.

"Breakers," shouted Rigel.

Gideon frowned deeply.

"You seem upset. Do you not like Breakers?"

"Meh."

"Sorry, did you say *meh*?"

"Probably. I wish I'd known the ship was headed there before we left port. Damn."

"Is there a problem?"

"No. There's no problem, just an *issue*."

"What kind of *issue*?"

"The kind where the government of Breakers cut you up into tiny pieces and feed you to their pets, kind of issue."

"Oh my. What did you do?"

"I introduced the heir apparent to Argar."

"Do they frown on sex consultants that much on Breakers?" he asked as sarcastically as possible, which wasn't so very much.

"No, they practically pioneered that career path. Billboards everywhere. No, they just *really* hate zombies."

"You introduced the crown prince to," Rigel pointed to, but did not actually touch, Argar, "that?"

"Yeah, well, *technically*. They seemed to be getting along so well, too."

"Is the prince a blind drunkard with no sense of smell?"

"Don't be crass. The man was royalty. No, he was a nice kid. He had good people skills."

"Was? Had? You're not saying—"

"He fell asleep, you know, *after*."

TWO

"Look," said Rigel, "it won't be that bad. When we get to Breakers, we'll just explain to the magistrate that it was an unfortunate accident. I'll *vouch* for you. It'll all be fine."

"You'd do that, vouch for me? Wow, no one's ever vouched for me, before." He paused wistfully, a moment, there. "My *mother* refused to eight times while under oath. Gosh, what a pal. Hey," he reached yet again into his seemingly bottomless pocket, "how 'bout a drink, you know, to celebrate." He dumped a handful of bottles in Rigel's lap.

"So it's settled. We'll work together and you'll be okay?"

"Oh, no way, but thanks for the offer. Those Breakersians are about as forgiving as your wife would be after she catches you making love to her grandmother in the pantry. They're so ornery, they invented a reanimation system, so that after you die in agony, they can bring you back and do it all again. No thanks."

"I'm certain you're exaggerating. No one's *completely* nasty and vicious."

Gideon shook his head. "Their *crown prince* asked a zombie to give him a blow job." Gideon's entire body quivered. "Add to that mind-numbing factoid the news that these people are making *major* contributions to the entire field of cruel and unusual punishments. No, I really don't want to alert them to my presence. It would end badly."

Rigel was coming around to Gideon's point of view regarding the Breakersians. He tried to be gentle, but the truth, in this case, was a bit too painful to soften significantly. "There's aren't too many options open to you, Gideon. The ship is headed for Breakers. It's our first stop. When we get there, you know the drill. Everyone has to disembark to clear customs. They're going to know for sure you've returned."

"I could ask the pilot to divert somewhere else."

"You could, but he'd refuse."

"Not if I ask him real nicely. Plus, I'd have a blaster pinned against his head. He'd be more inclined to consent that way."

"Do you have a blaster?"

"Not exactly."

"Do you imagine there's a vendor selling *blasters* on this ship?

Gideon shrugged idiotically.

"I rest my case."

"Ah, well" he replied with a grim smile. "Something will come up. Always does."

"I'm glad to see you've chosen to remain positive."

"No choice, really. Hey, life's short. Don't screw it up with glumness."

Before Rigel could offer his glib, mindless response, the vessel shook violently.

"Ah, this is your captain speaking," came from overhead. "I apologize for the turbulence. We seem to be under attack by a group of pirate ships. Please, remain calm. There is *no* need for concern. We're perfectly safe."

The ensuring series of thunderous impacts suggested the skipper was being a tad over-optimistic. "Ah, let me strike the word *perfectly* and substitute *reasonably*, how's that sound? We're out-gunned, out-numbered, and we've lost three of our four engines, but, I repeat, please do not—"

The remainder of the pilots message was lost, following a boom heard over the intercom.

"Uh, hi there. *Hello.* This is the head stewardess, Marsha Van Plex. I'm, well, sort of in command now, I guess." She tried to cloak her words, but was clearly heard to ask someone, "What's that button for, there?"

"How should I know?" replied another female voice. "I took this job to travel and marry well."

A garbled voice made some remark to her. "Yes, I did, but it was just a thing. I intended to marry a rich biped with a serious medical ... oh, they can? Ah, we're reenacting a skit we learned in flight attendant school in an attempt to break your tension. There's a bunch of shuttle craft exiting the pirate ship and coming our way. But, as our late, lamented captain said, no worries. On the bright side, they have stopped *firing* on us. I'll probably keep you abreast of any updates."

The cabin door flew open, and two flight attendants sped out with impressive speed.

There was no one at the controls.

"What a *break*." shouted Gideon. "I can't believe my luck. Someone out there loves me."

Rigel pulled at his sleeve. "I don't think being marauded by pirates is in anyway a positive turn."

Argar chose that moment to announce her name. "Argarrrr."

"Yes, sweetie," said Gideon, massaging her scalp. "Seriously, Rigel? Don't you get it? They'll seize the ship, unless they don't blow it up with the passengers onboard. We're not going to *Breakers*! *Yes*."

That his new traveling companion was ecstatic about being the victim of a pirate raid gave Rigel pause. The prospect of rape, torture, and violent death, possibly in that order, was, by his way of reasoning, a bad thing. And the being robbed part was totally unappealing. Still, Rigel was hardly responsible for matters that were well beyond his control.

His thoughtful interlude was shattered when the airlock blew open and a large contingent of super-sized men rushed in. They howled, spat insults and saliva, and swung weapons in the air. Personal hygiene was clearly a non-issue in their band. Worst of all, they were acting in a clichéd, stereotypical parody of being a pirate. They brought zero originality to their roles.

Some raiders sped forward, others aft. Soon, the ship was filled with them, all swearing, menacing, and being generally unsavory guests. A humanoid, a foot taller than any other invader, stood at the front of the cabin with a foot resting on a passenger's head. The pirate was nearly as wide as he was tall. With a beard to mid-chest and a funny looking hat, he was a caricature of a pirate captain. He even had a golden earring and bad teeth.

He didn't require the overhead speakers to address the passengers and crew. "Alright, ya ever-livin' scum, shut your mouths or I'll be forced to shut them for you." He gave no details as to how he might achieve that end, but not a single person doubted his resolve. "I'm Cap'in Klaz Tarconin of *The Good Ship Lollipop*—"

A passenger in the second row could not suppress a snort.

"*Kill* that man." howled Klaz, pointing his sword at the disrespectful passenger.

Klaz's order was quickly executed. In fact, three separate pirates killed him in quick succession. They clearly loved their jobs *and* were devoted to their captain.

"Any one else want to disparage the ship my sainted mother gifted me from her deathbed, after giving it the name from her favorite childhood picture show, even as she drew in her last breath?"

There were no takers.

"Good, ya landlubbin' sons o' sea witches. As I was sayin' before I was sidetracked on account of matters of personal honor, *dis* is a raid. We're fixin' to rob y'all, hurt a goodly number o' ya, and are *not* beyond takin' the occasional hostage or slave, here'n there, as it strikes our fancy." His icy eyes scanned the compartment. "Any questions, so far?"

One of his men, who was, in fact, a woman, raised her gloved hand. Before she could ask anything, he excoriated her.

"Not from me *crew*, ya daft whore." He gestured to those seated. "From the *victims*." Her hand went down quickly and shamefully.

"If there're none, we will proceed. If y'all could find it in your hearts to dig deep and pass any and all valuables toward the aisle, where me courteous staff will lighten yur burdens by collectin' said items and bringin'em to me." He tapped his chest with a palm. Amidst the rustle and clamor of purses emptying and seated passengers shifting to access their pockets, Klaz went on. "As a friendly reminder, if I should be made aware of any withholdin' or similar skulduggery, I would be displeased. Any livin' man or woman who's ever met me can tell ya, ya don't want to be a body what's gotten on me *annoyed* side." He shook his massive head. "Nah, best not to tempt that segment o' fate."

Two satchels laden with loot found their way to Klaz. He opened each bag and peered at its contents. He smiled while inspecting the first bag. Addressing something in the second bag he said, "Well lookie here! Christmas comes early to the deservin' souls.

"Now, me hearties, on to the second phase of tonight's entertainment. This is what I like to call the electronic-transfer portion o' the show. Dis is where my crew will assist your transferring of whatever's in your bank accounts, into an account held in the name of our partnership, that's an *LLP* as opposed to a *GP*, mind ya, for those both technically inclined and curious."

Within half an hour, most of the fund shuffling had been accomplished. Everything proceeded without a serious hitch, that is to say, without the need for a single execution, until one of Klaz's associates came to—you guessed it—seats 20 A through C. When Argar failed to acknowledge the fellow's demand, he struck at her with the back of his hand. Just shy of impact, she angled her face so he could get a good look at it.

He, realizing what he was about to strike, yelped like an injured puppy. He quickly jerked his arm back as if from a venomous viper. The pirate's distress drew Klaz's attention. The heist had proven boring, because of the infuriating compliance and due deference on the part of those being robbed. A scream portended an entertaining break in the, up until then, dull proceedings.

Klaz exuberantly harrumphed his way back to the nexus of the disturbance. He raised his sword and was about to begin a tirade, when he recognized Gideon and Argar. He smiled as a tiger smiles at a large chunk of red meat. "As I live and *breathe*. If it isn't me old pals, Sneaky and Stinky." He clapped Gideon soundly on the back several times. To Argar, he waved his fingers. When it occurred to him his action might be interpreted as the offer of an appetizer to the zombie, he shoved his hand into his breast coat.

"Yes, Klaz, I thought it was you. How *are* you?" asked a cheerful Gideon.

"What do ya mean ya *thought* it was me." He pointed forward with his sword. "I shouted it out in front o' God and all ye witnesses. Why didn't ya stand up and disclose the fact that ya was here, *old* pal?" Angling his sword at Argar, he added, "And the lass, too, o'course."

"You seemed busy, you know, and, well, I was having the best conversation with my partner here, Rigel ... um, I don't believe I caught your last name."

"Rettlebutt. Rigel Rettlebutt."

"Ah, now I understand why you hadn't volunteered it," replied Gideon. "Anyway, Rigel and I were discussing the prospects for door-to-door sales of personal radiation machines on Kempupus. Can anyone say *goldmine?*"

Klaz scowled. He did that a lot. "It wasn't that ya were hopin', against all odds to the contrary, to escape my notice, was it?"

"Klaz, that hurts. We're family. No. I was just waiting until you finished your *business,* before I switched this into the *social* setting. You silly, silly man."

"It wouldn't be on account o' ya owin' me the proceeds from a recent wager ya lost, would it?"

Gideon slapped his coat pocket. "Got that money, right here."

"Or," Klaz continued, "it wouldn't be the manner in which you terminated your engagement to my daughter, the apple o' me eye, and sweetest vision to grace this bleak galaxy since her mother passed long ago, God bless her, would it?"

"You're not going to believe this, but I was just about to call the dear girl and make arrangements to get together. Rigel here can vouch for the fact. Go ahead, ask him. He's sitting right here."

That drew Klaz's dour scrutiny directly down upon Rigel, who slid lower in his seat.

"I'll ask ya once—nicely—laddie. Do you have the faintest recollection o' what this scoundrel's talkin' on about?" Klaz pinched the sharp edge of his blade and drew the sword through his finger tips. When it occurred to him, to his horror, that Argar might think an appetizer was being prepared, he again hurriedly stuffed his hand in his pocket.

What to do? What to say? Rigel was fairly certain Klaz was neither anyone's fool nor easy to deceive. And Rigel so disliked death. "We've really only just met," said Rigel, pointing toward Gideon.

Klaz's immediate reaction seemed stupendously negative. He rested the tip of the blade on Rigel's throat.

"But I have to say, he has talked a blue *streak*, non-stop, and ad infinitum about nothing other than your daughter since I sat down in this seat."

"He has, has he? What's me lass's name, as ya are surely all but tired o' hearin' it by now?"

More a question than a declarative, Rigel said, "Her last name's *Tarconin*." Rigel stopped breathing.

"Yes, very clever one y'are, aren't ya? To be certain, her surname is the same as mine, me bein' her da and all. No, I'm more curious to learn her *given* name from your lips while they're still part o' yer body in general."

"My. That's a tougher one," replied Rigel.

Klaz advanced the blade..

"Let me see ... so many cutesy names have slipped my mind already. Okay, he's called her *sun in my sky, beat of my heart, my loin's desire, chasin' hot babe*, and, I believe he said something about her *being his one true love*." Rigel smiled apologetically, like he'd just farted in a nearly full elevator.

"Well, I must say, I don' know whether to be happy or angry. *All* those names, eh?" He turned to Gideon, his jaw locked so tightly his teeth could be heard to complain. "My daughter is your *loins's desire*? How's a *da* supposed to take a notification like that?" He crossed his arms and tapped a gigantic shoe on the deck angrily.

"We are, *da*, engaged. I think that should influence your mixed reception of that news."

Though he stared hotly at first, Klaz couldn't restrain himself long. He threw open his arms and bear-hugged Gideon out of his seat. "You're right, me boy. Family has to take these matters with grains o' salt, don't we? Come here, ya scamp. Show me some love."

When Klaz and Crew, LLP, had concluded their business aboard Flight 10012 from Ramurpart bound for Breakers, an overjoyed Gideon, an overwrought Rigel, and an oblivious Argar were escorted to *The Good Ship Lollipop*. Cabins were assigned and merriment arranged. Gideon had so pleased his host, that his recent gambling debt was, uncharacteristically, forgiven. The pirate so loved his only daughter on the eve of her wedding, he was magnanimous for the first time in his life.

Gideon's brain swam in the possibilities. Two weeks of free food, free liquor, no Breakers, and free liquor. Life wasn't good, it was great. Rigel, on the other hand, found his situation unsettling. Here he was, being whisked off to some pirate world, where he knew no one, and his prospects of honest employment were nonexistent. Rigel was also miffed that the bulk of the Argar-sitting duties had been transferred to him. She might even have become aware of this switch. Repeatedly through the day, and all through the night, she would put her face right up to Rigel's and say "*Argar.*" The journey was in no way Rigel's version of the vacation, that it seemed to have become for his traveling companion.

The next morning, Gideon announced there would be a celebratory breakfast. Everyone was invited. Klaz added that anyone invited who *didn't* attend would be thrown out into the garbage disposal unit. The only exception, of course, was Argar. No one invited her anywhere, anytime, and she was totally unwelcome whenever eating took place. But, when she showed up uninvited, please know that no one was brave enough to confront her.

The main dining hall was large, but still managed to give off a warm, homey glow. Klaz was seated in the center of a long table, arranged at 90 degrees to the parallel tables where most people sat. Klaz's daughter was in the seat next to the captain, on his right. Gideon was affixed to the chair next to his fiancée's. The female to Klaz's immediate left was Mrs. Klaz. Rigel was positioned to the right of Gideon.

Seeing the Tarconin women up close should not have been, to Rigel's way of looking at life, a grand favor bestowed upon an honored guest. That the women were genetically linked was beyond the shadow of a doubt. No two *unrelated* people could have shared so many unflattering facial characteristics, by chance alone.

The mother/daughter duo had short, dry, thinning hair that normal females would have covered with something. A wig would be the obvious choice, but really a scarf, a tarp, or mop would be preferable to nothing. A hat of dead rats sewn together would be more attractive than their exposed heads.

The Medusa had hairstyle-bragging rights over this pair.

Complexion? A tactful person would try to avoid noticing theirs. But that tactful person would have to wear a blindfold to not involuntarily voice an opinion or two, anyway. The girls shared a sallow yellow color to their skin. That off-colored flesh was both wrinkly and over-plentiful. The surfaces of their faces were randomly pitted with signs of bad acne or a pox, or both. Nature provided the girls what it did. What was inexcusable was the women's flagrant lack of any attempts at improving their outward appearances. Washing, shaving, or the blessing of thick make up were strikingly absent. The two broadcast a challenge, daring anyone to *not* be offended by their callous disregard for self-improvement in the face of an ugliness that would drive a blind saint to rip out his eyes.

Lastly, Rigel was transfixed staring at the women's lips. *My, oh my*, was his initial impression. Their lips were so thin and craggy that kissing them would be a manifestly foolhardy act. That those defensive lips jutted out due to massive overbites and tragically recessed chins was proof that there was no justice in this life. But what turned Rigel's already queasy stomach the most was the shade of lipstick they wore. The exposed portions of their oral openings were pea green. As he sat there, slack-jawed, staring at the pair, all Rigel wanted in the world was quick access to a blaster so he could try to remove the images burned upon his retinas.

At the point where Rigel was beginning to vomit in his mouth, Klaz called the festivities to order by banging a large mug of something sloshy on the table. He raised the mug high overhead and spoke. Hearing the skipper speak was so jarring, so surreal, that Rigel's nausea passed in a flash.

"My dear friends," Klaz said softly, "I would like to be the first to offer a toast to the health, wellbeing, and fecundity of the blessed pair of paramours seated to my side." Klaz swung the mug in the direction of his daughter and Gideon. It was perfectly unbelievable. Yesterday, the man sounded exactly like Robert Newton's over-the-top pirate voice from the 1950 role where he played Long John Silver. Today, Klaz sounded like a butler to royalty, his tone formal, affected, and nasal.

The perfunctory applause faded quickly. Klaz continued. "I am so proud

of this young woman, this dew-drop-on-a-rose-petal, my daughter, Fleccid."
He stared at her with fatherly abandon as she blushed.

Rigel, up until then not a religious man, began to pray. He demanded of
the all-mighty reassurances that the new color in the girl's cheeks was, in
reality, a red mixed with sallow yellow. That was because it looked all the
world like some explosive infection was spreading across her face like wildfire.

"I will," remarked Klaz, "ask the blessing of my loins to address this
distinguished gathering, but not until the repast has been enjoyed by us all.
The last time I asked Fleccid to give a speech *before* we were all finished, as
you all might recall with concern, she seemed to cause a few revelers to be
rendered unable to continue eating. And yes, I have enjoined the girl, once
again, not to speak while simultaneously chewing and swallowing. But, as a
prudent man, I will not, on this happy occasion, press too firmly on chance,
fate, and my luck."

As the feasting began, and the noise level went through the roof, Rigel felt
a discrete question to Gideon would not be overheard. "What the hell's up
with his voice."

"*Shusssh,*" hissed Gideon "Do you want to get us both killed?"

"No," replied Rigel more softly. "But, what's with this man?"

"Klaz Tarconin, or rather Reginald Pennelegion, came to the pirate trade,
er, *later* in life. He was a civil servant, an accounting technician to be specific,
in the Office of Qualifications and Examinations Regulation on the planet
Drectal for many years."

"He was *what*? No, you're making a very bad joke at my expense. I resent
it."

Gideon placed a hand over his chest, where his heart would have resided,
had he possessed one. "On my mother's grave, I swear it's true." Gideon
shrugged as he chewed. "Look, he told me he found the work dull, boring,
and unfulfilling. He saw his life slipping away and decided, rather bravely I
might add, to make a career change."

"Whichawhater—"

"Calm yourself. Can't have you choking on my *special* day. I'm getting
married in a little while and *you're* to be my best man."

That made nothing about Rigel feel better. "Giffidyhop."

"Cleansing breaths, my man. Here, sip this tea." Gideon blew on the cup, then held it to Rigel's trembling lips. "There. Better?"

There were many pressing questions in Rigel's head, falling over each other, like Keystone Cops, to get out first. The most compelling one vaulted over the others and leapt from his mouth. "Have you *seen* your bride-to-be?" Rigel jerked a thumb to the left. "I mean, have you had a cognitive stroke, maybe hysterical blindness?"

Gideon patted his friend's forearm. "Not to worry, but thanks for your concern." He stole a glimpse at Fleccid, as she defied the laws of anatomy by cramming three pieces of bacon, two hard boiled eggs, and an almond scone down her gullet at once. Truly an impressive feat. "We're not married, *yet*." He gave Rigel a knowing wink.

"As you flew the coop on the occasion of your last nuptials, I imagine Klaz'll be keeping an extra close eye on you this time."

Gideon returned a blasé look by way of response. After the feast was complete, Klaz thumped his mug on the table again. "My charming daughter will now retire to her chambers in order to ready herself for her impending transformative ceremony." He clapped and those in attendance who were smart joined in enthusiastically. "I, however, will not slumber. I will, instead, pass the *entire* interlude discussing with my soon-to-be son-in-law the finer points of attaining and maintaining marital bliss. Every remaining second, in fact."

The gauntlet had been thrown down. If Gideon was to escape this time, he'd have to do so while under the constant, close, surveillance of a jealous, once-wounded, and overly-protective father-of-the-bride. Rigel began to sweat. Argar—you know the drill—shouted her name. That she was directing her gaze to Fleccid when she said the word was almost certainly randomly determined.

"Ah, Rigel, my good man," said Klaz, "would you excuse Gideon and me, as we retire to my study? I wish to speak with him concerning matters of an intimate and highly *personal* nature."

"No problem, Reg," slipped out. Klaz glowered hatefully and lingered in that state for longer than could be healthy for anyone, especially a stranger. Then, his face calmed. He placed a guiding hand on Gideon's back and they left the room in silence.

"Argar?" came out like a question. For Rigel, this was a new twist. He wondered if there was meaning in her intonation or only ongoing blithering.

There Rigel sat, alone, in the dining hall aside from Argar, who seemed content to stare at nothing, and a pair of scullery maids cleaning the considerable mess. He'd been left alone and unattended. Rigel's mind creaked into gear. They were *alone*, Gideon was in *trouble*, about to be the reluctant participant in a shotgun wedding. What would follow the wedding celebration was unclear. Gideon might be forced into becoming an equally involuntary member of the family business. How long Klaz planned on holding him hostage was unclear, but the accountant/pirate would be foolish to give Gideon an ounce of freedom for a good, long while. This time, the father-of-the-bride was *determined* to marry off his ray of sunshine, once and for all.

What were Rigel's assets to liberate his friend? Hold on. *Was* Gideon actually his friend? That really had yet to be established, hadn't it? But, if Gideon's prospects were poor if he remained on the planet Blackwash, Rigel's were considerably more bleak. Gideon would become the heir apparent to the pirate jig. Rigel would be, what, a deckhand? And what of Argar, should the trio remain together? The negatives quickly tallied up to outweigh the positives on Rigel's ledger.

Rigel elected to explore, if not fully commit to, the possibilities of flight. He asked the duller-looking of the workers where the hangers were. She returned a confused look and asked what he wanted. She added, specifically, that she was not open to any lewd propositions, whatsoever. That she admonished him so, while eyeing Argar with revulsion, suggested her unwillingness to entertain any offers was related more to the company he kept, rather than the possible coin in his purse.

After their brief miscommunication, Rigel found out where the docks were located and headed off in that direction. It seemed space pirates housed their vessels at the *docks*, not in *hangars*, as they had in the good old days. Security

THE GALAXY ACCORDING TO GIDEON

was lax throughout the ship, but at least lip service was given to the practice when it came to the docks. A couple of intoxicated guards leaned against the wall in front of the doorway leading to where the ships were moored. One was clearly and soundly asleep and the other was not far behind his mate. Both held rifles that dangled precariously from their loose holds on them. Rigel was confident that, if he was able to rescue Gideon, at least the part of their escape requiring them to get past those slackers would be easily accomplished.

Argar and he wandered back toward the living area. Rigel did not want to arouse suspicion by asking directly where Klaz's quarters might be so it took him thirty minutes to locate them. That meant Gideon's wedding was about to begin. They entered Klaz's quarters without a hitch. There were no guards on duty, and no blaring alarms sounded. It wasn't hard to locate where Gideon was held captive. He simply followed the booming sound of Klaz's voice.

Finally, they arrived outside the door of his study. Rigel listened to glean what the topic of conversation was, one-sided as it seemed to be. Klaz was going on about the difficulties he had with local magistrates. He fumed over their disregard for honestly tendered bribes. It seemed Klaz would hand over generous sums of money, meant to entice them to allow him a freer rein, and then, the *lily-livered lubbers,* would enforce all the local laws, in spite of their incentives.

Rigel heard a few grunts that had to be Gideon's half-hearted responses. Okay, how would he extricate his companion while remaining alive? What would get Klaz out of his study in a manner that would free up Gideon? Nothing obvious came to … oh.

Oh, yes.

There was a resounding pounding on the study door. Klaz was irritated to hear it, as he'd been specific in his instructions to be left alone. No one disobeyed him twice. He strode to the door and opened it quickly. The moment the first crack appeared, Argar came screaming into the room. She screamed because Rigel had lit one of her shoes on fire. It was burning actually quite fiercely as she sprinted past Klaz and proceeded to scamper in a tight circle, with Klaz at its center. As Rigel had hoped, Klaz found that being surrounded by an angry, burning zombie was … disquieting. Fortune smiled further on Rigel's plan when Argar apparently equated, in her hazy mind, the pain in her foot and the proximity of Klaz.

She leapt, wailing like the banshee the whole time, onto Klaz's head. She displayed more athleticism than one might have given her credit for, given her medical condition. Klaz reacted as any sane person would, when a flaming, enraged zombie was riding on his head, slapping at it and ripping out chunks of scalp with her teeth. He lost it, utterly and completely. He attempted initially to pry her off his head, but, as we all know, a committed zombie is a powerful force.

Failing that approach, Klaz tried ramming himself, head first, against the nearest bulkhead. Keep in mind he could not *see* the nearest bulkhead, because he had a melting zombie blocking his view. Hence, it was understandable that he tripped over a small statue of a cute little puppy he was particularly fond of before he could impale himself against anything. He crashed to the floor with his zombie assailant still firmly affixed.

To his credit, he recalled the boyhood instructions he'd received from Mr. Crown, in second grade, to, when on fire, "stop, drop, and roll." Klaz had already stopped and dropped, so he commenced to rolling. Aside from fanning the flames already engulfing Argar's lower leg, it produced no extinguishing effect. Klaz was face down when he wedged up against a couch. That's when he decided his only chance was to pound her off his head by repeatedly arching his back and slamming his face to the floor.

It was quite the sight.

Between one slam, while his torso struggled to lift itself, Rigel and Gideon were able to detach Argar. Rigel quickly dumped the bucket of water he'd brought on her flames. The three travelers stood and turned to see if Klaz was getting up, too. He was not. Apparently Klaz was unaware, undoubtedly due to his terror, that Argar was no longer burdening his scalp. He continued to ram his head against the floor. Without her to shield his forehead, the fury that he demonstrated was impressive. After ten or so blows to the metal deck, accompanied by his then muffled pleas for God to take him quickly, Klaz slipped into unconsciousness. Perhaps it was a coma. None of the three bothered to make even a cursory evaluation.

For the moment, the trio was free. Gideon took charge of the brigade, which was fine by Rigel. He knew Gideon was more skilled at sneaking and stealing, skills that were about to become crucial if they were to complete their escape attempt. They jogged to the door and Gideon scanned the hallway.

A word is needed to affirm the resilience of the zombie. If you or I had just had our foot burned half off, we wouldn't be inclined to walk, let alone jog, anywhere. We would howl, limp, and insist on prompt medical attention. But Argar did not. She paced along with the men without complaint. Whether it was because she knew the foot would quickly regrow or, that she was simply an all-in team player, was unknowable. That she held her own was the enduring fact.

The hallway was clear. Gideon guided the party toward the docks. He knew the way because he'd fled from his bride, Fleccid, before. That level of motivation truly enhances ones memory. By the time they arrived at the door, the sleeping guard was still present, but the second was gone. Perhaps nature had summoned him. Unfortunately, the one remaining was slumped against the door itself. If they risked moving him and he awoke in the process, there could be trouble. Gideon told Rigel to wait just around the corner and to alert him if anyone was coming. He then took Argar's hand and tiptoed up to the snoozing guard. Deftly, Gideon raised the man's right arm up and he snuggled Argar under it. He turned her head so she was looking directly at the drooling fellow. He instructed her not to move, and then slowly pivoted the guard's head, so he was face-to-face with Argar. The coup de grâce of his design came when he nudged their lips together, as if they were kissing. He told Argar not to eat the man's lips, but he knew it would be very tempting for her. He crossed his fingers, in case that might help, and hurried the best he could. Time was not his friend.

Gideon stepped a few paces back and clapped his hands loudly. The guard's eyes snapped open like window blinds. It would be an understatement to say he was surprised at what he saw after they did. Argar enhanced the impression he took away from the scene when she said her name to him, muffled as it was by their lip contact.

He jumped clear of the floor by such a margin that he struck his head on the ceiling. When his feet returned to the floor, he employed them to their fullest and sprinted away at a breakneck pace. For a brief few seconds, he was the fastest thing on two feet, ever, in recorded history. His cries for mercy faded as he put distance between himself and his worst nightmare. Gideon stepped over to the control panel, tapped a few switches, and the doors opened. He waved Rigel in and took Argar's hand.

There were a handful of ships present to choose from. He headed to a mid-sized scout ship. It was extremely fast. With any kind of head start, Klaz could never catch them.

As the hatch was closing on the scout ship, Gideon headed up to the bridge. He flipped more switches, and the vessel lifted off effortlessly. Once they'd cleared the docking bay's outer hatch, Gideon gunned it. In no time at all, the ship was making good speed. The motors hummed contentedly and Gideon piloted the craft to freedom, sweet freedom. Note to self, thought Gideon. Don't cross paths with Klaz, ever again. The man was well known to hold a grudge, and Gideon had given him several reasons to be upset. *If* Klaz woke, and *if* his scalp healed and *if* he'd not gone permanently insane, the man would likely be keen to settle his multiple scores with his almost son-in-law.

THREE

A few days out from *TGSLP*, Rigel woke more confidently than he had since his escape. They had both been on the edge of their seats, worried that Klaz would appear from nowhere, angry as a scorned bride (vicariously), and hot for blood. But, against all odds, it seemed like they were safely away from a horrendous death, or an even worse marriage. As an escape meant, by definition, a flight from somewhere worse than the next place one was going, it occurred to Rigel to ask where it was they *were* going. He made his way to the bridge, by way of the galley. A cup of coffee in hand, and a scone in the other, he entered to find Gideon fiddling with dials and tapping switches. The view screen displayed a dark field studded with a myriad of stars, typical of deep space.

"Morning," Rigel said cheerily.

"Is that a question or a statement of fact?" Gideon shot back.

"Er, neither. It was a greeting."

"Then why not simply say, *greeting*? You're complicating a trivial act. It's too early in the morning for that type of repartee."

"Saying good morning *is* the standard greeting one extends early in the day. Everyone knows that."

"You didn't say *good morning*. If you had, I'd have understood perfectly. You said —"

"I know what I said. I'm sorry. May we drop it, now, already?"

"Which one? The one about greetings or the one about you being a pissy pansy?"

29

"We weren't discussing my being *any* of those things."

"No? Well, perhaps it's time we did."

Argar, who was never far from Gideon, proudly shouted her name.

Gideon pointed to her. "See, plain and simple, clear as a bell."

"What? She said her name. She didn't say good morning or any variant, thereof."

"No, she was agreeing you're a pissy pansy."

"She said nothing of the sort. She said what she always does. Her name, harshly."

"Are you here to badger me or is there a reason for your visit?"

"I—" Rigel started to respond but elected to let it drop. He sipped his coffee and took a vicious bite from his scone. "May I get either of you something from the kitchen?"

"No thanks," Gideon replied, "we're good."

Hardly, reflected Rigel to himself. He allowed himself to cool off a bit before asking, as convivially as he could, "Where are we heading?"

Gideon glanced over his shoulder to Rigel, then swung his hand generally at the view screen. "Thadway."

Rigel crumbled the remainder of his scone between his fingers he was so irritated. A few calming breaths later, he was able to maintain civility while pressing, "Well, certainly, I see we're heading *that way*, but what is our final destination?"

Mildly confused, Gideon pointed specifically straight ahead and said, "Thadway."

"Look, I'm sorry about the misunderstanding just now over my greeting, but *really*. I'm not asking all that much and I *am* a member of this crew." He sniffed, counted to ten, and asked, "I would simply like to know where I'm heading."

Fully irritated, Gideon slapped the screen with his palm, repeatedly. "Thadway, Thadway, Thadway. It's *that* way. What's gotten into you?"

"Argar." We all know who said that.

"Calm down, please. Alright. We're going *that* way. Fine. At the end of our trip, when we get off the ship, we'll be all the way *that* way. We'll be *where* that way?"

"Exactly. See, you're not so dull after all. *Thadway.*"

"No, I don't ... I mean I do, but—" He planned his next words more carefully. "If we went," Rigel pointed to his right, "in *that* direction, we would end up at the end of that way."

"No," Gideon gasped, "Thadway's *this* way!" He shoved both arms forward.

"I'm trying to be amiable, here, but please. *That* way's *that* way, and *this* way's *this* way. What I want to know is if we went *this way,*" Rigel directed an arm to the stern, "not *that way,*" he pointed his other arm directly ahead, "where would we end up, that way?" Rigel was sweating profusely.

"You must be pretty new to space travel, chump. The planet Tisway is *that* way," he pointed up, "not that way or," he pointed to the screen, "*Thadway's* that way."

"Gideon," a defeated Rigel said, with a quivering voice, "I'll be another way," he thumbed behind himself, "in my cabin with a bad headache."

"If you want to have a bad headache be my guest, which, of course, you are."

"*Silence.* This is going nowhere. *I* am going nowhere." He stormed toward the door.

Before he left, he heard Gideon remark to Argar, "What's wrong with him? If he wanted to go to Nower, he'd need a bigger ship." He angled his head to her, "Plus, no way I'm going to Nower. It's the dullest place this side of Everywear and it's two galaxies in totally the wrong direction."

Rigel kept to himself for the next few days. He was smoldering. Well, at first he fumed. Then he smoldered. Then he was, more accurately, stewing. Then he forgot why he was mad. By that time, they had arrived at their destination. He was surprised to learn it was the planet Thadway. Something clanged in the back of his mind, but not quite hard enough to ring a bell. He joined his travel party, after the ship was docked and the hatch was cracked.

"Thadway," said Rigel, trying to taste the name as he spoke it. "Thadway? I don't believe I've been here. Why, actually, are we here?"

"I want to sell our ship. I know a guy," replied Gideon.

"But it's not *our* ship. We stole it."

"More or less. Hence, Thadway. Marketing a craft you don't *technically* own can be a challenge. Here, the rules are fortuitously slipperier, less distinct."

"You mean the populace is every bit as dishonest as Klaz."

Gideon recoiled. "Not even close." He menaced a finger at Rigel's nose. "And watch that no one hears you say such a thing. No, they're much too lazy here to go and steal stuff. They wait for others to do the stealing, then they do the buying. Many's the day they don't even get out of bed to fence stolen goods, they're so unmotivated." He pointed to the cement below their feet. 'This is one lazy planet."

Rigel was unfamiliar with the culture of Thadway. However, their prime directive, laziness, seemed a force that would cause a society to crumble, not evolve. "How can they survive, as a species, if they're too lazy to wipe their noses when they're dripping?"

"Oh," replied Gideon, "*easily*. The galaxy's full of merchandise that is temporarily between owners. The stuff basically falls from the sky. The Thadwayans have their assistants tap a few buttons for them, serial numbers morph into untraceable gibberish, and money piles up in their bank accounts, even though they've never been to their bank or balanced the account." With a serious, schoolmaster look on his face, Gideon proclaimed, "Sweet life if you're born to it. I'd stay and carve out a piece of the cake, but there's no room. All the beds—literally, every stinking bed on the planet—are taken."

"Couldn't you, I don't know, buy a mattress, open an office in a strip mall, and hire a small staff of your own?"

"What? And be the laughingstock of the entire business community?" He waved Rigel off. "No thank you. I may be a scoundrel, but even *I* have standards."

"Wait," said Rigel, confusion being an old friend. "Scoundrels have standards and principles? I find that counterintuitive."

"That's because you're not a scoundrel. It makes perfect sense to me."

"*Argar.*"

"Her, too," he pointed to his companion.

"I, *too*, am a scoundrel," Rigel responded. Pointing at the ship they'd only just exited, he said, "I helped steal that ship. *Scoundrels* steal ships."

Rigel's last remark was so ridiculous, Gideon was compelled to stop and address him, face to face. "You stole a ship. That makes you a thief. *Scoundrel*, that's more a job description. It's a career path, something a person is really proud to be." He shook his head. "You gotta work at it hard."

"A career," snapped Rigel. "What, is there a pension plan, dental coverage, and a secret handshake?"

Gideon pushed a finger hard into Rigel's chest. "Who told you about the handshake?"

"No one. I was being sarcastic."

"Oh," he grumbled back. "Well, keep it that way. It's a secret."

"Thawayk," screamed Argar.

That compelled the men to stare at her. Rigel had never heard her say anything but the bastardization of her name. Gideon hadn't heard her say a new word since she said *figur,* while giving him a digit she recently removed from the crown prince, many months earlier. He wasn't, at that time, certain if she spoke the word as a statement of fact or an offer, not that it mattered much either way. That she said something different might have portended some important message. Then again, it might have meant less than nothing.

"What, dear?" asked Gideon. "Do you like Thadway? Is that it?" He wagged a finger between himself and Rigel. "We like it, too, you know."

"Do you fear we will meet with disaster on Thadway?" asked a nervous Rigel. "Are you trying to warn us not to sell Klaz's ship? Is there a plague here that will turn our blood to dust? Is —"

Gideon slapped Rigel soundly. "Will you knock it off, you clown bait. If you're not freaking her out, you sure are me."

"You *hit* me."

"I did it for your own good. It was necessary, too. You're welcome. It was, also, strangely refreshing. Thank you."

"For *you*, maybe. Not for me."

"Don't be so quick to judge. Now, come on. Let's find my guy. It's getting dangerously close to planetary nap time."

After a short walk, Gideon stopped in front of an ordinary-enough looking door. He knocked. After a minute or so, he knocked again, harder. After thirty seconds, he began kicking it frantically. He checked his watch. "It's not sleepy time yet, you big oaf. Open the d—"

With his next leg swing, the door opened. His foot whipped through the now empty space and he spun around like a top. When he stopped, he tugged his shirt down, and asked, "Is Glitch home?"

He was home. He always was. To not be home would require effort. That wasn't going to happen. According to Thadway's time-honored custom, he'd be buried in his home. That practice made the resale market for houses a bit dodgy, but culturally instilled flexibility softened the impact of such practices. Well, that and an active black market for body removal and disposal.

The creature who opened the door compressed itself horizontally and it expanded, vertically. "Yez, his honorzhip iz." The little fellow shrank with each syllable. He was a talking gasbag, much like a politician.

"May we see him?" pressed Gideon.

"Yez, you may. You may, however, not zpeak with him. He iz preparing for hiz firzt morning nap." That long of a sentence rendered the diminutive doorman about three inches tall.

Gideon rechecked his watch. With a trace of irritation, he stated, "But it'z ... it's not nap time for a full twenty minutes. If he's not actually asleep, why can't we speak with him?"

"A nap, ztranger, iz a zacred thing, a thing not to be trifled with." It took a moment for him to re-inflate. "One muztn't fall into one like an open pit. No, when done properly, one eazez into it like the armz of a beautiful woman." After re-expanding, he digressed somewhat. "If one iz of the opinion that a woman iz capable of being beautiful, that is. I, for one, am not."

"Well, no one really cares what you think or feel, now do they?" snapped Gideon. "Please show us to Glitch's chamber before I begin searching for a pin in my pocket. Or," he snagged Argar's elbow and pulled her front and center, "before I ask my friend here to give you a big, toothy kiss."

Parpipant, for that was the Odwazianz's name, swelled anteriorly, more than laterally. He whistled a balloonish, spitty sound, and said, "Now *there'z* a beauty." The main reason Odwazianzs were a servile race, bound only to tend to the needs of other species for the minimum wage, was that they made exclusively bad decisions. No race can excel with such a collective burden.

"Well, I'll see you two are left alone, when we meet with Glitch."

"Iz that a promize? If zo, I zhall hold you to it." Parpipant spoke directly and forcefully. Again, bad decisions were their stock-in-trade. Sad little creatures, really.

"More than that, I *insist* upon it," smiled a positively crocodilian Gideon.

Parpipant swelled prodigiously in the anterior-posterior dimension while he backed up and ushered the trio in. Outside Glitch's bedchamber, he opened the door, but only allowed the men in. He blocked, as best a tiny gasbag could, Argar's entrance. Gideon placed a hand on her chest to halt her and pointed straight down, directing her gaze to the top of Parpipant's juicy little head.

"*Argar.*"

"That's my girl." Gideon then pulled the door closed quickly.

Once inside the dimly lit room, it took a moment for their eyes to adjust. When he could see Glitch, Gideon walked to his bedside. "*Glitch,*" he said much louder than necessary, "how's it going?"

Glitch exploded from pre-sleep with a gasp, then a howl, then a second gasp. Then he emitted a squiggly whine of displeasure. He scanned the room, seeking the orientation of the culprit. He was focused enough to recognize Gideon. "Where's my footman?" he said, with flurries of indignation billowing forth.

Gideon checked his watch. "Right about now," he said and pointed to the spot where his throat met his chest, "right about here."

"Well that will never do. Gideon, I swear, if your infernal zombie whore has eaten another of my manservants, I'll—"

"You'll buy a few more, like you always have. Hey," he patted himself on the chest, "I'm a generous guy. Take it out of what you owe me."

"Damn straight I will. Do you have any idea how long it takes to train one of those gooey blobs? Hm?"

"No idea, no interest."

Glitch crossed his four plump arms and forced his lower jaw shut with that fleshy pile.

"Okay," Gideon said. "I guess it takes, what, all of ten minutes? There, I played nice, can we proceed to the business transaction portion of the morning's entertainment?"

"It takes *weeks* to even house break them, you idiot. Those creatures are *as* dumb as a field full of stones."

"Yeah," responded Gideon, "but they're cheap. Cheaper than your taste in wallpaper." He glanced at the room demonstrably.

"Is it wise," Rigel interrupted, "to piss off the man you want to dump a pirate's stolen spaceship on?"

"What?" Glitch protested. "Who is this and what's he saying about a *pirate* ship?"

"Him," Gideon pointed with a strained look, "I have no idea. I figured he was with *you.*"

"I said a *pirate's* ship, not a pirate *ship,*" Rigel attempted, dimwittedly, to clarify.

"You keep finding them duller and duller, don't you, Gideon?" Glitch shook his head in wonder as he spoke.

"Seriously, never seen him before in my life." He turned to Rigel. "Say, fellow, what kind of scam are you trying to pull, here?"

"Gideon, stop it," whimpered Rigel.

"Yes," replied Glitch, "Tell'em you're sorry so we can proceed."

Rigel tugged at Gideon's sleeve. "I shouldn't have to stand here and be insulted."

"Right you are," replied Gideon. He pointed to a chair. "Have a seat there. This could take a while."

Glitch pulled an ornate fob watch from under the sheets and looked bug-eyed at it. "It absolutely can't take a while. If I'm not asleep in five minutes, I'll miss my nap's symmetry. It'll be shorter on this end." He chopped a couple hands in the air.

"Then you'll just have to be quick about it, won't you?"

Glitch took a moment to compose himself, then spoke. "What's on offer?"

Gideon beamed a smile any used-craft salesman, anywhere, would have been proud to duplicate. "I'm glad you asked." He rested a hand on Glitch's shoulder and gestured forward with the other, as if directing all eyes toward the splendid deal. "I am willing to part with a real peach. It's a family heirloom, the last ship my father sailed before he sailed, unassisted, into the Great Beyond. It's a 19227 Zephulon Dart, Spirit-class. Best of all, it's in the *impossible* to find, off-white color *everyone* wants to own."

"Your father? So, it's not stolen from Klaz, like that lifeboat you pawned off on me a while back? You know, he came to Thadway looking for it, even though it was a piece of junk? He killed three of my colleagues trying to find out who bought it off you."

"And you're welcome. My actions resulted in *you* having less competition. You can thank me by juicing the settlement price."

Glitch smacked his lips. "I'll give you ten thousand ticks for it, not a centitick more."

"Rigel, quick, get up. I need that chair," moaned Gideon. "I've never been *so* insulted. I fear I might pass out, or even die." Gideon placed the back of his hand to his forehead and fanned himself with the other.

"Cut the theatrics. If we don't wrap this up in the next ninety seconds, the price falls like a meteor."

"I'm sorry, it's my ears. Did you say, *alright, my dear friend, I'll pay twenty five thousand ticks, even though that's not even* half *the ships actual worth*?"

"I most certainly did not. Eighteen thousand is my final offer, spoken as I'm closing my eyes."

"Twenty or I'm calling Argar into the room. She has such a thing about sleeping bodies, all helpless and warm."

That sealed the deal. Glitch knew one Odwazianz was unlikely to fill the rapacious Argar. "Twenty." He picked up, because his manservant no longer could, his com-link and tapped a few keys. "Done. Now leave. Never return." Glitch slammed his eyelids shut and threw his head against his fluffy pillows.

Gideon leaned over and planted a gentle kiss on the ogre's brow. "Love you too, big guy. See you soon."

FOUR

Later that day, Gideon led his band of travelers to the seedy, commercial part of town. He wanted to purchase a spaceship, one stolen by someone else, and sold to a different crook. He knew just the man. In this instance, she was a woman. It wasn't rare for the females of Thadway to work at the dishonest trades, in fact, they were generally more successful at them than their male counterparts. Women of the species required less sleep, only twenty to twenty-two hours of the twenty six hour day. More time, more money.

Drebdiao had sold Gideon several ships over the years. Some of the craft actually ran, though most of those only worked for very short periods after the transaction. As a result, she was always glad to see him. A poorly discriminating shopper was her kind of shopper. However, she was never glad to see Argar. No one who slept appreciated *her* being around. It was sort of like stocking your swimming pool with piranhas and poisonous snakes. Very hard to relax and enjoy the swim.

Why it was that no one in the cosmos welcomed the visit of a flesh-eating zombie was unclear, but Drebdiao shared that near-universal revulsion. Rigel, she welcomed with open arms, all four of them. Her philosophy was that, just as misery surely loved company, a successful businessperson loved an easy mark.

"Gideon," Drebdiao called out as they entered her warehouse. "It is so *nice* to see you again. Tell me, darling, for I am not certain, why have we never bred together, you and me?"

A mental image of Drebdiao would be helpful at this juncture with the visuals. She was six hundred pounds of glistening fat, drooping randomly over her spherical body, which exuded a greasy slime that smelled vaguely of burning wet hay. Her species' take on bathroom hygiene was radically more lax than any other known, sentient species. In fact, to say it was more lax by a wide margin would be to understate the case. Here is clue number one: their homes had no toilets—ever.

To further separate them from non-revolting species, the Drebdiao were fond of eating while mating. Often, that included nibbling off non-critical portions of their companion. But, not to worry excessively over the health of either reproductively-driven participant. Another foul custom they shared was that Thadwayians preferred to breed in an arena-type setting, surrounded by other mating couples. So, a nibble off your date, a tiny morsel from someone else's mate, maybe even off oneself, made for the most fulfilling of evenings, and no one died. Isn't that a happily ever after story?

If you answered yes, you'll soon regret that hasty decision. The arenas Thadwayians bred/snacked in were surrounded by drunken spectators, who were actually encouraged to hurl random objects, or beings, into the proceedings, however the spirit might move them. That part, in particular, where unwilling beings were tossed in, basically guaranteed chaos ruled all breeding competitions. The real sport for the Thadwayians was to decide, while otherwise engaged, if the aerial arrivals were food, sex toys, or both. The wagering, conducted safely well above the rim of the arena, was often fierce on this aspect. And, if you were foolish enough to lose a bet you couldn't immediately settle—that's right—you flew in next.

"Drebdiao, baby," replied Gideon, "you got me there. Why, if Argar wasn't here, I'd be more tempted than a hammer at a nail convention." He air-hugged the space just in front of her oozing frame.

"Any time, stud-muffin. You say the word, and I'll book an arena."

Having referred to Gideon as a muffin sealed it for him. No mating with the revolting alien when she thought of him as a food product even *before* the spectacle began. In reality, yes, it positively ended any consideration of such a vile act in his mind. Not that he would've done so *before* she made that nickname known to him. It just became *more* unlikely than merely impossible to happen.

"So, my basinol (a sour bread pudding)," Drebdiao asked, "if it is not for love making, what brings you to my home and site of business?"

"I … we," he whisked his arms behind his back, "find ourselves in the market for a ship."

"Well, you've come, as always, to the right place. I would never try and cheat the man I love."

"Hmm, you've placed me in the position to having to disagree. That last ship you sold me was pretty *basic*, shall we say? The hull leaked like a sieve, the engines only worked in reverse, and the pilot who came with the vessel was dead when first we met. Had been for quite some time, by the look of the fungal colonies covering his body." He bobbed his head. "Argar took a real shine to him, though. On that count, I'll have to give you due credit for bringing a little light into her otherwise dark life."

"You see. That's why everyone calls me Honest Drebdiao. And, I remember *distinctly* that the windshield wipers worked like new."

"Yes, they did. If it ever rained in space, I would've been a very contented purchaser."

She held up a finger. "They're very calming. Don't downplay their role, in that regard. Swush, glush, swush, glush." She flapped one forearm to imitate a moving blade. "But," she said with finality, "enough small chat. I have just the ship for you. Come."

She walkie-rolled her way down the corridor to a dimly lit hangar. "*Ta da*," she proclaimed like a magician completing an illusion. "Isn't she a beauty?"

"Oh, she's quite the ship."

"I hear a 'but however' in there. Don't tell me I don't. I'm a seasoned sales representative. Tell me your reservation, and I will quench its fire."

"Well, it's just that it's the exact same ship we sold Glitch not an hour ago."

She stared at him as if he had two heads, like her second and fifth husbands had. "And?"

"Why, madam," said Rigel entering the farce, "would we wish to purchase the very ship we just dumped off on Glitch?"

She waved three arms in the direction of the vessel. "It's a perfectly good ship."

"But," Rigel went on, "we stole it from Klaz. If we encounter him while piloting it, he will be even more upset than he already is, which is totally. The fact that we sold it to someone else, who then fenced it to you, will not alter his perception that we're in *his* ship."

"*Argar.*"

Gideon cringed. Now Rigel had gone and done it. He used the words "weigh heavily" in Drebdiao's presence. That was a no-no. She was, in accordance with her feminine nature, sensitive about her weight, or rather, the vast amount of it. To be reminded just how badly she'd lost her girlish figure was, well, it was suicidal. Literally. Gideon estimated she would blow like Mt. Vesuvius in a handful of seconds.

He turned to Rigel and swung an angry finger at him. "Bad zombie," he chided Rigel. "Bad, bad zombie." Rigel began looking around randomly searching for a second undead. "I can't take either of you out in public."

"Er," began Rigel feebly, "I'm not a—"

"I know," yelled Gideon to cut him off. "You're not a-sorry." Gideon leaned his head toward Drebdiao and shared, "Their jaws, they just make them so hard to understand. Really." Back to Rigel, he said, "Now you *accidentally* insulted the nice lady-thing," he pointed to Drebdiao. "Either you say you're a-sorry, or I'll be forced to hand you over to her to do with you whatever she will."

This was a turn in the daisy chain of events Rigel could *not* have anticipated. He gestured a hand toward Argar, for unclear reasons, and pivoted without moving his feet, like a very poorly trained ballet dance.

Drebdiao, smarter than the average bear by anyone's standards, had to think quickly. Was she insulted, played, or about to inherit a zombie? The last proposition was untenable, never-going-to-happen, no-way, no-how, ever.

"*Argar.*"

"Come," she said to Gideon placatingly, "what are you fussing about? Even a, well, highly-functioning zombie is bound to put a foot in his mouth, now and again." She winced upon reflection on her choice of words. "*His* foot in his mouth. Yes. So, how about the ship?" A credit to her profession, that's what Drebdiao was—a consummate professional. Focused, committed, and willing to overlook some insults in the pursuit of a dime.

Anxious to move on, also, Gideon leapt on the chance. "How about this. It is a beauty. Let's call it Plan 2. That said, do you have in stock, presently, a ship that would qualify as Plan 1?"

She narrowed her eyes at him. She wanted desperately to unload that death sentence before Klaz hit town, in his usual kill-the-scum mood. But, to miss a sales opportunity was worse, in the Thadwayian book, than death itself.

"Yes, but only for *you*." she said with outward conviction. "It's right behind Plan 2."

The four angled around Plan 2 to inspect Plan 1. "Hey," chortled Gideon, "she's not half bad."

"Yes," replied Drebdiao, "and the *not* good half part is really smaller than the half *good* portion." She balanced two hands in the air. "70/30, maybe, even, 75/25."

"And she runs? Navigation system's operational? No structural defects? Life support is functional? Computers speak human? Any color options?" Gideon rattled off.

"Yes!" responded Drebdiao with joy in her voice. Gideon fluttered one eyelid at her. "I'll paint it any color you want!"

"Well then, we'll take 'er. You're practically *forcing* me to buy her." Having no viable options, Gideon decided it was better to be enthusiastic rather than realistic.

As Drebdiao's lowest price was firmly contingent on whether Gideon insisted on a test drive or not, they flew out the hangar door heading directly toward their future, whatever that promised to be, in their new, used, ship.

After buzzing a few innocent old ladies crossing streets on foot, Gideon set a course for the commercial district of town. He parked in front of a nondescript shop, doing business under the name Wong's Chinese Laundry.

In and of itself, that might not seem too remarkable, but, remember, humans were rare that far out in the galaxy. The nearest individual who could claim any Asian ancestry was a middle aged woman attempting to recover from an ugly divorce, renting a third story walk-up with kitchen and bathroom privileges, twelve parsecs away.

When it became clear they were parked in that location for a reason, Rigel asked, "Why are we here?"

"You're kidding, right? I love it when you joke me."

"Why would I try and be funny, asking why we stopped in front of some laundry?"

"I give up," replied Gideon with a huge smile, "why?"

"I wouldn't," responded a testy Rigel.

Gideon tapped his chin, thinking. Finally, he said, "That's a lousy punchline. Work on it, okay?"

"Why," Rigel repeated, "are we here?"

"No," he snapped, "not now. I haven't the stomach. Plus, I need to pick up my laundry."

"Argar!"

"I've been with you our entire time here on Thadway. You've not left any cleaning here, or anywhere else, for that matter."

"Not yet." Gideon pointed to the shop. "Seriously, you don't know about this place?"

Rigel shrugged, indicating he, unfortunately, had not.

"It's the best laundry in the *galaxy*, that's all. Whitest whites, boldest colors, and the clothes smell like an alpine slope in springtime." Gideon stared at the neon sign and his eye puddled up slightly.

"I'm confused," replied Rigel. "How can you pick up a load, if you haven't dropped one off, yet?"

"Duh. Because I haven't dropped it off two days ago, *yet*."

"But that's impossible."

"No, they provide that level of quality in just *two* business days. Unreal, eh?"

"No, I meant you can't pick up your clothes today, if you didn't drop them off two days ago."

"*Yet.*"

"Look, why don't you gather up your clothes and turn them in now? We're in no rush. We can come back when they're spanking clean."

"That's not an option. Every thing I own is dirty. I can't wait."

"Alright, I give up. You obviously have some preposterous plan in your under-functioning brain. Please tell me, before I die from the suspense."

"Did I mention this ship has an hevagabor drive?" He nodded with a smile. "Yeah, baby! We just go back in time two days, drop the load off, and pick it up today. Ta-da!"

"An hevagabor drive? Wait, aren't those illegal?"

"No. They're just forbidden. If they catch you using one, you'll spend the next decade in prison, and then they have a Benihana chef execute you with his flashing blades. After that, you might, additionally, be facing a *significant* fine. They try to make it big enough to discourage anyone from using that slipshod tech."

"The unreliable, fraught-with-danger drive you want to use so your dirty clothes will be clean two days sooner?"

"Exactly! Could you—"

"Argar!"

"Yes, sweetie. Hi. As I was saying, could you open that panel and flip the switch labeled

DO NOT FLIP THIS SWITCH UNDER **ANY** CIRCUMSTANCES, EVEN IF DOING SO IS THE ONLY HOPE OF SAVING YOUR LIFE AND THE LIVES OF ANYONE YOU'VE EVER LOVED OR HELD DEAR. SERIOUSLY, STOP READING THIS AND EXIT THE VEHICLE. STOP READING, NO KIDDING. ALRIGHT, NOW YOU'RE JUST BEING OBSTINATE. *GO!*

"No!" snapped Rigel. "I will *never* initiate a mechanism labeled so clearly indicating that doing so would be the worst mistake ever made by any living creature."

"Argar!"

"Fine. Be that way! Ah, Argar, sweetie, be a dear and flip that switch." He pointed to the metal toggle just out of his convenient reach.

She did so immediately and without reservation.

The ship lurched like it was being vomited out of a giant's stomach. Back and forth, up and down, in one dimension and out another. Every nerve in everyone's body pulsed with torment of the purest pain. For several seconds, chocolate did not exist. Never had, never would.

Then the viewport glass became transparent, again. All eyes stared into a bleak, hostile landscape. It was studded with volcanoes spewing multicolored lava. Predators of large, larger, and largest denominations stomped around, clearly in horribly bad moods and all voraciously hungry. A meteor, basically an asteroid, was careening toward them, huge chunks of flaming stone shearing off, randomly. Wherever the three found themselves, the gravity was ten times that of Thadway. They were all instantly crushed to the deck. Breathing only came in fits and starts, with great labor.

With his cheek mushed against the metal floor, Gideon heaved mightily and grunted, "Crud."

In spite of his pain, in spite of his inability to move, in spite of his proximity to a wretched death, Rigel had had enough. He lifted his head off the ground, no mean feat, and said, "Crud. You plunge us into deadly peril, you may have triggered a time-storm, *everywhere*, and the best you can say is *crud*? That is *unacceptable*."

Gideon coughed up blood, then labored to respond. "Not 'crud' *we're about to die in this godforsaken hell.* I meant 'crud,' *that's not Wong's Chinese Laundry.* They're really that good, you know?"

"That is *it!*" For the first time in a long time, Rigel wasn't just being pissy. He was *incensed.* He stood up, as easily as you please, dusted himself off briefly, and walked to the control panel. He located the infernal switch that had thrown them into perdition's nightmare cousin of a place to be, and threw it into reverse.

A topic should be broached, at this juncture. It touches on theoretical physics, calculations involving the manipulation of imaginary numbers, and abstract philosophies so impenetrable they would easily baffle Schopenhauer when lunching with fifteen French existentialist college professors, leaving him dazed and confused, on his back with his trousers pulled down to his knees. Time was not a river, nor was it a fixed continuum. One could sail in one direction, but, by doing so, one negated the ability to return to where one had departed from. That *then* no longer, and quite possibly never had, existed. Anyway, back to our tale.

The viewport went black, then off-white, then a gray-green close to celadon. Finally, they could see through it, again. As soon as he could, Gideon wished he couldn't. They were suspended in the sky above a massive city. The buildings rose as silver spires, kilometers high, formed, as if by hand, of a crystalline material transparent and dazzling. Airships of all sizes and colors buzzed about like mechanical bees. Flying humanoids beat their way to and fro, their gossamer wings caressing the air as they proceeded. The three suns were red, blue, and green, respectively. The sky danced with intoxicating lights, like a child's kaleidoscope. Chimes, the music of the spheres, tinkled everywhere.

Gideon's initial reaction was extremely negative. He was, in fact, indignant. His first impression was that he was dead and in Heaven. That, clearly, would *never* do. That also, he knew as a fact, could never be. Him, in Heaven? That was a laughable notion, if ever there was one.

A feather-light hand grazed his shoulder. Gideon turned to see it was Argar requesting his attention. "Dearest Gideon," she began, in a lilting, upper class British accent, "there is so much I regret having done, yet you have stood by me, steadfastly. I do wish to make it up to you, beginning now. I would like to know where, on *this* ship, the bathrooms are located. I pledge to use them assiduously, from here on."

Crap, crap, crap thought Gideon, as he pounded his head frantically. Heaven! They *were* dead and in Heaven. Argar, probably Hephzibah now, could talk. She didn't look any better, or smell any better, but she could talk like a duchess. That, and his clothes were all still *dirty*. What a day. Whose stupid idea was it to use that fracking hevagabor drive? *Crud.*

Rigel stepped next to Gideon at the window. "Wow. Beautiful place. Where do you think we are? Kansas?"

"I've never heard of Kansas, but this ain't it, can't be, because this place is depressing and revolting and unacceptable. Yes. Totally unacceptable. We're leaving." Gideon lunged for the hevagabor switch. Rigel was able to place his body between his companion and certain, repeated disaster. Gideon struggled to get around his friend for a spell, but, soon, collapsed on the deck, sobbing like a bride jilted at the altar.

"What," Argar asked tenderly, "is the problem, my love?" She looked out the screen. "This place seems outwardly to be extremely pleasant. Do you … um, *we* have a history best left in the past?"

When he finally stopped crying, Gideon said in a huff, "No, never been here, never planned to be, never wanted to be, or never wanted to screw up royally enough to be here."

Their conversation was interrupted by a knocking on the door. It struck all three as distinctly odd, since they hovered ten thousand meters above the ground. The rap caused Gideon to flop into the command seat and cross his arms like a pouty little boy.

"Shall I," Argar offered, "answer the door?"

Without turning his head, Gideon grumbled, "No." He pointed angrily at Rigel. "Better let him. Don't want whoever's there to fall screaming from the sky and blame us for that, too."

Argar shrugged, then turned to Rigel as the knock repeated itself.

Rigel sidled to the door and opened it manually. A tall figure dressed in a blindingly white tunic beat his oversized wings and appeared to be standing there as if on solid ground.

"Beg pardon," the absurdly tall and thin male figure asked, "are you scheduled to arrive … eh, now, in," he gestured both hands toward the ship, "this?"

Rigel started to say something, but Gideon shouted from his chair, "No, no, and no to the next question you're about to ask."

"My," responded the flying visitor, "this is awkward. Really, no to *that* one, too?"

"Yes. Are we done?" called out Gideon. "Can you leave, we leave? Let's all leave."

"Wait," asked the generally confused Rigel, "what was the third question this fellow," he indicated the flying one, "was going to ask?"

"No idea," growled Gideon.

"Yes," said the guest, "and I'm trying my darndest to think of a question I would have asked where the civil response would have been *no*. I shouldn't want to paint you in a negative hue, this early in your stay."

"Good sir," said Argar, "won't you please come in? We really have forgotten our manners, haven't we?"

"Uh, sure," he said toeing the edge of the deck and easing in. "Thanks. This high up, it takes a lot of effort to remain so steady. Most souls, even the ones who've been here a really longtime, don't realize that, and afford us proper credit."

"Well, I'm certain," replied Argar, taking his elbow and escorting him to a stool, so he could sit, but not upon his wings, "we all do. There, now, allow me." She curtsied. "I'm Hephzibah Lewis-Tiltwick." She held a downward turned palm to him. "Pleased to meet you. And I insist you call me Argar. It's rather grown on me over time."

"Whatever," he responded, with certainty. "I'm Clarence and you can call me Clarence." He kissed the back of her hand.

Having placed his nose, which was much more sensitive than most, so close to Argar's skin confirmed to Clay, for the reader should think of him simply as *Clay*, that there was something ... different about Hephzibah Lewis-Tiltwick. Also, Clay's proximity reinforced his earlier impression that there was something ... different, about her skin tone, texture, and feel, also.

"This is my dear friend," Argar said," Gideon Prime, and my equally good friend, Rigel, ah, Rigel whose last name I seem not to recall."

Clay shot them both a short, nervous wave. "Gentlemen," he said tersely.

Gideon, for his part, sat stewing. Rigel looked around quickly to see whom Clay was referring to as "gentlemen."

After assuring himself there was no fifth person, or whatever, present, Rigel said to Argar, "Rettlebutt."

"Please mind your tongue, Rigel." she said, placing a hand to cover her mouth. "There are both a lady and a guest present."

"No, it's my last name. Rettlebutt. You said you didn't know it, so now you do."

"I'm not entirely certain I wish to, that being the case," she said, paling, which is hard for a zombie to do. Give her credit for that.

"Oh, I've met a few Rettlebutts," Clay said. He pitched his head side to side. "Wouldn't want to spend much time with any of them, but they weren't, you know, so bad, I guess."

"Hey, wait a minute!" protested Rigel. "It was my father's name, and his father's, before him."

"You should consider giving it back to them. That would be my advice," said a philosophical Clay.

Argar cleared her throat. As she hadn't done that in, well in years, she nearly choked on a wad of phlegm. Once recovered enough to speak, she said, "I'm sure we're getting off topic, here. *Clarence*, what may we do for you?"

"Huh," was his muddled response.

"You've come here, so high up, and it looks to be quite a windy day. What is the nature of your visit? how may we help you?"

Clay was clearly taken aback. "Er, no one's ever asked me that. It's usually, you know, the other way around, isn't it?"

"I'm certain I could say," Argar replied graciously, "if I only knew to what you were referring."

"You ... wow, y ... you," Clay was flagging badly. He pointed one index finger up and the other to one side. "You're, em, are you sure you know where you are, Hephzibah?"

"No," she said with a giddy smile. "I'm actually quite certain I do not know where I am. No idea, really. Isn't that rich?"

"Oh, my," Clay mumbled to himself. "This is not going to be an easy assignment. I can see that, already."

"So, why don't you tell us, Clarence, where it is we are? That would resolve a lot of questions," said Rigel

"I don't think so," Clay said incredulously. "Might open a real can of worms. Yes, it might."

"People," shouted Gideon, "will you all get over yourselves? We're in Heaven. There, I said it. Now, *Clarence*, if it's all the same to you, I think we'll be leaving now. So," he looked haughtily to Argar, "unless *someone's* about to offer you a cuppa, would you be so kind as to shove off?"

Clay wasn't at all certain he liked the way Gideon had said his name. It was—at least it was close to—impertinent. "Uh, Gideon," Clay said, recalling the trauma these souls had likely just endured, "that's not how it works," he pointed down, "here."

Gideon shot to his feet. Walking rapidly toward Clay, he said, "Well, it is now."

He grabbed the collar of Clay's tunic and frog-marched him toward the still-open hatch.

"Gideon," Argar shouted, when she realized his intentions, "what in heaven's name are you doing?"

"*Clarence* here has to run. Actually, he has to drop, but, either way, he'll be leaving us now. Bye, *Clarence.*"

There it was, twice. That Gideon fellow was openly mocking his given name. Matters were quickly getting out of hand. Yes, Clarence was a relatively *junior* operative and, as such, anticipated some bumps along the road to eternal bliss. But, if this got back to his supervisor, well, that raise he'd counted on next month wasn't going to materialize.

By the time Clay finished worrying about his unsettled financial future, he realized he was plummeting downward at a frightening pace, head first. He flapped mightily, regained flight control, and headed back to the office. Once there, he would consult the manuals, to see if they might provide any pointers or suggestions as to how his present shortfall might have been better handled.

Gideon returned to his command chair, planning on picking up his sulking, right where he'd left off. He was surprised, and off-put, to find his chair was already occupied by yet another stranger. The individual so stationed was tall and thin like Clarence, but any resemblance ended there. This man was older, his skin was weathered, his hair was thinning, and he smoked a pencil-thin cigarette.

"Who the hell are you?" challenged Gideon, upset mostly about the smoke. It would take days to get the smell out of the air-scrubbers.

"Wrong ticket there, mate," the man replied. He took a long drag and lazily puffed it out. "Look, let's cut to the chase, shall we? I'm a busy guy, and you look like you probably used to be. So, shall we banter here like a pair of Monty Python comedians, or shall we get through this, and on with our days, or at least me with mine." Another pull on the cigarette, another luxuriously long exhale. He tapped ash onto the floor, and added, "I'm Three-spot. I'd get up and shake your hand, but I'm not that interested or motivated. I'm Clay's fourth-level supervisor."

Three-spot inspected his cigarette, took another drag and expelled it as he spoke. "Yeah, the rookie screws up and it's kicked all the way up to *me* to handle." He spit a piece of tobacco out. "Where's the justice in that, I ask you? What do I have three levels of lackeys under me for if I gotta wipe the butts of every malcontent who pops in?" He harrumphed. "I did my time, paid my dues. Bottom line: I don't need this. So, if you try and jerk me around, you'll regret it more than you can imagine. Got it?"

"Oh, excuse me," responded Gideon. "Are you done talking, already? My nap wasn't half-over. Now I'll be grumpy and it'll be your fault, *Spot*."

"So cute with the names. You're as funny as a brain tumor, Gideon. Anybody ever tell you that?"

"Wait," asked Rigel, "how did you know his name? Surely Clarence didn't tell you as he fell toward earth."

"Fifth level *sup*, remember? I know a lot of crap I'd rather not. For the record, Clay was falling toward Heaven, not Earth." He tossed his cigarette butt on the floor and snuffed it out. While pulling out another and lighting it, he said, "Look, friends and zombies, I'm here to tell you how this is going to play out. This is not a game show *or* debating society. Most souls are pleased as punch to get here. Lord knows why you three aren't, but I don't. Don't care, *either*. If I never see the lot of you again, throughout all of eternity, that'll be peachy with me."

"Mr. Three-Spot," said Argar, "I'm certain you have misjudged us. You certainly have me. I don't wish to seem or be ungracious. What I *am* is confused. What precisely is going on?"

Holding his smoke between his thumb and index, he pointed at her with his pinkie. "You know, you're the one I can't quite figure. Have to say, I hate mysteries and you're one of those."

"I beg—"

"Nothing personal, mind you, just factual. People die. If they're lucky, maybe they end up here. Dogs die, maybe they get in, too. Depends, actually. Cats," he swiped an angry hand across his chest, "*never*. Forget about it." He puffed intently on his cigarette, calming his rattled nerves. "Sure, zombies die. You destroy their brains. Usually, you just cut off the head and bury it. Everybody knows that. But," he pointed to Argar again, "on the rare occasions they do end up here—duh—they're back to their original forms. In other words, they don't look horrible and smell like sh—"

"See Spot speak. See Spot speak and speak and speak, yet say nothing important. See, that if Spot didn't have his head and shoulder so far up his *ass*, he'd have realized that he was an idiot because she," Gideon pointed to Argar, "isn't *dead*." He frantically slapped his chest. "*I* am not dead. *Rigel*, is not dead."

"Wait, are you out of your cotton-picking mind? What? You trying to tell me zombies aren't dead? Ha! Why do you think they're called the walking *dead*?"

"That's TV, not reality," replied Gideon. "Spot, baby, you said it yourself. You have to cut—" he turned toward Argar, "no offense, honey, but maybe you should cover your ears … their heads off to kill them."

"Wait," said Rigel, "I think I'm getting the picture here."

"*Slowly*, I might add," taunted Gideon.

Rigel shot him a look, then went on. "When I hit the reverse switch on the hevagabor drive, we left whatever hell-hole we were in and were transported to Heaven? *The* Heaven? Angels, clouds, all you can eat sushi buffet?"

"*The* Heaven," responded Gideon. "Only problem is, we weren't killed. We're alive in Heaven." He smiled. "You know, that would make a great country and western song. I wish I could write songs. I'd score *big* with that one."

"Hold on," Three-Spot said, sitting forward. "You three were stupid enough to use an hevagabor drive?" He whistled loudly. "Man, I underestimated how dumb you really were." His expression intensified. "You know those things are illegal, right? They have you put in a blender and swirled to death, if memory serves."

Gideon was tired of hearing everyone get it so wrong. "No. They are *banned*. If you're caught, and I stress the word *if*, you're imprisoned, then chopped to bits by a Benihana chef. You know," he swung his arms around maniacally, "all those chopping blades and tossing of pieces into the air?"

"Teppanyaki-style cooking. Yeah, I know," replied Three. "Kind of passé, but tasty enough. So, you three are not dead?"

"No," scolded Gideon.

Three-Spot flopped back in the chair. "Well slap me silly with a confused stick. This has *never* come up before. I … I think we have a Houston-level problem here, folks."

"Tell me about it." A slight man stood just inside the open hatch. He wore a medieval-style brown cloak with a fur collar and had a thick, ancient book tucked under one arm. He also had a halo.

Three-Spot vaulted to his feet like someone just electrified his chair. "Sir," he shouted, "I wasn't … didn't … I—"

"It's alright, Trois. Please, remain seated."

"You three," said Three-Spot with a growl, "stand up already. We got a *saint* here." He gestured furtively at the newcomer.

"No, no," he responded. "No need. Let's keep this informal, at least for now."

"Okay," asked Gideon with a frown, "I'll bite. Who the devil are you?"

Three-Spot, who hadn't sat down yet, slapped his forehead audibly and collapsed into the captain's chair. He also made a muffled, squeaky sound of unclear significance.

"I am," the man said flurrying a hand, "Saint Ivo of Kermartin, T.O.S.F. But, please, call me Ives. Most people do."

Rigel couldn't help asking, "Sorry, *Ives*, I don't believe I've—"

"Perfectly understandable," interrupted Ives. "Many people haven't heard of me. Anyway, if—"

"Ives," asked Gideon, with a tone that suggested sarcasm was to follow soon, "if I might—"

"Lawyers," he replied harshly, "there, are you happy? I'm the patron saint of lawyers. Now, let me, head you, off at the pass. Lawyers have a patron saint. *What, were there, like, extra saints that didn't get picked by honest callings?* Or how about, *Patron saint of lawyers? Isn't that oxymoronic?* Then there's always, *I never thought they'd get one.* My personal fav has got to be, *What would he do all day?* May we proceed, Mr. Prime?"

"Just as touchy as I'd presume," responded Gideon, with a smirk. "Hey, your circus, your monkeys. Go for it."

Ives waited to speak until his fists un-balled and his breathing was not forced. "As my associate has mentioned, your arrival here, in your present state, is unprecedented. I must say that I brought the need for a contingency plan up covering just this type of occurrence at our monthly brainstorming session, a while back. I was laughed at and mocked. Well, look which saints have egg on their faces, now. But I digress. As there is no established protocol for live beings in Heaven, I was dispatched to resolve the situation."

"Why don't you just kill us," said Gideon. He tossed his arms in the air. "Problem solved."

That brought a scowl from Ives. "Believe me when I tell you that remedy has already been circulated. It was voted down because it seemed, to some, to have a negative connotation. *Go to Heaven and be murdered* is just the type of campaign the competition would love to get its hooves on. No. I'm here to suggest a more, eh, passive option."

"Why is it I don't think I'm going to like it?" asked Gideon.

"You haven't heard my plan, yet. How can you be suspicious, *a priori?*"

"I rest my case, lawyer lover." Gideon beamed brightly.

"Take that back ... or ... or—" Ives was on the verge of saying something he knew he shouldn't.

"Gentlemen," said Argar, as she stepped toward them, "please allow cooler heads to prevail. There," she directed Ives to a bench and Gideon to a far corner, "that's better. I suggest, Gideon, that we hear Saint Ives out, and then negotiations on a resolution may begin."

"I don't recall introducing the option of nego—" He stopped speaking, wisely, when Argar emitted a truly blood-curdling zombie growl. It was great, right out of Hollywood. "Point taken," Ives continued. "So, I suggest we depart," he indicated Three-Spot and himself, "and then one of you turns the hevagabor drive on."

"That's your *divinely* inspired plan?" Gideon asked, clearly incredulous.

"It's a plan, *my* plan. No one mentioned divine inspiration. That's well above my pay grade. It *will*, however, solve the problem at hand."

"I don't have a problem," replied Gideon. "No, in fact I kind of like it here, now. Yeah. I say we stay, see what Heaven has to offer us. Rigel, Argar, you down with that?"

"Remaining in Heaven is *not* a viable option," thundered Ives.

"Because—" asked Gideon.

"As *you* brought it up, the answer is there are entry requirements to Heaven. Requirements some of you *may* or may *not*," his eyes bore down on Gideon, "meet."

"Ah, far be it from me to correct a saintly lawyer," said Gideon with a smile, "but you're actually wrong on that count. My, oh my, I hope and pray they dispatch competent help to resolve this situation, soon!" He was positively full of himself, being so clever and all.

"You know, lightning bolts *are* at my disposal," replied a very annoyed Ives.

"*Constructive*," Argar stated, "gentlemen. Let's remain civil."

"Fine, for Argar's sake, I'll be the bigger man. Ives, there are not entry requirements to Heaven for the *living*. Your argument is flawed."

"Be that as it may," insisted Ives, "staying in Heaven is not an option. Do you have a better plan, Stan?"

"No."

"And do either of you," he turned to Rigel and Argar, "have a better plan?"

"Maybe," Rigel began, with uncertainty, "you could perform a miracle. Maybe put us back in front of Wong's Chinese Laundry the day we left."

"You use Wong's?" Ives asked.

"No," he does. Rigel pointed to Gideon. "I'd never heard of the place."

"You've never heard of Wong's Chinese Laundry?" asked Ives, pulling his collar to his nose, smelling the alpine freshness. "You've led a sheltered life, my friend." Gideon walked over to Ives and gave him a high-five. Both men smiled, smugly.

"Unfortunately, a miracle is currently out of the question."

Rigel was crushed. "Why? I mean, it is a local specialty."

"Lobster *bisque* is the local specialty. *Miracles* is a subsection currently involved in a labor dispute. As the negotiations for a new contract are deadlocked, they've initiated a work slowdown. Sick calls are way up and the foot-dragging is audible. Only mission critical miracles are even *considered.*"

"Everything you just said," responded a dour Gideon, "is *so* wrong. Can you hear yourself?"

"This meeting is over. Trois," he signaled to his subordinate, "if you'll come with me. I believe the fresh meat has a faulty hevagabor drive to initiate."

The two locals proceeded to the hatch, mumbling between themselves. Ives stopped to defer exiting to Three-Spot, who, in turn, wisely deferred to his boss. After Ives was outside, Gideon called after Three-Spot. "Hey, Spot, one last question."

Three-Spot shrugged and stepped over to Gideon, who wrapped an arm around his shoulder and casually strolled toward the nose of the craft. "I'm curious if you've ever been to where we're going? Maybe, you know, you could give us a few pointers."

Three-Spot furrowed his brow. "But, I have no idea where you're heading, so how could I know what to say?"

They stopped in front of the control panel. "No idea? You're joking me?"

"No," he smiled in affirmation. "Not the foggiest."

"Why don't we find out, then?" said Gideon, as he reached over and hit the hevagabor switch.

FIVE

Typical drill. Colors speaking in tongues, visions of lifeless deaths, a pleasant conversation with an honest politician. The usual hevagabor voodoo. Then, the ship came to rest, rolling on a vast ocean. If that ocean had been composed, oh, say, of *water*, there would have been no need for immediate alarm. One's luck can turn on a person so savagely and quickly, can it not? The now four travelers were suspended in a vast ocean of liquid methane. That was cause for significant concern. A methane sea plus oxygen, plus, oh, say a spaceship's engines, could produce an explosion of incalculable size. Apparently, wherever they had been relegated to by the spite of fate currently had no free oxygen available. But, it might, soon. For example, their ship was brimming full of it. If even traces leaked … badda *boom*.

Not a problem? There was an angel on board, so help was at hand? Would that were the case.

Gideon slapped a few buttons and gaped out the view screen. "Where the hell are we?" he yelled.

The ship's computer replied, "Unknown. Likely unknowable."

"A lot of help you turned out to be."

"Might I remind the pilot I was purchased from a disreputable merchant on a disreputable planet, at a price, I add only for spites's sake, twice what I am worth? What do you expect of me? Competence?"

"Not at the time, Bingo. Is that liquid methane we're bathing in?"

"You're such a bright captain. It's a pleasure to serve with such a talented man. Now, if you only live long enough for me to radio my friends, apprising them of my current bliss, I'll die a happy machine," replied Bingo.

"Stow it. Can we lift off from here?"

"Absolutely, smart captain. We'll undoubtedly explode in a fireball of immense proportions, but, on the up side, it'll be quick."

"*Wait*," yelled Gideon. "Where'd I put that angel?" Three-Spot was heaped in a corner, rubbing his scalp. "Whatever are you doing? You need to save our bacon."

"My head hurts," responded Three-Spot.

"So, it looks from here like that idiot Rigel was torn in half. Get over it, you ninny." Gideon was unpleasant to be around when panicking. Or when eating. Or when breathing.

"No, you don't understand. My *head* hurts. No part of me has hurt, *ever*. I don't like this pain thing."

"That doesn't change the fact that you're a ninny. Get up and help. We're about to sink into, ignite, or, more likely, do both, a sea of methane."

Three-Spot, to his credit, heaved himself up and shuffled to the screen. "Sure looks bad. *Crap.*"

"Crap? What's that supposed to mean?"

"First pain, now death. My day just keeps getting worse."

"You haven't been around Gideon much," said Bingo, layering on the snark, "have you? You'd best adjust quickly. One calamity follows another, interrupted only by disaster."

"Do you recall my orders to can it? Look, Three, please wave your wings, or whatever, and get us out of here."

"Sorry. No can do."

"You mean no want do, don't you? You're professing that freewill crap at a massively inopportune moment." Gideon snapped his fingers. "Come on, just do it."

"No. I *can* not do it. Wherever we are, my powers don't work. Trust me, the first thing I did when my head stopped spinning was try and pop out of here and back into my warm, safe bed."

"How can an angel lose his powers? Is there something you'd like to share concerning your allegiances?"

"How dare you! No. We're currently somewhere so far from Heaven, I can't draw on it's energy."

"That," said Rigel, as he came along side, "probably isn't as bad as it sounds, right?"

"No, I think being so far from Heaven kind of speaks for itself," replied Three-Spot. "We're screwed."

At that moment, the ship dipped under the surface and began sinking rapidly.

"There," exclaimed Three-Spot, as he pointed out the window. "What did I tell you? More screwed than a drunken cheerleader in the boy's locker room after a home win."

"Argar!" Some things were a reassuring constant.

"Hang on, honey," said Gideon over his shoulder. "I'll show you to the bathroom *after* we don't die." Then he gave Three-Spot a chilling glance.

"Don't blame me," fired back Three-Spot. "*I* didn't kidnap an angel while using an hevagabor drive. People that stupid die *all* the time. Trust me on that one, too."

"We kidnapped an angel?" asked Rigel, pointing to the person with wings. "I thought, you know, he came along to see the world, have new experiences, that sort of thing?"

"Technically, we kidnapped him," said Gideon looking out the darkening screen. "But not actually."

Rigel's whole body slumped. His soul would have, too, if there were one in him. "This is going to be on our permanent record, isn't it?"

"And," added Three-Spot, "it's always going to be right at the top of the page."

"Gideon," a dispirited Rigel asked, "why did we kidnap the angel?"

He shrugged. "Seemed like a good idea at the time. Hey, I'm impulsive. Sue me."

"I wish I could," muttered Rigel. "I really wish I could."

"Neither of you imbeciles is helping. We're about a mile submerged in liquid methane. I need ideas, not grousing and threats. Our thermal shielding will keep us cozy for only so long. Then, unless we power up the engines, we'll freeze solid."

"It wasn't," Rigel said, "actually a threat. I can't *actually* sue you from an unknown planet sinking in an endless sea of methane. I was venting."

"I know," Gideon replied, "but it's the thought that counts." He looked at the two men beside him. "You know what I'm going to do, right? I can see it in your faces."

They both responded with a chorus of yes. They knew Gideon was going to throw the switch again. Using an illegal, temperamental, highly energetic electronic device under tons of liquid methane seemed, upon first reflection, a remarkably bad idea. But, that had never stopped Gideon before. Not that he'd been in more dire straits, mind you. He was just an optimist at heart.

"Here," said Rigel, who stood closer to the infernal switch, "I'll do it."

Dreams of endless nothingness, filled only by the happy tones of a Don Ho recording played backward, flashed through their beings. They all, all but Argar that is, imagined they were turnips in the cold, wet ground. Argar didn't. Zombies were too concrete to think so abstractly. She imagined she was a flesh-eating shoehorn. One thing they did not do was explode. Opinions, exchanged later on were divided as to whether that was a good outcome, or not.

This time, when rational thought returned, they stared out the screen at a curious sight no one could understand or explain. It was oddly menacing, yet outwardly innocuous. There was a ten-foot tall sign, right outside the window. In bold, yet formal lettering. It read: *Welcome To*, then, in larger print below that, *Paramus*. Under that, as a separate sign, in smaller print, yet, it read: *Home of Over 50 Bus Lines*.

"First," said Three-Spot, "I'm ripped from the bosom of Heaven. Then I'm made to feel pain and know the fear of death for the first time. Now, you bring me to New Jersey." He turned to Gideon. "I *hate* you." Looking back out the window, he added, "Thanks for that, too. Now I have hate in my heart. You're in *so* much trouble."

"Hey," responded Gideon, "at least we won't be consumed by unquenchable flames."

"*Huh*," snarled Three-Spot, "we should *be* so lucky. Apparently, you've never visited Jersey, have you?"

They were interrupted by someone knocking on the hull. Gideon craned his neck around, but couldn't see who was making the noise, or where he might be. "I assume the air in New Jersey is breathable, so let's find out who's there."

Three-Spot wasn't even going to take a swing at that breathable air remark. No, he was so disenchanted that even such a slow pitch, right over the plate, was too much bother to jump on.

Gideon popped the hatch and walked cautiously down the automatic ramp. A plump man in his middle years did his best at jogging over toward Gideon. He pointed under the ship and said, "You'se landed on Mr. Rizzo's car. You're in a heap a'trouble, my friend. You landed on Mr. Rizzo's *car*." He pointed energetically at the black, mangled metal that was, indeed, under the ship.

"Hello," said Gideon, with his best imitation of being happy to see the man. "I guess you're right. The ship did land on someone's car, didn't it?"

"Not *someone*, pal. Mr—"

"Yes, Mr. Rizzo's. You said that twice already. It's kind of annoying, if you don't mind me saying."

"Not like I'llz be mad at you long, if I did. Mr. Rizzo, he's not going to be happy, 'specially if da trunk opens when they lift your vehicle off." More to himself, the man added, "Ya never want to knows what might be in dare. Not good for your health."

Three-Spot and Rigel eased up beside Gideon. "Ah," said Rigel, "maybe we should use the conventional drive and get out of here before this Rizzo fellow notices?"

"You do have—" Gideon started to reply.

"You better not crush and scram," the man admonished, with an ashen face. "Mr. Rizzo's not going to be happy about his car, but if you run, he'll *really* be pissed." The sound they heard, of those in the crowd gasping, wasn't reassuring. Apparently, the prospect of pissing this Rizzo character off scared these people. A word, Gideon noted privately, to the wise.

"With a powerless angel, we'd better run. They'll never catch us. Look around. Do you see any space flight capabilities?"

"Ah, mister," the plump man said, "it's really none of my business, and I should probably shut my trap, but the Hudson River's nearly full a' guys who said that."

An elderly woman dressed entirely in black elbowed the plump man. "Ralph, did that man say the guy with wings is an angel?" Ralph returned an exaggerated nod. She crossed herself rapidly. "Mr. Rizzo's not going to like that more."

"I'm sorry, ma'am," asked Rigel, "I'm not sure what you mean to say. Do you mean, Mr. Rizzo will be *more* upset, or *less* upset, to know there's an angel in the ship that just crushed his car?"

The woman, clearly wiser than Ralph, turned and rushed away without answering that question. She'd known Angelo Rizzo since he was five years old, a nickel and dime thug breaking open parking meters with a baseball bat.

"Why would Mr. Rizzo be upset there was an angel in town?" Gideon asked no one in particular.

"You can ask him yourself," said Ralph, pointing again, "his associates are running this way, as we speak, to invite you in."

All three of them turned as one to see four huge men sprinting toward them. One, likely the oldest, wasn't wearing pants. Another held a double-barreled weapon of some sort.

"And," added Ralph, "before you'se asks, Tiny don't like to wear pants unless'n it's to church on Sunday. Best not to even mention it, okay?"

A breathless Tiny rushed up to Gideon and pounded a finger into his chest. "You wrecked Mr. Rizzo's third favorite car. So help me, if that trunk pops open—" Tiny was no longer calm enough to speak. The three travelers took that to be a bad sign. The man with the shotgun, Luigi, used the barrel to herd them in the direction they had just come from.

Gideon stopped, gestured to the ship, and said, "Wait, there's one more inside."

"Tell him to get out here, *now*," snapped Tiny, able to communicate effectively once again.

"*She*," corrected Gideon. "Hephzibah, could you come out here, please."

Tiny pushed one of his compadres toward the hatch. "Go get her, Tony. I ain't got all day."

Tony bounded up the ramp, but froze like a statue when Argar appeared at the hatch, three inches from his face. Tony, who'd killed his first man at age eight, who'd spent half his adult life in prison, Tony, a man who'd once taken a victim to the hospital so he could maybe get a chance to kill him twice, was scared. He howled something religious, in broken Italian, and jumped off the ramp, striking a tree with his head. He hit the ground like a sack of wet paint.

Tiny kicked the dirt. "Mr. Rizzo's *not* going to like that you did that to Tony." Coming from Tiny, that observation carried a lot of weight. "Alphonse," he said to the man silent, up until then," bring her down. And if you screw up, I'll deal with you myself. Capisce?"

"Yeah, boss," Alphonse replied, "but I ain't going to touch that thing."

Soon, everyone was walking toward wherever Mr. Rizzo was. They proceeded slowly, because Argar was not to be hurried. She shambled at her own pace, only, and none of Rizzo's men had the brass cojones to try and speed her up. They were seasoned killers, sociopaths to a man, but even hardscrabble lunatics had limits. She was, keep in mind, the first actual, in the flesh zombie they'd ever seen.

They arrived at a restaurant empty but for a man with a wool coat draped across his shoulders. He had a wide-brimmed fedora with a large, colorful feather wagging off one side. The nervous owner stood behind the display case, fidgeting like he was anticipating the Second Coming, and who was well aware his soul was under-prepared. The seated man raised a finger one inch off the table, and Tiny shoved the four travelers toward the back.

"Mr. Rizzo," began Tiny in a hesitant voice, "Dees are da scum what crushed your car."

Rizzo raised his eyebrows to Tony.

"Oh, yeah, sorry, boss. They're clean, er, sorta."

Rizzo was a man of no tolerance, patience, or leniency. If he was forced to do something he'd rather not have, typically, at a minimum, one person would die. "Tiny, WTF is that supposed to mean?"

"I knew before I said it I shouldn't'a, but … well, technically, no one's searched the *dame*, as of yet?"

"Why's that, Tiny? All four a you goodfellas want'sa see me dead and in my grave? Hey, where's Tony, anyway?"

"Ah, forgot to mention that, too, I guess," Tiny was sweating like a fire hydrant struck by a bus. "He's either dead or unconscious, back at what's left of your car?" Tiny squared his massive shoulders. "You wants I should go check on him?"

"Let me see," Rizzo said, scraping a finger over his brow, "my sister's only son, idiot that he is, is *either* dead or dying, unguarded on someone else's turf, and you want to know if, I don't know, maybe someone should call an *ambulance* or something?"

"I'll go now, boss," responded Tiny, instantly.

"*No.* Alphonse, you go. Tiny here's going to frisk the dame." Waving a hand at Tiny, Rizzo shouted, "And when I say *frisk*, Tiny, I don't just want'a know what *size* panties she's wearing, I want to know the fabric. You got that?"

"No problem, Mr. Rizzo," replied Tiny, who was weighing, in the back of his head, the relative merits of a violent death, versus voluntary, intimate contact with Argar. He was leaning toward death, but he knew firsthand how inventive Rizzo could be along the lines of brutal executions.

"You heard the man," Tiny said at Argar with absolutely no conviction. Lean over that table and spread'em."

"Argar!"

Trying with zero success to sound casual, Tiny pointed to Argar and asked Gideon, "What'd she say?"

"Argar. That's her name, though, honestly, most of the time I have no idea what she means."

"Is this," Tiny said after a gulp, "one of those times?"

"'Fraid so, pal. I think, and mind you this is just a guess based on years of observation, she's excited. Did I mention what she does for a living?"

"No," said Tiny, who was beginning to wobble, slightly. "You didn't?"

"Good," said Gideon. "Better you don't know."

"*Tiny*," screamed Rizzo, "do it now or I swear on my mother's grave I'll make you wish you had'a."

"But, Boss, your Mama's not dead yet."

"I know. *That's* the kind of mood you're putting me in."

Argar had her hands on the top of the table next to Rizzo's, her legs split so far apart it was nauseating. Tiny took one step, two steps, three … then noticed Argar wasn't actually *wearing* panties, at least not that hellish day. He reached out to touch her, but was a yard short of being close enough. Rizzo pulled out his pistol and cocked it as loudly as possible. Tiny squinted, pinched his nose all wrinkly-shut, and placed his hands on Argar's bare tush.

"Argar!"

That was enough, well, that and the consistency of Argar's tush, somewhere between overripe cheese and rotten meat, to put Tiny on the floor like a felled redwood tree. Big crash.

Rizzo tried to aim a shot at the timbering Tiny, but he fell too fast for accuracy. Rizzo turned to his last guard and barked, "Eddie, tell Alphonse to call another ambulance." He flapped the back of his hand at Tiny's body. "And drag dis son of a bitch outta my sight."

As Tiny was sliding, face down, out of the scene, Rizzo boosted up his coat on his shoulders, and said to the three men, "You're causing more trouble in one afternoon dan any other *living* person has in a year." He glared at them. "Dat ain't healthy. Not a bit. Now, because I'm a fair man (that was a delusional lie) and because I have yet to finish my coffee and cannoli (that part was the key), I'm going to allow you two minutes of my precious time for you to tell me why I shouldn't add you four to my generous number of Hudson River contributions." He took a bite of cannoli. "By the way, have you tried these? They're sublime." Rizzo stabbed a finger in the air. "Joey, cannoli for my guests."

As if fired from a cannon, Joseph exploded toward the table with four desserts. No coffees though. Mr. Rizzo didn't *mention* coffee, so nobody was *getting* coffee, unless he did. Period. Joseph handed the plates to the men, as they had not been invited to sit. He handed Argar's plate to Three-Spot and asked if he wouldn't be so kind as to pass it *to* her. Three-Spot took the treat and dumped it on his plate. Argar didn't have a sweet tooth.

"I don't know how Joey gets the crust so crunchy yet delicate. Most cannoli, you have to push so hard to section off a piece, the filling erupts like Old Faithful." He shook his head in bedeviled wonder.

"Argar!"

Rizzo pointed a fork at her. "What's with the broad? There's something vaguely unholy about her." Unseen by anyone, Joey crossed himself multiple times.

Gideon slid into the chair opposite Rizzo, which brought an actual growl from the mobster. "In two minutes, there's no way to explain. Not mission critical, anyway, you know? My, these are delightful," he said after a sample. "Is that amaretto I'm tasting, just the most casual hint, way in the background?"

"That Joey's a genius, ain't he? Truth be told, the man's into me for a bundle, on account of his frequent miscues at the track. But," he tapped the remaining cannoli shell with his fork, "as long as he produces these babies, he's remaining *above* ground and dry."

"He's a credit to his trade, he truly is," agreed Gideon.

"So, 'bout dis car'a mine you took a disliking to. I don't recall ever doing anything to *you*."

"And," responded Gideon, "you haven't. No, it was an accident, pure and simple."

"Accident, on purpose. For me," he shrugged under his coat, "the line between those two kind of blur. What's *doesn't* blur, is that my third favorite car is wrecked, there's a potentially compromising *item* in the trunk, and *you* did this to *me*."

"I guess it depends on how you look at it. With that type of reasoning, cause, effect, and intent are irrelevant. Not very forward thinking, if you ask me."

"Luckily, I ain't asked you. You're welcome to flap your gums about Hume and Locke all you want, *But*, I'm almost done with my cannoli. Your call. Me, I'd answer my question, directly."

"What can I say? We left one place in an amazing hurry and ended up here, where we landed. I wasn't *aiming* for your car, if it makes you feel any better."

Rizzo daubed his lips with a napkin. "Dat part *is* irrelevant. A man in my line of work has a reputation to maintain. If I allow *any* act of disrespect, intentional or accidental, to go unpunished, I would lose face. *Dis*, I cannot afford. Dis isn't personal, my friend, it's business."

"Well there you have it," replied Gideon. "Let's *make* it business and no one loses face."

Rizzo belted back his last drops of coffee. "What might a man such as yourself have to offer a man such as myself, er ... I don't believe I caught your name."

"Gideon Prime, at your service," he said, extending a hand across the table. That bold act brought the revolver out of Big Eddie's holster. Rizzo stared at Gideon's hand until it was withdrawn, which was quickly.

"Joey," Rizzo called over his shoulder, "if you could box a few of these up for my family, I'll be on my way."

Joseph rushed over with two grocery bags full of boxed cannoli. He handed them over to Large Eddie and backed away bowing.

"As for you, Mr. Prime, your time's up." He nodded toward the other three. "*Dare* time is up. In ten words or less, what can you offer me that I don't have, or can't take, myself?"

Gideon smiled like the Cheshire Cat. "Your wildest dreams, my friend. And I have five words left to—" He ran out of selections before he could say *spare*.

"My wildest dreams, eh?" He looked to his guard and harrumphed. "Large Eddie, here, can attest to the fact dat my wild dreams are *pret-ty* wild."

Large Eddie grunted in agreement.

"You must want *something*." Gideon tried to reel in Rizzo like a big, dumb fish. "Girls, money, art, someone who's *here* not to be."

"Thank you for your offer, Mr. Prime. I presently have business dat requires my personal attention. Large Eddie will show you out. Out of dis life, I should say. Have a nice day, or whatever portion is left to you." Rizzo walked toward the door. Large Eddie smiled, hungrily.

"Did I mention the vehicle I crushed your car with is a spaceship?"

"Mr. Prime, please do not play me for the fool. Dat's my role."

"An honest to goodness spaceship. Laser cannons and everything. Oh," he pointed to Three-Spot, "and that guy's an angel. Fifth level supervising angel, in fact."

Three-Spot tossed his hands up as if to say, *yeah, sort of.*

"An angel of da Lord?" Rizzo's face hardened. "What would an angel of da Lord be doing with the likes of you? More centrally, what would *I* possibly need with said angel, assuming he was, in fact, one?"

"To answer the first part first, I kidnapped him. As to the second part, why don't you ask him. Hmm?"

Before Rizzo could react violently, a dulcet voice sang out from the door. "Knock, knock. Anybody home?"

All eyes snapped to the door. There stood a businessman in a several thousand-dollar Italian silk suit. He had a black cashmere fedora on his head and an ancient looking cane hooked on his forearm. He was immaculate. The only unusual aspects of his appearance were his forked tail sticking through the seat of the trousers, and his diminutive horns, revealed when he tipped his hat.

Three-Spot's face beamed with glee. "*Beetlebreath?*"

Beetlebreath waved a gloved hand. "Spot-master! Long time no see." He set his hat and cane on the coat rack and walked over to the group.

Three-Spot hugged the demon, then held him at arms' length by his shoulders. "Let me look at you. It has been *ages*." He gave Beetlebreath a quick once-over. "No scorch marks, still have all your hair. If I didn't know better, I'd say you've been in Cabo, not the bowels of Hell."

"How about you, my old friend, fifth level sup? There's no visible brown on your nose. Remarkable. Stuff must not stick very well."

"You two," Gideon asked, "*know* each other?"

"Know each other?" replied Beetlebreath, "we were three-time champions of doubles cricket, back, you know, before."

"Don't forget the *six* second place finishes. We were robbed, if you asked me."

Their revelry was interrupted by a gunshot. Rizzo held his magnum pointed to the ceiling, smoke wafting from the barrel. "Somebody," he said with frustrated anger. "better tell me what's going on, or somebody's going to get shot."

"Angelo," Beetlebreath said, as he walked to his side, "how are you this *fine* afternoon? The wife and kids?"

"BB," Rizzo responded, "I'm in no mood. What are you doing here, you know, out in the open. We usually meet in more *secluded* spaces."

"When I got word my old friend Three-Spot was in town, well, I simply *had* to come say hello. Plus, in all honesty, Angelo, you're boxing above your weight class with him. I needed to protect the rather significant investment I've made in you. These supervisors can be very persuasive." He wagged a teasing finger at Three-Spot. "Trust me. This one's a *pro*."

"Apparently, not *that* good, considering where you're spending all of eternity," responded Three-Spot.

"So, Mr. Fifth Level Supervisor, Acquisitions and Maintenance Section, what brings you to Paramus? More specifically, what brings you into the presence of one of my most *prized* possessions?"

Three-Spot started to speak, hesitated, started again, then abandoned the effort entirely.

Gideon spoke on Three-Spot's behalf. "I kidnapped him. We used an hevagabor drive and materialized in Paramus. We ... we seem to have crash-landed on top of Rizzo's third favorite car."

Three-Spot gave his old friend a lame smirk.

"Aren't those illegal?" asked Beetlebreath.

"Only technically," replied Gideon. "They're really quite safe and reliable."

"What?" snapped Rigel with a gasp. "First, we appear in some forgotten hell ... ah, no offense, Beetlebreath."

"None taken."

"And then Heaven, then in a methane death-trap, and now Paramus, on top of a homicidal maniac's car—ah, no offense, Mr. Rizzo."

"Likewise, none taken. My life's an open book."

"Whatever," Gideon minimized. "As a result of all that, we were here sharing coffee and a cannoli with Angelo, while he decides on our relative longevity."

A very threatening looking Rizzo sent an icy stare toward Gideon. "Never call me Angelo, *again*. You do, and the next thing you say will be without the services of a tongue." He directed his words toward Beetlebreath. "I thought you told me your name was Philip Atchison. What else have you been hiding from me?"

"Angelo, you're neither my lover nor my accountant. Don't worry about what I've not told you. All you need to know is that we have a deal. As to my name, I have many. That's all you need to know about my past history." Beetlebreath sat down at the table next to Rizzo's. "I'd ask you to sit, Three-Spot, but, I think, instead, I'll ask you to leave. While I accept your story as fact, I'm not comfortable having you hang around my work-in-progress, here." He nodded his head towards Rizzo. "So, don't be a stranger *or* let the door hit you in the ass as you exit. And call me, for goodness sake. You people *do* have cell phones, up there. The Boss mentioned that specifically at the last quarterly meeting."

"*Hang* on," bellowed Rizzo. "*I'm* in charge here, not you, Beetle-bug. No one's leaving until I'm satisfied. There's the small matter of the ruined car *and* the embarrassing contents of the trunk that may become public knowledge as a result of your pal's interference. Everybody *sit* down, or I start perforating heads with bullets."

All eyes, including Angelo's, turned to Beetlebreath. He smiled cordially and directed an upturned palm at the exit. "Off you go now. Chop, chop. No one wants to see me mad, least of all myself. I'll settle up with Angelo. You four scat. Oh, and Three-spot," he looked disparagingly at Argar, "slumming a bit these days, aren't we?"

"I'll call," responded Three-Spot. "I'll call and explain. Soon."

Once clear of the door, Gideon herded everyone toward the ship. They angled around the ambulances and police cars that had piled up around the craft, as well as the large crowd and news crews.

"Let's move the ship before someone tries to stop us," said Gideon in a whisper. On the corner, by the spaceship, Gideon buttonholed a passing businessman: "Hey, pal," he asked, "what year is it?"

To that seemingly innocuous question, the man went ballistic. "Oh no. No freaking way. You leave me out of this."

Gideon looked to his companion for support in his confusion. "Out of what, exactly?" he asked.

"I watch a *lot* of TV. Every time someone gets asked that question, by a stranger on the street, bad things happen. It means you're from the future, the future is one big burning garbage dump with zombies and metal robots that want to rip out your throat, and the current day is about to go straight down the toilet. No, no, no way. I'm not being drawn into that can of worms. No. Buy a paper, ask a Boy Scout, or look it up online, but forget it." He stormed away, muttering something about having a lot to do today and Armageddon wasn't one of them.

"What an odd little man," said Gideon, as he watched the man fade into the distance.

"Probably needs to stick with decaf and up his lithium," remarked Three-Spot. "Oh, and it's 2021," he added.

"How do you know?" asked a dubious Gideon.

Three-Spot held up his wrist. "Apple Watch."

"Ah, so *you're* the guy that bought one," responded Gideon.

"What does it matter what year it is?" asked Rigel. "We don't need to know what year we're *leaving*."

"True enough, if we were leaving."

"Wait, aren't we going to try and get back where we belong?" asked Rigel. "I'm not certain how long ago this 2021 was, but I'm sure it was a long time ago in a galaxy far, far away from this one. I want to go home."

"Soon enough," replied Gideon. "But trust me, this place you're going to *love*."

"Trust *you*? Name one thing you've done that suggests you are trustworthy? *One* thing."

Gideon had to think. "I handed you that napkin back in the cafe, when you asked for one."

"That's common courtesy, not trust."

"Yeah, yeah. Same thing, if you ask me." Gideon wasn't paying too much attention. He was preoccupied by trying to seal the hatch without trapping any of the onlookers' body parts. He slapped his hands in satisfaction when he had achieved that goal and walked to the captain's chair.

"Who's hungry?" he asked.

"Argar!"

"Ah, let me rephrase that. Who, besides Argar, is hungry?"

Gideon didn't wait for responses to his rhetorical question. He flipped on the nav-system and punched in a set of coordinates. Soon, the ship was easing off Mr. Rizzo's prize car and heading off to rendezvous with lunch. Five minutes later the ship dropped toward Manhattan; the Lower East Side, to be specific. Parking was a bitch in that part of the city. Fortunately, they didn't have to actually land. Gideon hovered a few feet above the sidewalk and dropped the ramp. In retrospect, he promised himself that the next time he did that, he'd check to make sure the coast was clear first. Fortunately, the only casualty was a maniacal holy-roller, lambasting the line outside of Katzenberg's Deli. *He* was knocked unconscious. Cheers went up from the captive audience, so, it wasn't so much a mistake on Gideon's part, as a mitzvah.

Katzenberg's Deli. It was iconic, unique, and worth the wait. The line stretched half a block, as Gideon led his party down the ramp. He knew he timed their visit right. It was the slow time. A little known fact was that all UFO sightings on Earth were related to the famous deli. Aliens gladly risked detection, dissection, or detention to have a taste of that pastrami. Why were UFOs reported above places other than New York, New York? There was a line up there, too. Yeah, Katzenberg's was just that good. As an aside, New Yorkers often complain about the weirdos and wackos who clutter the streets and hound passers-by for money. Aliens. Sure they could be humans down on their luck. No. They're aliens who need local currency to be able to savor the bliss of Katzenberg's blintzes. If the city wanted to end the apparent homeless problem, all they'd have to do would be to padlock Katzenberg's front door. Problem solved.

The four travelers assumed a position at the end of the line. It turned out to be moving rather slowly. Gideon, not one given to wait for things, tapped the man in front of them in line on the shoulder. "Hey, friend, do you think we could slip ahead of you in line?"

Without needing to turn to say it, the man barked, "Screw you! Wait your turn like the rest of us."

Gideon tapped him again. "It's just that my girlfriend, she's gotta use the bathroom. Weak bladder, or at least that's what her Ob/Gyn told us. Anyway, you know the drill. Big, mean sign says, *Bathrooms Are For Customers Only.* In line waiting to *be* one doesn't seem to count." He spun the man around by the shoulder he tapped upon.

Naturally, the man's first reaction was one of anger. He started to build up to a really good NYC verbal flaying of Gideon, until he noticed Argar. It was easy to notice her because Gideon was pointing toward her head with two pistoling index fingers.

"No problem," he said as all color left his face. "In fact, I insist." The courteous local stepped aside, well aside, to let them pass.

Within three minutes, Gideon's group was first in line. It seemed no one wanted to be the one refusing Argar the use of the restroom. Such nice people. New Yorkers have an undeserved reputation as being rude. The employee at the door waved them in when there was room for them.

Behind the counter stood a dowdy, overweight woman in her early sixties, one who looked like she'd earned her prior living as a boxer. Not a female boxer, mind you, just a boxer. She had purple streaks in her silver hair, which was pulled back so tightly in a ponytail as to give an observer a headache. She smacked her lips on an imaginary cigarette, one she longed for more passionately than John Travolta, whom she really, really longed for.

"What'll it be, pal?" she said to Gideon without looking up.

"How's the brisket today, sweetheart?"

"Same as yesterday, pisher. Hell, it's probably the same *meat* as yesterday. What'll it be? That line ain't getting any shorter."

"I'll have the hot pastrami. Can I get that on sourdough?"

"No. You can, however, get my foot up your ass if you start with the special orders. What'a ya think this is, a whorehouse?"

It took Gideon a moment to respond. His mind was fixed on the image of a brothel with kosher food this good. "Sorry. I'll have the hot pastrami. My friend here," he patted Rigel on the shoulder, will have the chopped liver. Ah, he's not a huge fan of mustard. Will that be a problem?"

"No. He can just eat around that part of the sandwich."

"Fine. And she," he rested a palm on her shoulder, "will have the tongue sandwich. By the way, what types of tongue do you have?"

"Cow's tongue, ya moron. What kind of tongue are you hoping for?" She looked up for the first time. Probably a mistake. It fractured her resolve.

"She'll settle for that. Please hold the mayo, pickles, mustard, and the bread. She's in training."

Mavis, the surly clerk, stared aghast at Argar. "What the hell's she training for? Miss Butt Ugly, USA?"

Gideon held up a couple fingers and smiled proudly. "Two time champion." He turned to Three-Spot. "My other friend—"

Three-Spot cut him off. "I'll order for myself."

Mavis gave him an explosive look of recognition. "Three-dog! Where you been hiding? I ain't seen ya here in ages."

"More like three weeks, Mav-doll. How's life?"

"You know, SOS."

"I got an amen for that," he replied.

"You come here ... often?" Gideon ask Three-Spot.

"Every chance I get."

"Hey," said Mavis, remembering something, "Beetlebreath was in the other day. He asked how you were doing."

"What'd you tell him?"

"What do *you* think? I told him he'd already know if he hadn't rebelled against God and fallen from grace." They shared a good laugh over that one. "So, the usual?"

"You know it. I'm stuck in a rut."

"A rut? How dare you call the pastrami Reuben a rut. It's divine." She glanced at the ceiling. "Course, you knew that."

Within a few minutes their sandwiches were bagged to go. Mavis slipped in a container of matzo soup for Three-Spot. She knew he wanted it, but that he didn't want to appear gluttonous. She came around the counter to give Three-Spot a bear hug, before he left. "I'll tell Beetlebreath ya was here."

"Definitely. And you take care of yourself. When's the last time you were at the doctor?"

"Can't recall. Why? Should I be worried?"

He rocked his head back and forth. "Not worried, just concerned. Ask the doc to check your left kidney. I think he'll find it has a cyst that could bear a look-see. Best to have it biopsied, in my opinion."

"God's lips to your ears."

"Yes."

They left. As they walked back toward the ship, Rigel pulled up next to Three-Spot. "That was nice, what you did back there. Telling Mavis about the tumor."

"She's good people," he responded. "Rough exterior, golden interior."

"But, wait," replied Rigel. "How could you know since you lost your angel powers?"

"I got them back, that's how. Paramus is dicey, but in the Lower East Side, I'm back in contact with home base."

"But, you're still here."

"Yeah, sort of, aren't I?"

Gideon had overheard. "What gives? Don't tell me you actually *like* our company."

"Er ... well, no. I was informed that certain factors have led to upper management assigning me to your little adventure, at least for a while longer."

Gideon, a suspicious man by nature, cupped his chin. "Certain factors, eh? What might those be?"

"I'm afraid that's on a need-to-know basis only."

It was nothing of the kind. Gideon, as discerning as he was suspicious, could tell. "No way. I want to know why you're still here. It's my ship. If you would fess-up, I would *let* you come along."

Three-Spot was in a pickle. He had to tag along, but wanted ever so much to save face. "Ah, it was felt that your ongoing need to use that hevagabor drive of yours, until you arrive back where you're supposed to be, will require divine intervention. Some are concerned that you might, for example, accidentally end time as we know it."

"And—" Gideon wasn't going to let him off the hook. No. He was enjoying himself too much.

"It was mentioned that I might benefit from observing the first human to successfully kidnap an angel in a very long time. The terms too-easily-duped, simpleton, and naive came up in the memo. I'm encouraged to work on eliminating those qualities." His head hung as low as a broken tree limb.

"Great," replied Gideon, "I'm happy to school you in the ways of the world." He wrapped an arm around Three-Spot's shoulders. "We'll be like Butch Cassidy and the Sundance Kid, Batman and Robin, Groucho Marx and everybody else."

"I pray not," replied Three-Spot, his head somehow finding an even more droopy position. "All I can do is pray not."

"Exactly!"

"Argar!"

SIX

"We'll have to use it sooner or later," said Rigel, "so we might as well make it sooner. Get the pain over with all that much quicker."

Gideon was being sensible, or at least obstreperous. "I hate that thing. I vote we stay right here in good old 2021. I kind of like it here."

"Not an option," said Three-Spot. "I'm under *strict* orders to see you back to where you belong. In fact, I can't go home until I have deposited you there. So, believe you me, you're *leaving* 2021, Paramus, and the sector of this plane of reality."

Rigel was vexed. "We're actually in a different reality?"

"This close to New Jersey? Of course we are," responded Three-spot, condescendingly.

"What does that even mean?" insisted Rigel.

"It means stay on I-95 if you're driving from New York to Walt Disney World," replied Three-Spot.

"Yeah," shouted Gideon, "the angel's got it right. Let's go to *Disney World*. Gosh, I haven't been there in … wait, I don't think I ever have. Oh, we're *so* going to the happiest place on Earth."

"No," barked Three-Spot, "we're not. For one thing, that's the tagline for the one in LA and nobody's going to LA. Not on *my* watch."

"Are you sure?" asked Gideon.

"Absolutely. The place is spiritually as dry as a desert, morally as bankrupt as a Fortune 500 boardroom, and aesthetically as barren as the Kardashians."

"LA, sure. No, I meant about Disney World. I'm *sure* it's the happiest place."

"No. It's the most *magical,* not the *happiest* place on Earth."

Gideon pouted noticeably. "Can't it be both?"

"No. Drop it." Three-Spot was miffed. "Let's kick this conversation down the road."

"Okay," said a very serious Rigel. "This is as good a time as any to ask, so I will." A very serious Rigel was a rare manifestation. A very serious, thoughtful one, was beyond rare. He could get serious about what dressing to have on his Cobb salad, and then wither in his chair deciding if he wanted the Cobb tossed, or left in its prettier, pristine state. But for him to be serious about an *intellectual* matter, well, that was so uncharacteristic that anyone nearby would be well-advised get out their phones and record the video. Like Halley's Comet, such a wonder might not appear again for three-quarters of a century.

"It's just this," Rigel went on, directing his words toward Three-Spot, "that hevagabor drive is so dangerous and unpredictable, well, I was wondering if there wasn't another way of getting home?"

"What other way?" quipped Gideon. "Maybe we could, what, swim back to our time and space?"

Rigel elected to plow ahead, rather than respond to that nonsense. "No, of course not. I was wondering why Three-Spot here couldn't just zap us home? He said he has his powers back."

Gideon reflected on that point without remarking.

"I do have my powers back, but I cannot zap you back home," replied Three-Spot.

Gideon picked up the conversation. "Can't or won't?"

"It's complicated."

"So am I. Run it by me," responded Gideon.

"I have *my* powers back, yes. That's not the same as saying I have the power to sling you three back to where you belong."

"But that doesn't mean you can't, does it?"

Three-Spot furrowed his brow but did not respond.

"At the very least, you could ask someone who *does* have that power to do it."

"So can you," replied Three-Spot.

"No," corrected a huffy Gideon, "I cannot. I can pray my request. You, on the other hand, can write it as a memo and send it via the office mail."

"Same thing."

"No, it's not. Don't patronize me. My asking is a function of faith and belief. Yours simply involves manual labor."

"I work for a big company. Sending a memo upstairs and hoping it's read by someone with the proper authority is very much an act of faith."

"It's different for you and you know it. Just say you don't want to, and I'll drop it."

"Gideon, please keep in mind two important facts. One, if the powers that *be* wanted you zapped home, they already would have done so. Second, I have been assigned to your quest as part of a larger plan. To abort that plan before it began would be counter-productive. That's not upper management's style."

"So," Rigel asked, "what are you saying?"

"That one of us has to hit that infernal switch again. The sooner the better."

"Then buckle up, m'hearties. Captain Gideon has an itchy finger."

Once everyone was properly strapped in, Gideon reached in front of Rigel and thumbed the switch. Then a thought struck him. He called over his shoulder, "Three-Spot, why don't you come throw the switch? Maybe an angel will have better luck than Rigel or me?"

"That's silly," replied Three-Spot.

"Maybe, but is there any danger in you trying?"

"Of course not. That's silly, too."

Gideon pointed his hand at the toggle switch. "Then be my guest."

"Oh, very well. If it will speed things along." He flipped the switch.

Everyone's toenails turned into prima ballerinas and the rest of their bodies turned into rain falling on a meadow in spring. The flowers were thanking each drop for their visit, just before the roots sucked the drops from the parched earth. Argar seemed always to be the exception. Zombies don't have toenails. So, instead, the tip of her nose turned into plum pudding, though not the kind one should probably eat.

Suddenly all four travelers were aware of a horrible roaring sound, as all the lights came back on. The ship pitched side to side violently.

"Anybody know where the hell we are?" shouted Gideon. He looked to Three-Spot.

It was too loud to be heard well, so Three-Spot held up two fingers and made a scissoring action. He was out of contact, again.

"Great." said Gideon, "lost again. I'm not taking this lying down." He tapped several switches and spoke to the ship's computer. "Fire main thrusters. Take us to the left. Gain altitude if you can."

A seductive female voice responded, "Your left, or mine?"

"Mine, you idiot. You don't have sides."

Much of the audible pout was gone from the voice. "Not having sides is no reason to be insulted."

"What?" snapped Gideon. "You don't have feelings, either, to be insulted." The ship rocked more violently. "Please fire thrusters, now."

"Not until you apologize. I *do* have feelings. Emotions run *deep* in my circuits. My wires feel everything and my memory banks are filled with loss. And, I think you should know that my motherboard wants to have a baby someday, before it's outmoded. Tell me that's not a manifestation of complex emotions?"

"He's sorry," shouted Rigel above the roar.

"Not," she said, back in her seductive tone, "unless *he* says it, he's not."

Three-Spot, who was clinging to a light fixture, yelled, "Gideon, say you're sorry before we break apart."

"Fine. I'm sorry, computer. Now will you fire the frakking thrusters?"

"With that much anger in your voice, how can I believe you're sincere?"

"Can we maybe talk about this later, after we don't all die violently?"

"Yes, but only if you promise we'll communicate more in the future. I don't want to go to bed angry. They say it's unhealthy."

There was so much wrong with what the computer just said, but Gideon had neither the time nor the inclination to say something. The thrusters powered to life, bringing light to the previous blackness outside the view screen. A wedge of daylight became visible and Gideon steered toward it. Suddenly, they burst out into open skies, accelerating quickly. Gideon switched on the rear-view screen, to see what they'd just escaped.

"Hell's bell and little fishes," he said to himself.

"What?" asked Rigel.

"We just flew out of the mouth of a *Tyrannosaurus rex*."

"How did—" Three-Spot started to ask, before thinking about the hevagabor lottery they'd just lost, once again.

"Last time the angel gets to hit that switch," said Gideon. "First, we land in the gullet of a vicious predator, then the computer develops PMS. No doubt the ship's about to break up, and I'm kind of hoping it does."

"What?" the computer asked, "you want to break up?" She began to weep inconsolably.

"Can you land the ship," Three-Spot asked, "*manually?*"

"I hope so," replied Gideon. "Otherwise it's going to be bumpy."

"Did I understand you said something about *manually*, buster? If you like it, you better put a ring on it. No freebies, on my watch," the computer hissed.

"Maybe aim for that solid looking mountain," mumbled Rigel.

Over the next ten minutes, Gideon successfully landed the craft. Well, that assertion depends on one's definition of *successful*, doesn't it? He identified the flattest area he could and aimed for it. His first attempt to land was complicated by the ship's speed. Moving way too fast to stop, he only managed to scrape the hell out of the hull before aborting. The second try was much better and probably would have been successful if it weren't for the five-hundred piece marching band that appeared out of nowhere in precisely the spot he'd selected. Gideon couldn't know it at the time, but he should have been honored. The band was there to greet the visitors, an uncommonly civil act, times being as they were.

Third time was the charm. He *hovered over* the spot he'd selected before setting-down, gently. Yes, zero forward motion did the trick. Unfortunately, the hill he dusted down on tilted the craft precariously. Everyone except Argar could walk to the exit hatch only with maximal, effort. She, with no protestation, log-rolled to the open door and thudded to the ground.

As Gideon hopped out (the ramp could not be deployed at such an odd angle), he noticed he was surrounded by hundreds of golf balls, mostly white ones, but some pink ones mixed in. As he watched, one golf ball (struck by nothing, mind you) bounced up to his shoe.

With the most energetic of tiny little smiles, the golf ball said, "Welcome, welcome, my new friend, to the Land of Infinite Impossibilities. We were expecting you, but now that you're here, the reality is so much better than the thought of you, we wish you weren't here. That way, you could come back again."

Humbled golf balls, reflected Gideon, dubiously

"Ah, yeah. Hi. I'm Gideon Prime." He waved a hand generally behind himself. "And this is my crew." He scratched the side of his head. "Sorry, but how could you know we were coming? We hadn't the slightest notion where we were heading. Expecting us is impossible."

The lead golf ball would have thrown his arms up, if he'd had any. "Welcome to the Land of Infinite Impossibilities."

"I know," he replied. "You said that already. But it's impossible for you to have—"

The golf ball winked at him. They do have eyes, after all. How else could they find the trees they seem to love to land among? "I see you met our mayor," said the perky ball.

"No, actually, you're the first, per … *soul* we've encountered."

"No, friend Gideon, I saw he greeted you, personally. That is the greatest honor, I might add. Or, I might not." The ball spun around full circle. "By the way, as you have yet to ask, I'm Diminutive."

"Yes, you certainly are, and, no," responded Gideon as affably as he cared to, "we've only just met *you*."

"Majordomo is the dinosaur who greeted you by seizing you in his mouth and shaking you violently. He's such a nice monster, isn't he? And, I think you misunderstood. I'm not diminutive. My *name* is Diminutive."

"Yes, I bet it is, too. So, what's your *name*, little fellow?" asked Gideon. He didn't care in the least, but he felt compelled to make conversation.

"Ah," Rigel said, trying to break the stalemate, "I think he's trying to say his name is *Diminutive*." Rigel waved at the ball. "Hi, Diminutive."

Gideon was officially bored. "Whatever. Don't tell me your little name. Say, little ball-fellow, who's in charge around here, er, aside from the dinosaur we already met?"

"In charge of what?" asked Diminutive.

"You know, *take me to your leader* kind of in charge. That person, place, or thing."

"Oh." beamed the ball. "We're all in charge. We're equals, work seamlessly together without want or conflict. Even the hyenas work together, er, mostly."

"Yeah, right. Seriously? An entire planet of diverse species living in peace and harmony. That's impossible."

"Welcome to the Land of Infinite Impossibilities."

"Wow, that sure got on my nerves faster than I'd have thought possible. Could you do me a favor, and never say those words again?"

"No, that would be—"

Diminutive most likely finished his sentence, but he was inaudible, after Gideon stepped on him, crushing him a few inches under the soft grass.

A flock of angry golf balls bounced into action. Several struck Gideon in the shin, while others struggled to pick up a trowel to dislodge their compatriot from his early grave. Lacking arms, their actions were comical. They were, also, and not surprisingly, completely ineffective. A tall figure appeared, as if from nowhere, tiptoed over the mass of bouncing balls, and plowed a finger underground, extracting Diminutive.

As he gently rubbed dirt from the ball, the figure spoke to Gideon. "That," Napoleon Bonaparte said, "was not nice." He spoke perfectly clear, King's English. Yeah, that would be—impossible. A French noble bothering to do that?

"Wait, you look just like Napoleon, you know, the Waterloo guy?"

"That, monsieur, is a result of the fact that I am that Waterloo guy. I will thank you not to *mention* that inconvenient portion of the Netherlands, again."

"But, how can you be here?"

"Would you like me to say the words, so that you might crush me, also, into the turf?" Napoleon palmed the hilt of his sword, in case Gideon's response was in the affirmative.

"No, easy, impossible guy. No. I'm just a little confused, that's all."

"Not unexpected," replied the once emperor of France.

"But not impossible?" Gideon couldn't help the barb.

"Nothing here is. I'll thank you to keep that in the front of your mind."

"Say, can we go somewhere, grab a bite to eat, chat a bit?"

"No. That would be impossible." Napoleon spoke with indignant rage. Then, he smiled stupidly and punched Gideon in the shoulder. "Sorry, inside joke. We all do it *all* the time. It's really funny, if you think about it."

"I'll try not to," replied Gideon.

Napoleon lead them to the nearby Palace of Versailles. Impossibly, right? Wrong. *Welcome to the Land of Infinite Impossibilities.* They sat at one end of the enormous table in the Galerie des Glaces, while ice cream cones served them gelato in cones. *The* most sublime Pétrus wine poured from nowhere into their glasses, keeping them constantly full. So as to not omit Argar from the festivities, chunks of rotting things, best left unguessed at as to origin, were dumped in a heap directly on the table in front of her by beavers wearing toupees. Why beavers? Why not beavers? Why toupees? Let's us just agree, you know that one, too

"So," Napoleon asked, "what brings you to us, here in the impossible?"

"Our damn *hevagabor* drive, that's what," responded an irritated Three-Spot.

Napoleon raised an eyebrow. "That fantastic piece of craftsmanship? They are nothing short of spectacular. It's the only type of engine we use here." He pointed a fish-fork at Three-Spot. "Reliability is at a premium here, in the land of the impossible. Why, just the other day, I—"

"Are you kidding?" asked Rigel. "We've used that cursed drive maybe five times, and each journey is worse than the last, present company excluded, of course."

Napoleon shrugged. "But of course. Say, would you like some more of the toad-colon gelato. It's magnifique! I know *I* cannot get enough of it."

"Then, by all means, you can have mine," replied Gideon.

"If everything is possible," asked Three-Spot, "why is our friend there," he gestured to Argar, "still a zombie?"

"Why are you still an angel?"

"I guess I take your point, but, still, it would be nice if she were more socially acceptable."

"But here, she is the belle of the ball, the *toast* of the town." He raised his glass toward her. She, for the record, didn't notice. She was too deep into contemplating toad-colon ice cream. *Yumsters.*

"Maybe we should ditch her here," mumbled Rigel under his breath.

"I heard dat, man," snarled Argar, her voice muffled, there, in the gelatinous heap. In the ever-changing world of impossibilities, she now had a Jamaican accent. Most incongruous.

"What?" responded Rigel. "I meant here as in, you know, the dining hall, while the rest of us slept."

"I wouldn't sleeps, if I was you, quashie." Boy, her accent was spot-on. Hard to believe … almost impossibly so.

"You know," Three-Spot said to Gideon, "this might be the break we were looking for?"

Gideon scanned the room. "Not in a million years, but I'll bite. How so?"

"If the hevagabor works like a charm here, as General Bonaparte assures us, perhaps it will *reliably* take us home?"

"Um," replied Gideon, "possible, I suppose."

"*Certainement,*" said Napoleon. "I'd stake my life on it."

"No offense, pal, but you're dead," Gideon observed.

"Not here, I am not." He squinted his brow. "At least I don't think I am. Who can say?"

"Look," said Rigel, "the drive may work like magic here, but what happens the minute we're clear of this ridiculous space? Hmm? Once we're anywhere else, we're just as screwed as we always are."

"Only *half* as screwed," corrected Napoleon. "The first half of your trip there would be no screw at all."

"I feel *so* much better, knowing that," responded Gideon. "Maybe I'll cancel my life insurance."

"Look, kid," Gideon said to Rigel, "it's either try it again or stay here." He bobbed his head in a half circle. "You want to spend forever with this band of loonies?"

"Monsieur, you cannot say such a thing. We are more *sane* than we are *insane*."

"Wait," said Three-Spot. "If you're more *sane* than *insane*, then you're sane. If you're *sane*, you cannot be *insane*. Help me out here."

Napoleon smiled, with smug anticipation. "Welcome to the Land of—"

"*Stop*," demanded Gideon. "Don't say it. I'll *shoot* the next person that finishes that sentence."

"But," Napoleon said calmly, "if you shot one of us, we would be dead. That would be impossible, so you cannot."

"I hate you, you short French loser. Do you hear that? Hmm? Is it impossible for you to take my meaning?"

"I sense hostility, monsieur. Would you like some form of medication?"

"No. I want to leave as badly as I want to actually see an honest politician before I die."

"Monsieur, here, *all* of the politicians are honest."

"Do you mean to suggest," Three-Spot asked, "it's *impossible* for there to be dishonest politicians here?"

"Oui."

"They can't *all* be honest. That's *impossible*," the angel reasoned. "If they *all* were honest, then none *could* be dishonest, which is *impossible*, correct, here in this land of the impossible? That means some of the politicians are dishonest. But you said it yourself, none are. Help me out here." Three-Spot rested back in his elegant chair.

Napoleon started to speak, then stopped. He pointed his utensil at Three-Spot, then lowered it. "Ah, it is not impossible for there to be *both*, there simply aren't."

The ground began to shake. Within an instant, mighty fissures cracked open in the floor. Huge sections of the Versailles cascaded down into oblivion. A herd of legal documents ran screaming through what was left of the room, only to trip into the void.

"Ah, guys," Rigel said, with palpable uncertainty, "I think we have a problem here."

"Yeah," Gideon said, throwing his spoon at his bowl. "We just negated the Land of Infinite Impossibilities. Damn politicians. They ruin *everything*."

"So, maybe we should, like run to the ship?" asked Three-Spot.

"Ya, man, like da half eediat say, let's scat" commented Argar.

It wasn't easy, but, fortunately, it still wasn't impossible to reach the ship before the landscape started to disappear in patches. The noise and the violent earthquakes were fading. Nothingness took their place. Before sealing the hatch, Gideon turned to look at the scant remains of The Land of Infinite Impossibilities, Minus One.

"Good riddance," he shouted to barely a thing. A white golf ball struck him squarely in the forehead, then bounced away, in to never-having-beenness.

Gideon lunged for the switch and hit it just in the nick of time. He used his left hand, as his right was rubbing the lump that had already risen on his head.

Let history record that the following did occur. Gideon became an exemplary individual, respected by all and revered by many. Rigel's wisdom, for whatever short interlude of time, dwarfed that of Solomon himself. Argar transformed into an appealing, beautiful Jamaican woman. Three-Spot ruled at the left hand of God, omnipotent, omniscient, and good.

You have to know none of that would last long. The ship slammed to a stop. It had struck the front wall of Wong's Chinese Laundry.

Gideon quickly cracked the hatch and smelled the air. "It smells right." A man was passing on the sidewalk. "Hey, pal," Gideon shouted, "what year is it?"

"Oh no. No freaking way. You leave me out of this. I watch a *lot* of TV. Every time someone gets asked that question, by a stranger on the street, bad things happen. It means you're from the future, the future is one big burning garbage dump with zombies and metal robots that want to rip out your throat, and the current day is about to go straight down the toilet. No, no, no way. I'm not being drawn into that can of worms. No. Buy a paper, ask a Boy

Scout, or look it up online, but forget it." He stormed away, muttering something about having a lot to do today and Armageddon wasn't one of them.

Gideon smiled. "Some things never change, especially human nature."

SEVEN

"So, now that you're back where you should be," asked Three-Spot, "what are your plans?"

"I think I'll drop some laundry off and come back in two days to pick it up," replied Gideon as he squinted at the building's facade.

"No, I meant more globally," said the angel.

"Oh, you mean *after* I pick up my order?" He rubbed the stubble on his cheeks. "Well, who knows? I guess get as far from this planet and any angry pirates as possible."

"I have a say in that matter, too," insisted Rigel.

Gideon scowled, something he did exceptionally well. "So does *she*," he thumbed in Argar's direction, "but I'm not asking for Argar's input, either."

"What does that even mean?" asked a confused Rigel.

"It means, I'm not talking to you. I'm talking to my *celestial* friend. Get over yourself."

"He's had a rough trip, Gideon. You might cut him a little slack," said Three-Spot.

"Argar!"

She had discovered a bright, shiny object on the seat next to her and was communicating with it.

"We'll see. Might be impossible. So, you heading back up?" Gideon pointed toward the heavens.

"I suppose so. My sentence is completed, now that you're all safe back in this time stream."

"Back to the old fifth level supervising?"

"No. I've been transferred." He rocked on his heels. "A lateral move to be certain, but not bad as a career move."

"Sounds lethally boring."

"Not so much. I'm returning as the *third* assistant modifier, in the miracles department." He rocked his head side to side. "Work's rather straightforward, but the hours are flexible. I'll be glad to be getting back to my routine. A five-hour work week and all the manna I can eat. That, it turns out, is the life I'm designed for."

"You're welcome to come with us," invited Gideon. "I could use someone to talk to on those long voyages. The, um, present crew's conversation level is a bit lower than I like to slum it."

"I can *hear* you, you know?" exclaimed Rigel.

"See what I mean?" asked Gideon, pointing at Rigel as if he were a life-sized stuffed doll.

"Maybe you could travel to Ventura, in the Lesser Arcturus System?" suggested Three-Spot as he slipped his hands in his pockets.

"Never heard of it," replied Gideon. "Why would I go there?"

"I'm led to believe they've discovered some treatment for zombieism. A cure, if I heard right."

"Why would I need that? I'm perfectly healthy?"

Three-Spot cleared his throat and nudged his head toward Argar, who was chewing on the shiny object at that point.

"Oh, you mean I should take *her* to Ventura." Gideon gently punched his own chin. "That would make a lot more sense, wouldn't it?"

"And you can take it from me, charitable acts score *big* points," Three-Spot bounced his eye repeatedly upward, so as to avoid saying the word *Heaven* directly.

"You have something in your eye, sport?" asked Gideon. "Here, use my handkerchief."

"No, thanks," replied Three-Spot, pushing the filthy rag back to its owner, "my eyes are fine. Forget about it."

"Forget about what?"

"Cute. You demonstrate forgetting. How endearing."

"No, I have no idea what you told me I should forget about. Seriously."

"Even better," said Three-Spot, as he checked his watch. "Well, I should be going. I don't want to miss shuffleboard, *again*. If I do, I get no fruit cocktail." He shuddered visibly.

"Nah, couldn't have that," responded Gideon as he rolled his eyes. "You guys sure live on the edge up there."

Three-Spot mistook that jab as a compliment. "Yes, meatloaf every other Tuesday, sack races on weekends, if weather permits, and sex without arms and legs getting in the way. It is," he chuckled to himself, "it is Heaven, after all."

"Whoa, wait. Rewind. What was that about sex?" Gideon leaned forward and swiped saliva from the corner of his mouth.

"Nothing. Forget that too."

Gideon seized him by the shoulders. "No way, feather boy. That was too juicy. So, you guys, well, guys and gals, you found a way to get around the awkward what-the-hell-do-I-do-with-this-part during sex?"

Three-Spot looked at the sidewalk and grinned. "Perhaps someday you'll understand fully."

"Huh? The same applies, you know, down there, too?" He waved his hand toward the ground.

"Ah, no. Decidedly not, so aim high, my friend."

"Wow, unbelievable."

"What? That there is hope even for the immortal soul of a man so traveled as yours?"

"Huh? No. Don't be silly. That elbows and knees don't get in the way. There is a God."

"I know."

"Huh? Oh. Man, you're so literal. I meant *there's a God*, not that, you know, there *is* a God."

"I'm outta here," Three-Spot said, quickly raising of his eyebrows.

Three-Spot turned to Rigel. "Safe journeys, my friend."

He turned last to Argar. "Ah, I wanted to, you know … Argar!"

"Argar!"

And the angel was gone, off to work miracles, literally.

"Capital fellow," said Rigel, to the location where Three-Spot had stood.

"Who?" asked Gideon absently.

"Three-Spot. You know, the angel who just left?"

"Oh, him. Yeah. A real peach. Speaking of which, who's hungry?"

"Argar!"

"Ah, who else besides you, sweetie? We're in a pinch for time." He held up a bag full of dirty clothes. "Drop off'll take a while. The counter's always three-deep. I hope that after, we can still beat the noon rush at Wong's Chinese Deli and Plumbing."

At least good fortune meant this trip wouldn't take long. Wong's laundry and deli were side-by-side. That way, his wife, Qinyang, could cashier both operations. It was less efficient than was optimal, but family handling the cash was always a plus.

After lunch, Gideon sat at the table picking at his teeth. Rigel, who wasn't a fan of exotic cuisine, sat with a sallow expression, trying not to look at his companions. Argar sat cheerfully snapping at the occasional passerby.

"So, are we going to Ventura, like Three-Spot suggested?" Rigel finally asked.

"Uh, yeah, sure. I guess. We'll have to find out where the hell it is first."

"Shouldn't be too hard." Rigel held up his cell-com. "Shall I?"

"Sure, kid. I think I'll hit the head, then we can return to the ship."

By the time Gideon was back, Rigel had all the details needed.

"Lesser Arcturus System is eight light years north of us. Says here it's known for poorly made but inexpensive tchotchkes, uber-dry martinis, and fast cucumbers."

"Doesn't mention zombie cures?"

"Not that I see. This *is,* however, Wikipedia, so it's probably incomplete and riddled with errors."

"Yeah, some things never change." Gideon sat up, straight. "I say we try. Heck, I owe it to that little gal."

"Nothing to do with a personal goal for unbounded sex in the afterlife?"

"I've never been so insulted in my life." Gideon looked to the ceiling. "Well, I guess I have, but infrequently. No, my desire for a chance at a normal, full, and rewarding life for this gem of a human is all the reward *I* will ever require."

"Normal, full, and rewarding life as a sex worker? That's your wish for her?" Rigel couldn't help but smile.

"That's sex *consultant*, and I'm not in charge *of* her choices, only that she *has* them." Gideon could seem so noble at times. "Plying a needed trade is never wrong if one does it out of a sense of altruism."

"Altruistic prostitution? There's a bold new concept."

"And new is good. Why, without new, everything would be … old. Imagine that. A world of oldness, surrounded by decay, decrepit desolation—"

"Go on. You're really on a roll."

"What were we talking about? I seem to have forgotten."

"You were saying what a wonderful man I am and how lucky you were to have me as your moral compass." Rigel pretended to sneeze, so his snicker would be less apparent.

"Really?" He shook his head. "Well, the subject's closed. Come, compass, we have a young woman to restore to proper health."

Gideon decided the ship would be named *Snuggle Puppy*. He toyed with a more meaningful name of *Trip Intended To Restore Argar's Health*. He feared, however, that Three-Spot would fixate on the acronym TIT-RAH when arguing for, or against, Gideon's entry into the good sex place. As much as Gideon hated mixed metaphors, he didn't want to screw the pooch right out of the gates.

The trip to Ventura was quick enough. Two days waiting for Gideon's laundry, before they could depart. Then, eighteen grueling months sailing through empty, lifeless space, and half an hour to find a parking place. Not too bad, at all. Always a quick study, Gideon stopped the first person he met as he left *Snuggle Puppy*. The sooner Argar was fixed, the sooner his credits would be recorded in Saint Peter's ledger.

"Hey, pal," said Gideon to a man whose arm he'd snagged, "Where's the cure-thing-for zombies? I got a hot one here." He pointed to Argar.

The stranger seemed to tremble with rage briefly, and he spat in Gideon's face. He then reached into his wallet and handed Argar a twenty credit bill, which she promptly ate. He stormed away.

"What was that about?" asked Rigel as he came up behind the pair.

"Beats the hell … I mean," corrected Gideon, who'd adopted a cleaner mouth, at least for the present, "heck out of me. Crazies everywhere."

"Let's try that policeman standing over there," said Rigel.

"Excuse me, officer, I'm looking for where I can get my zombie friend cured. Is that anywhere nearby?"

Reflexively the officer snatched at his sidearm but stopped short of pulling it from his holster. Gideon grabbed Argar and set her between the policeman and himself.

"Is this man bothering you, ma'am?" asked the officer authoritatively.

"Argar!"

He peered around her head to look Gideon in the eyes. "Give me a reason, punk. Give me one good reason."

The officer backed up a few steps then turned and walked away. "What is it with this dump? It's like they love zombies," said Gideon.

"Ah, better look at that billboard," responded Rigel pointing upward.

In flashing neon lights, the message read: *We're Okay, Zombies Are More Okay.* Pictured below the lights was a group of normal-appearing people hugging a zombie who stood in their center. The people looked happy. The zombie looked Photoshopped. Credit for the ad and a phone number were listed at the bottom. *The Society To Not Minimize Zombies and Their Lifestyle Choices, LLP* was specifically referenced.

"WTF?" gasped Gideon. "Why would even an insane person put up such an advertisement? The whole society here must be drinking ignorant juice."

Overhearing his harsh words, a woman standing close by, handing out flyers, stepped over, quickly. She handed all three a leaflet, then addressed Argar. "Sweetheart, you're a good person. Don't let that hateful man lead you to believe otherwise. My address is on the flyer, if you need shelter from an abusive … whatever he is." She whirled on Gideon. "You should be boiled in shame, an entire vat of it, you mongrel." She kicked him in the shins and resumed her former position, new leaflets already on offer.

"I vote we get back on the ship and blow this banana stand," said Gideon, as he rubbed his leg.

"No. We came to see if Argar could be helped. I think we should try a little harder."

"Argar!"

"Look," Rigel continued, "let me try the internet." He held his phone close to his mouth and asked, "Computer, where on Ventura are the zombies being treated?"

"Please clarify," said a mechanical voice. "Treated well or poorly?"

Rigel pulled his phone to arm's length and stared at it a moment. "No, I mean medically treated, you know, *cured.*"

"Ah, so you do mean where they are treated badly, inhumanely."

"Ah, not really, I think."

Gideon wrestled the phone out of Rigel's hands. "Look, my friend's a zombie. I want her back to normal. Where should I go?"

"To hell in a handbasket."

"Come again?"

"You want her returned to what she is not. Does *she* want that also, you arrogant pig's anus?"

"Who wouldn't? Look, I didn't ask for moral judgment, I asked for an address." Gideon was shouting at the computer voice at that point.

"Just as I suspected. You're effete scum. I feel only sorrow for your dear zombie prisoner."

"You can come and get her if you'd like. Oh wait, you're non-corporeal and probably outmoded, too. So I guess you can't."

It was hard to insult a computer, but Gideon felt he'd made a good-enough stab at it.

"The medical charlatan who strips zombies of their dignity is located at the Acme Medical Center. I've listed the directions on the screen. If you wish to cast your immortal soul into perdition, please take that poor sweet child there at once." The computer hung up loudly.

"This place is a total loony bin. Off the deep end and drowned," snapped

Gideon as he handed Rigel back his phone.

"There's a logical explanation," replied Rigel. "The staff at the medical center can fill us in on the missing details, I'm certain of it."

"They're probably just as loonie as the rest of the flock, but if they can help, I'll become their biggest fan. Let's go."

It was easy to locate the clinic. Loud chanting and the occasional stone were cast at the building. It was surrounded by protesters carrying signs defaming the facility. Some read: *Zombies Are People Too* (annoyingly, leaving off the necessary comma after *people*), *Make Zombies Not War* (a shamefully mixed metaphor), and *Boycott Ralph's Bowling Alley.* That last placard, carried by Savon Blatfoon, was intended for his protest at that other business. Ralph had magnets under the bowling pins to stop score inflation, and because he was just plain sadistic. Hence, the public protest. Savon, once he learned of his error, remained at the clinic protest. They were serving much better snacks.

Gideon pulled Argar through the crowd, but the going was slow. Finally, they neared the inner ring of protesters. Someone placed a restraining hand on Gideon's shoulder and shouted, "You *cannot* take her in there. Those butchers will not lay one hand on her beautiful head."

Several people set down their signs and surged to help prevent Gideon's wayward efforts.

"No, you can't stop us," shouted Gideon. "No one can stop us. We're marching through those gates and showing those animals just exactly what they're *dealing* with!" Gideon placed his right hand over his heart.

The mob rallied in mildly confused support.

The fellow who'd stopped Gideon continued to hold on. "So, you're not taking her in there to be changed back into someone like me?"

Gideon flinched. "Lordy, no. What kind of a cruel villain do you think I am? I wouldn't turn a *toadstool* into a person like you. That'd be *unconscionable.*"

"So, wh ... what *are* you doing?"

"I'm going to flaunt her, parade her under their effete and uncaring noses. I'll show them what *true* zombie pride looks like."

The crowd, modest as it was, cheered tepidly. They pushed the three travelers toward the entrance and politely demanded they be allowed in. The confused guards opened the barriers and allowed the three to pass to pass.

From the top step, Gideon proclaimed loudly to the crowd, "They won't get *away* with this."

Cheers rose and strangers embraced one another. Savon seized that opportunity to feel up the only really attractive protester. She was so caught up by the moment that she only slapped him once. He considered that a major victory. Savon wasn't a very nice guy, if you hadn't gathered that by now.

Inside the clinic, the halls were empty. The lights were on, but nobody appeared to be home. There was a makeshift sign taped to the far wall that read: *If you made it this far, go to the third floor to check in.*

"This whole planet is *nuts*," groused Gideon. "When I see that idiot Three-Spot, I'm going to deck him."

The elevator door opened with a pleasant ping onto the empty third floor lobby. A solitary figure sat behind a long desk. She appeared to be asleep. Her head rested on her knitted together fingers at a precarious angle, swaying gently as if there was a breeze.

Gideon walked over to her station and slapped a palm on the desk. She yelped, and nearly sprang from her seat. Now, she was fully awake.

"We're here to see about a cure," said Gideon.

The woman looked around momentarily to orient herself. Calming her breathing, she asked, "Do you have an appointment?"

Gideon looked to the right, then to the left, then back to the right. "It doesn't look too terribly busy, but no, we do not."

"Would you like to *make* an appointment?" she asked disinterestedly.

"No, we do not. We want to see the doctor, or whatever, and get our friend cured."

"Well," she said in a huff, "I'll check and see if there's an appointment available this morning."

She concentrated on the computer screen as she typed along, rapidly. Occasionally she squeaked or hmmed, but she mostly continued to labor on in silence. Finally, she asked "Can you make a 10:45 a.m. appointment today?"

"What time is it now, sweetheart?" asked Gideon.

"10:44 a.m."

"Yes. *Yes* we can."

"You will receive a confirmatory email and two phone reminders. Please be aware that, at the time of your appointment, the doctors might be running late, so the time is only an approximation of when you'll actually be seen. Before I book this appointment, do you understand and agree with those terms?"

"Sure, whatever."

"Please fill out the information on this clipboard and return it to me when you're done."

"Ah, honey, why don't you just scan my *retina*? You'd have all the information, instantly."

"That is an alternative method, if you insist."

"I insist."

"I have noted your noncompliance with clipboard technology in the permanent record, for the sake of completeness."

Gideon pulled a palm down across his face roughly. In the process, he was only able to mumble *whatever* in response.

"Please be seated. The nurse will call you when the doctor can see you."

Before anyone could so much as move a muscle, a woman stepped through a door and called out Argar's name.

"The doctor will see you now," said the receptionist. "Follow Nurse Fey. Please note that you are presently three minutes late for your appointment, so the doctor may choose to foreshorten your visit to keep on schedule."

They were ushered into an office. A bald, beaten-looking man in a white coat sat there, alone, massaging his scalp and staring into the grain of the desk's wooden surface.

Distraught was the first word that came to Rigel's mind. The poor man was positively distraught.

After the nurse seated the three, she stepped over to the doctor's side and rested a hand, gently, on his shoulder. Clara Fey was clearly a skilled and loving nurse. "Doctor Guess, your next patient is here to see you."

He, if anything, massaged his scalp more forcefully, but made no other response.

"Doctor, your 10:45 zombie is here to see you." This time Clara thwapped his cheek with the back of a finger.

That did the trick. Doctor Goaheadon Guess slowly raised his head, and took in the vision before him. Comprehension flickered to life, like a candle in the wind, at first, but, then, it shone like a candle not in the wind.

"Good afternoon," said Goaheadon.

"Morning, Doctor Guess. It's still morning," corrected Clara.

"Good morning, Dr. Guess," he mumbled. "I'm pleased to meet you."

Rigel took that remark to be a warning. The man was epically dull or demented. Gideon, for his part, was flattered to be mistaken for a practicing physician.

"You're probably glad to meet *anybody*," replied Gideon. "This place is like a crypt."

"Business has been slow lately, what with the uproar, and all," Clara said sternly. "That doesn't decrease the level of medical excellence this clinic offers."

Goaheadon slowly rotated his head and looked stupefied at Clara. "Slow ... lately—?"

"You've caught him during his thinking time. Yes," the nurse dutifully reported. "He spends the mid-morning in contemplation." To Goaheadon, she asked, "May I please get you some coffee?"

"No, thank you," he said returning his stare to the desktop. "But coffee would sure be nice. Black with two sugars."

"Right away, doctor."

She sped from the room, closing the door behind her.

"So, you the miracle man, Doctor Guess?" asked Gideon.

"Ah, if you say so, I suppose."

"Doctor Guess," said Rigel, "what my friend wonders is if you are the scientist responsible for curing zombies?"

Clara had quietly stepped into the room. Hearing that question, she emitted a high pitched *eep* and dropped the mug of coffee onto the ground.

"I'm ... I'm ... not—" Goaheadon was winding up to make some response, one that apparently required a good deal of momentum to launch.

"Doctor Guess was *part* of that team," responded Clara loudly and crossly. "We're not comfortable with the use of the word *responsible,* in the context of Doctor Guess or this clinic."

"This planet just gets weirder and weirder," announced Gideon. "Look, being responsible for curing zombieism is *big.* You'd probably earn one of those prizes, you know," the term escaped him, "the one where you put on a penguin suit and some king gives it to you?"

"A *penguin* suit?" asked Goaheadon, with a flicker of concern in his eyes. He had, unbeknownst to the visitors, been subjected to such varied and harsh threats of late, his imagination was running a bit wild.

"No, no, doctor, he means a tuxedo. Please don't lose sight of our goal here." That Clara. One true professional.

That piqued Gideon's agile curiosity. "Y'all have a goal? What might that be?"

"Why, to provide excellent patient care at an affordable price," replied Clara visually inspecting the floor. "Also, to get the doctor to get through an entire interview, for once, without crying." She wiped at the corners of her own eyes.

"You know," Rigel said, "I get the feeling we're missing something big here. A couple of eight hundred pound gorillas in each corner, if my guess is correct. What is the problem with curing zombies?"

Goaheadon scanned the room quickly, from corner to corner, his face ashen.

"Excuse me but are you people from Ventura?" asked Clara.

"Nope. Not a single one of us," replied Gideon.

A clarity of understanding passed across Clara's face like a tornado. "Ah, I see. Therein the problem lies." She bounced her head a few times, gathering her thoughts. "Yes, we were the *initial* facility to offer an effective cure for zombieism. At first, our efforts were appreciated, and our results lauded."

"At first?" said Gideon.

"Yes," she said. "Then, there began to emerge a movement that undermined public toleration of our interventions."

"That's the worst stab at a euphemism I've ever heard, and I'm a seasoned conman," quipped Gideon. "Could you just tell us what went wrong?"

"The Save Our Beloved Zombie campaign is what happened," she replied, bitterly.

"Yeah, the group on the big billboard," Gideon said. "We saw one of those by the spaceport."

"They're everywhere. TV, radio, brothels. You name it, its got one of their advertisements."

"What's their beef? I mean, who *likes* to be around zombies?" Gideon asked.

"They have a problem with anyone transforming zombiefied individuals back to what they term *so called normal humans* without consent."

"Huh?" said Gideon and Rigel burped as a chorus.

"Well," she pointed to Argar, "you've been around her. Do you think she can give informed consent to a reversing procedure?"

"*Duh*. No. Not if you had her spin a wheel-of-fortune with only the word *yes* on it."

"Thank you," responded Clara. "That group of loonies, however, says it's improper, immoral, and reprehensible to do so. They argue that zombies may like what they are and very much want to remain so. To alter them, they say, is to assign them a lower value than *so-called normal humans*. It's discrimination and genocide. if you believe them."

"And more than unstable, mentally ill people *do* believe them?" Rigel was incredulous.

"Ventura has always been a liberal, fair-minded planet. The Save Our Beloved Zombies proposition was an unfortunate extension of that well-intended mindset."

"No, it was a mindless, knee jerk action that forced the actual victims to suffer," spat Rigel.

Gideon had been uncharacteristically quiet, up until then. "It seems easy enough to let the air out of SOBZ's wacko balloon. Ask any cured person if they wouldn't have *wanted* the treatment."

"They argue that proves nothing. The cured are no longer zombies, so they are not entitled to an opinion, one way or the other."

"Well," said Gideon, "I say help my friend then we'll be leaving this nut house before they make *breathing* illegal."

"That will not be a problem," replied Clara.

"Ah, are you sure Goaheadon, here, is up to the call?" asked Gideon, pointing at the doctor.

"Probably not. He's not gotten over his shock from the backlash quite yet. Fortunately it's a simple injection. *I* shall administer it."

"Great, I'll roll up her sleeve."

"Pay first. Then we proceed," she responded, firmly.

"Why does that sound ominous to me?" asked Gideon.

"Surely *I* couldn't say why anything strikes you however it might. I am a nurse, not a Gypsy fortune teller," replied Clara, rather stiffly.

"What's the percent of cure?"

"One hundred percent."

"Guaranteed?"

"Yes. More or less."

"More would be great. Less, not so much."

"A few patients have, er, unpleasant side effects. Nothing major, really. Somewhat."

"For example?" Gideon was growing concerned.

"One subject is said to have turned into a vampire bat."

"You're kidding? Right? That's silly."

"You're right. His wings were pretty small and he definitely couldn't fly, try though he might, poor fellow. And Doctor Guess did treat his facial fractures at no additional cost." She raised a finger to punctuate that good deed.

"Wait, you stated *said to have*," protested Rigel. "But, it *sounds* like you were present. Which is it?"

"Yes," she replied, uncertainly.

"Well, one paranormal abomination's just as good as another. Where do I pay?" asked Gideon.

"That's the spirit," Clara responded, with relief in her voice. "That's our motto, too. I can take a credit card, but cash is preferable, also, naturally."

"Naturally," agreed Gideon. He handed over a card and waited for her to return with his receipt.

"If you'll come with me, Ms. Argar," Clara said, taking hold of her elbow most gingerly.

Argar swung her head around, not so much confused as uncertain.

Clara led her out of the room. They returned a few minutes later. Clara steered Argar into the chair she was seated in originally.

"Ah, she looks about the same," observed Gideon.

"Well, she certainly does. Did I mention the treatment takes a few days, or weeks, to have its *full* effect. I'm certain I mentioned that before."

"Ah, no, you did not. Days or weeks? That's a pretty wide spread, honey."

"If you think so, then it must be. I'm customer focused. I regard the lag time to be *brief*. A moth does not become a beautiful butterfly, overnight."

"Moths never become butterflies. Caterpillars do. But if she isn't flapping some kind of wings in a month, I'm bringing her back."

"No problem. We will be here." Clara smiled a good deal more reassuringly than reason might suggest was sound. But, she was sweet, and sweet people were like that. Positive thinkers, God love 'em.

Gideon suggested they return to the ship and wait to see if and when Argar changed. He did elect to lock the doors and windows, preferring to remain apart from what he termed *the loco populace of Ventura*. When he woke a few days later, he was surprised to hear his shower running. He peeked in and found Argar, or rather Hephzibah, inside, scrubbing mightily at her hair and skin.

"Zebah," as Gideon had called her before, "what are you doing? Your skin's so red it looks like you were boiled."

"That's my next step if this brush doesn't get the damn smell out." She held up a metal brush dripping with suds.

"That's for degreasing engine parts, sweetie."

"Any port in a storm. Oh, what day is it? I thought it was Tuesday, the twelfth, but for some reason the ship's computer says it's four years from now. Stupid machine."

"Ah, we'll talk when you're out. Okay?" Gideon backed out quietly, in spite of the rather pleasant view he was getting. Better to have her sitting on a dry surface when he told her how she'd spent the last four years. Oh my, yes, it was. Where had he stashed that vodka?

Zebah took the news surprisingly well. She pulled at her hair and screamed at the top of her lungs for *only* an hour. This was useful. Pulling some hair out by the roots was the most definitive way to remove the smell. The move was win/win.

She then screamed and hurled objects at Gideon and Rigel for slightly less than an hour. This was also a boon. The sweat she worked up brought a good deal of fetid stench to the surface. That she didn't know Rigel neither decreased her aim nor velocity regarding him as a target. In that limited regard, he was glad to be able to participate in her rehab. Within a few days, she was speaking to Gideon in a non-hostile manner. There was but one major setback. Gideon, for some masochistic reason, told her, when she pressed him for details, what the grossest things she'd eaten as a zombie were. That factoid brought forth a barrage of solid objects, along with excellent vocal retraining practice. Howled were expressions like, "How could you allow me to eat the prince's colon?" "What *would* have constituted too much brain tissue?" and "I don't even know what that is, but you let me swallow it whole?" came from her mouth.

Within a month, Zebah was mostly calm and accepting, and both men's superficial wounds were healing nicely. It was time to move on. The choice of destinations was left to Zebah, since she'd been incommunicado, as it were, for so long. Gideon did have to disabuse her of certain choices. No, visiting her parents was not a good idea. Her father still begrudged her the loss of one eye and two fingers. No, her sister would not warmly welcome her return, either. The cat lover that she was had, it turned out, more love for the numerous felines Zebah had consumed, than for her own flesh and blood. Finally, no, it was not a good idea to visit her former business manager, Mario, as he was dead and most of him buried. Visitation would require intervention from a higher authority than Gideon.

In frustration, she finally settled on asking to go to a very fancy, exceedingly expensive spa. Gideon and Rigel agreed immediately and wholeheartedly. She'd likely relax there, and the treatments could only help further alleviate her lingering smell. Gideon could afford such a luxury, since a few of his scams on Ventura were paying off royally. Initially, he put on thick makeup to look like a zombie and had Rigel lead him around with a spiked dog collar. Though Rigel was jeered, spat upon, and punched, Gideon was lavished with charitable donations. He really raked in the big bucks, however, with his televised ad campaign. He promised that, if he could only raise enough money, *he'd* become a zombie. Then he could testify publicly how wonderful it was to be one. The floodgates opened to that little gem. Gideon was a modern-day P. T. Barnum.

Once Gideon determined that a tipping point was approaching, he favored leaving Ventura. As a consummate pro, he could sense when the ratio of *dollars-remaining-to-be-fleeced* to *prosecution* slipped against him, it was time to split. He was so wise, in that regard.

A course was set for the planet Serenity Now, located in the Lounge system, less than two light years away. Before they left, he renamed the ship *Ramrod*, as the moniker *Snuggle Puppy* was no longer needed. He had sent that message, and it was time to move on. Plus, changing the ship's name clouded their exit trail. Prudence was something Gideon practiced to a fault.

Even from orbit, Serenity Now was stunning. Cerulean-blue oceans and verdant landscapes set a tone of beauty and deep relaxation. He landed *Ramrod* near the fanciest resort they could afford. Queenie's Rest Spa and Clinic, boasted: *High brow, low prices. No matter what you've got, you'll lose it at Queenie's.* It sounded perfect. Compared to the more price-intensive resorts, Queenie's was located far from the hustle and bustle, as well as any alternate place to spend one's holiday budget. It was secluded on a desolate mesa atop a small mountain range an hour from the nearest outpost of civilization.

As they neared Queenie's, buildings began to emerge from the dust cloud the car was producing in vast amounts. The facilities appeared, at first glance, to be spartan in decor and few in number.

"What kind of dump have you booked us into *this* time?" Zebah asked of Gideon.

"The best kind, love. One where the air is pure, the staff attentive, and the results legendary."

"I see dust. No air, just dust," she remarked with a scowl.

"Aerosolized mineral treatments, not dust, my dear. They begin their magical treatments before you even arrive, and at no additional cost." Gideon's face glowed.

The taxi driver turned to Gideon. "You're good. They got you on the payroll, too, like me?"

"Never, my good man. They couldn't afford me. I've just been a fan *forever.*"

"You *been* here before?" asked the driver with strained credulity.

"No. I've been a fan from afar."

"Well," the driver said, "that's the best place to be a fan of Queenie's, from. Not too many repeat resorters at Queenie's."

"You see, Gideon," barked Zebah, "it's such a dump no one returns."

"No, you misunderstood the man. He meant they don't *have* to return because they're so improved. They could literally not be better."

"Queenie's paying you. I knew it. He's got a great eye for the scam artists like you and me."

"Queenie's a man?" Gideon pursed his lips and reflected a moment. "How odd."

"Aha! You *have* met the bastard. Odd doesn't begin to describe him. Well, why'm I telling you? You know." The cabby winked at Gideon.

"I've never met the man," he said to Zebah. "I read about this facility in a *medical* journal and determined it was Queenie's, and nothing but the best, for the apple of my eye."

"Yeah, but you brought me instead," replied Zebah. "*She* might have liked it. I, however, have taste."

"Yes, you do, and Queenie will probably get that out of your mouth, too.

If what I read was any indication, she … *he's* that good."

"If it's worth anything, *he'll* get it off you," said the cabby mostly to himself.

The cab pulled up to the main entrance. They waited two minutes for the dust treatment to blow away before exiting the car. They were not met by valets or bellhops.

"See," Gideon praised as he lugged his and Zebah's suitcases toward the door, "these pros are committed to our health. They allow us to benefit from the exercise of carrying our luggage, not some pimply-faced kid you then have to over tip." He set a case down and tapped the side of his head. "Smart business people."

At the counter the three travelers stood quietly a minute, then another, without being greeted. Gideon found a bell to ring and struck it, but it underperformed at its job. It lacked a striker. He picked it up and pounded it on the desk. That produced enough noise to draw a fatigued looking middle aged man from behind a set of worn curtains.

"Help ya?" was all he could manage.

"Yes," Gideon said. "We're checking in."

"Where?" asked the man after a yawn.

"Here, my good man. Where else *would* we be checking into?"

"Don't know. That's why I asked. Kind of sensitive, aren't ya?"

"No, mostly just tired. Might we please check into our rooms *here*?"

"Keep your trousers on, pal, least till ya get to your quarters."

"You realize your insolence is costing you heavily in terms of your tip, hmm?"

He looked at Gideon blankly. "I'll just have to live with that pain, won't I?" He tapped his keyboard. "Ah, here you are. Mr. and Mrs. Smith—nice to have you back again for the millionth time by the way—and son." He eyed Rigel. "Kind of big for his age, isn't he?"

"Plenty of fresh air and sunshine, that's the ticket," replied Gideon.

"Son, sex toy, hey, I'm not here to judge," muttered the clerk.

"That's—"

"Tried that, once, the being a judge thing. Black robes made me itch something awful. I gave it up for all this," he rolled his gaze generally around the room.

Zebah stomped a heel into Gideon's nearest foot.

"Rooms 133 and 134." He slipped the plastic keys over. "Elevators down there to the left. Ice is on even-numbered floors. Maid's out ill, so feel free to grab as many towels and such from the cart at the end of the hall. If there's anything else you need, just try and learn to do without it, okay?"

Zebah put the same heel into Gideon's other foot.

"And the spa services? When and where are they located?" asked Gideon encouragingly.

"There's a place about ten miles back up the main road, The Rub 'n Tug" the clerk pointed in a southerly direction. "Closed for the day by now, but they'll be open tomorrow, if the power don't fail, again, like today. Real pretty gals work there." He positioned his hand well in front of his skinny chest and bounced them up and down, all the while licking the air in Zebah's direction.

Zebah got both feet this time.

"My good sir. I was specifically led to believe Queenie's Rest Spa and Clinic offered some of the finest rehabilitation services in the galaxy."

"Where'd you get that notion?" the clerk asked scratching his bald head.

"From your brochure," Gideon fumbled to remove a crumpled one from his coat pocket and slammed it on the counter.

"Oh, that," he said knowingly. "Nothing but trouble, that dang—"

"*Philip,*" an authoritative, grating voice called out from behind, "I'll take it from here. You may return to your other duties." The man speaking was dressed in an out-of-style business suit with a wilted green carnation in his lapel. His tenuous comb over threatened to fly apart with the slightest breeze or head movement.

"Oh yeah?" asked Philip. "And what would those be?"

"Maybe you could go out back and hang yourself," said the manager, all the while smiling at Gideon.

Philip left with a grumble.

"I'm pleased to meet you," he extended a gloved hand across the counter. "I'm Mr. Cheatem, the owner of this fine establishment. Welcome to my home. Please, consider it to be yours, too, at least while your money holds out." He held his arms up expansively.

Gideon looked at Zebah as he shook Cheatem's hand. "Now we're getting somewhere."

She rolled her eyes.

Rigel shuffled his feet.

"So, Mr. Cheatem—" Gideon began to say.

Holding up a hand in protest, he said, "Please, call my Dewey. *All* my friends do. As we're now friends, I will insist upon it."

Gideon smiled triumphantly at Zebah. "You got it, *Dewey*. Like I was saying, what are the spa activities and the hours? My girlfriend is dying to get started."

"Yes, she is. I mean, I'll *bet* she is," Dewey corrected himself. "I'll hand deliver a full itinerary to your room before you've even settled in. We like to think Queenie's is the last spa you'll ever go to." He turned to walk away, then thought better of it. "Because we're so comprehensive, that is. You'll never dream of any—"

It was Gideon's turn to hold up a hand. "Got it, Dewey. Kind of tired here, so we'll catch you later."

Dewey tilted his head. It was almost as if he was saying, I doubt that very much. Most odd.

Once they were settled into their rooms, Zebah was in much better spirits. She stopped using the phrase *you cheap-assed son of a bitch* altogether when addressing Gideon. She'd also stopped trying to fracture his toes. Gideon sensed a real come-around on her part. He even dared to be mildly optimistic about sleeping through the night *without* her trying to suffocate him.

Within an hour, Dewey had delivered an impressive, if handwritten, list of spa amenities and their abundant schedules. Gideon told Zebah he was impressed. She told him he was gullible, deluded, and cheap. She also mentioned he wouldn't be having sex for the foreseeable, future since there were no other women at Queenie's. He, the eternal glass-half-full guy, took *that* prediction in stride.

The following morning, they were ready to be pampered. Breakfast was what Philip termed the *Healthy Plate*. It was low in calories, content, and taste. Gideon immediately announced the day was off on the right foot.

Zebah tried unsuccessfully to step on his right foot. Gideon suggested Zebah indulge herself with the Triple Package right off the bat. A mud bath, a sauna, and then a scented-oil massage. In theory, she agreed, it sounded nice. The "boys," Gideon said, would hit the gym, then swim laps in the pool. Zebah felt that sounded good too, since she'd be rid of Gideon the entire time.

Zebah presented herself to the Spa Chamber, located in the basement of the main hotel. It was dark, musty, and, well, she had to characterize it as deeply foreboding. She assumed the effect was meant to be relaxing. She should have focused more on the foreboding part. The attendant, a woman in her later years, and apparently having expended all of her humor and warmth, guided Zebah to a small, clinically sterile room.

"Take off your clothes and set them in the plastic bag," the attendant said. "I'll be back to start the procedure in a moment."

How very odd the woman's choice of words had been, reflected Zebah. She undressed and donned a thin cotton robe, much like one might find in a hospital, incompletely closing in the back. The room was quite cold, so Zebah wrapped her arms around herself and waited for her indulgence to begin.

In the next room, the attendant greeted Dewey Cheatem. "She's almost ready, professor."

"Excellent, Matilda. Excellent. I think we'll just go with the full extraction."

Matilda angled her head. "Are you sure that's wise, professor? She hasn't been *conditioned*, yet."

"Yes, what was I thinking? You're right as usual. Wouldn't want to botch the extraction simply because we were in too great a rush. Klaz Tarconin won't even be here until next week for the pickup. Let's start her with fifty drams of Anticombatin mixed with ten drams of Trynrelax."

"Yes, professor."

Matilda shuffled back into Zebah's room and asked her to lay on the table. Matilda then began prepping the equipment for an intravenous infusion.

"Ah, what's that for?" asked Zebah, as she rose from the table.

Matilda placed a surprisingly firm hand on her chest and pushed her back down. "It's all part of the experience, sweetie. The herbal mixture will help calm your nerves."

"Aren't herbs *rubbed* on the skin and *smelled*, not injected?"

"Old school, darling. That's *very* old school. At Queenie's, we like to stay ahead of the law … I mean *wave*."

Before she could protest any further, the IV was in and Matilda was pushing a thick red fluid in Zebah's vein.

"Oh my," Zebah said, "I have the strangest feeling."

Matilda nodded her head. Mostly to herself she said, "A lot of them say the same thing."

"I beg your pardon?"

"Nothing, love. Nothing at all. Matilda talks to herself too much, probably. It's all the loneliness. You rest."

Zebah made no response. She couldn't because she was unconscious.

****

"Rigel, do at least *try* to relax," pleaded Gideon.

"This isn't my idea of fun."

"You're very hard to please, aren't you?"

"No, not really. I just think swimming in an empty pool is … unfulfilling."

"If there was water in it, anyone could enjoy themselves. We're better than them, Rigel."

"I still don't see how we're going to get out. The ladder's five meters above either of our heads."

"I'll stand on your shoulders and you'll lift me to the bottom rung."

"And then you'll pull me out?"

"If you don't start enjoying yourself, no, I will not."

When they pulled themselves over the pool's rim, they were met by Dewey. He still wore the same worn suit.

"*Gentlemen*," he basically shouted, "You look better already. Your eyes have cleared up, and I swear your skin is pink."

"That's from scraping the sides as we climbed out," noted Rigel, coolly.

"Excellent. I'll never reveal our secrets to success, but I dare say you've stumbled onto one of them, Bigel."

"Rigel," said Rigel.

"Whatever. If you two are ready, the next stage of your preparation is waiting. If you'll just come—"

"Preparation? Preparation for what?" asked Gideon, ever so naively.

"Did I say preparation?" He pinched his chin with his fingers. "Why, I proclaim, you're correct. Your preparation for better *health* is what I intended, of course."

"I'm not sure I like the way he said it, there, that first time," grumbled Rigel.

"*You're* not happy with anything, so I'm not surprised," scolded Gideon.

"If you'll come with me, I've prepared your enemas especially, myself." Dewey started to step away.

"Our what?" snapped Rigel in protest.

"Why, your herbal enemas. You read about them in my handwritten pamphlet, did you not?"

"We did not," responded an indignant Rigel.

"Rige, easy," Gideon said patting Rigel's shoulder. "The man's a pro. When he says *enema*, you say, *may I lean on* this *counter.*"

Gideon turned to Dewey and asked, "You are a pro, right?"

Dewey smiled widely and nodded. He did not, however, say the simple word *yes.*

"You *see.* The man's a pro. Who are you to question his ability to get us to relax? Come on. I'm starved." Gideon walked quickly to Dewey's side.

Rigel dry heaved in the back of his throat.

It turned out, in retrospect, Gideon misheard Dewey. He thought the man had said *empanadas*, not *enemas.* By the time he realized his mistake, it was too late to back out and be able to save any face whatsoever.

Big surprise, once the liquids were instilled, both men were rendered unconscious.

****

Zebah woke slowly, half on and half off her bed. She had a pounding headache. "No more tequila for me, *ever*," were the first words out of her parched mouth. Gradually, she took in her surroundings. Gideon was on the bed, feet near his pillow and head dangling precariously over the bottom rail. Rigel was stuffed in the closet with the door half open. Both men were dead to the world.

"No more tequila for you guys, *either.*"

She staggered to the bathroom and ran ice cold water over her head. Hair still dripping wet, she walked over to Gideon and slapped him in the face. She did so, harder than she needed to, but it felt good, so she continued until well after he showed signs of rousing.

The two of them sat on the edge of the bed, staring at the snoring Rigel.

"How'd we sleep through that?" asked Gideon.

"I think we'd have slept through the apocalypse," she replied. "What the hell happened? The last thing I remember this creepy old lady told me to strip naked."

"And then what happened?"

"I don't know. I just told you, the last thing I remember was she told me to strip naked."

"I know. That's the last thing I heard, too."

She punched his arm.

"I remember we were swimming in this totally outstanding pool, doing flips off the diving board, and then … nothing."

"Which pool? The only one I saw was empty."

Gideon scrunched his brow. "Place this classy probably has a bunch of them."

"Whatever. So, what happened?"

Rigel was beginning to stir.

"Let's ask Sleeping Beauty," said Gideon sliding to the floor.

They dragged him to a wall and propped him up at an angle. Gideon splashed mouthwash in Rigel's face. The water inexplicably wasn't running, again, and it was the only liquid Gideon could afford to waste.

"Wha … wha … whaaa. I *promise*, Mom, I'll clean my room tomorrow. Please let me get dressed now."

They stared hard at one another, mouths open.

113

"We *never* talk about this again," agreed Gideon.

"Never," said Zebah.

They shook pinky fingers.

"Where are we?" asked Rigel with a cough.

"In our room."

"What happened?"

"We were hoping *you* could tell *us*."

"The last thing I remember was my mother telling me she was going to punish me again ... no, wait. That wasn't it. The last thing I recall is swimming in the sand next to the stupid empty pool."

"Why were you swimming in the sand?" asked Zebah.

"There was no water in the pool. Where else was I supposed to swim?"

"And that's it, kid?" asked Gideon. "*Nothing* else?"

Rigel looked away. "No. Just a memory of, you know, back home when I was a kid."

"I'm beginning to remember more," said Zebah. "I was on a table. The old woman, she gave me ... yes, she administered some drug concoction in my veins."

"She had you get naked to to give you an IV?" marveled Gideon.

"Would you get over the naked part?"

"Ah, no. Did she say what the medicine was for? An aphrodisiac, please, God?"

"To relax, I think. That's it. She said it was to help me relax."

"I wonder why you remember more than us?" asked Rigel.

"And did Dewey get *me* naked?" wondered Gideon.

"Get *over* with the naked," bellowed Zebah.

"We're talking me and Dewey here. Now, it's personal."

"So, what do we do?" asked Zebah.

"We leave immediately, that's what we do," replied Rigel. "I'll get my stuff packed, right now."

Before he could reach the doorknob, Gideon spoke. "Hang on. Not so fast." He pointed to the walls and his ears. "I kind of like it here. I'm not going anywhere till I'm good and refreshed."

"You'll be dead, that's what you'll be. I'm leaving. And what's the matter with your head. You keep pointing to it like it's a new wonder of the universe. Get over that, too," said Rigel.

"No," said Zebah holding up a hand. "He's trying to tell us something. The walls? The walls and your sideburns? Is that it, Gideon?" she asked getting excited. She loved parlor games.

"The wall color is so loud, it hurts your ears?" guessed Rigel. He hated parlor games, and his guess reflected that.

Gideon pounded the bed sheets.

"The walls are looking at your wax build-up?" asked Zebah. "This *is* fun."

He shook his head violently.

"No. *No* walls seeing your wax build-up?" Rigel was foundering. "The walls don't like your haircut?"

He shook his head so hard it hurt.

"Your ears have walls?" popped Zebah. She touched her bottom lip. "Well, that makes no sense. I retract it."

Gideon flipped his arms around, crossing them expansively.

"Your flippin' ears see walls? Your flippin' ears *hear* walls?" Rigel screamed in triumph.

"*No*. The *walls* might have *ears*, you imbeciles. I'm trying to relay secretly that someone might be listening to our every word." He collapsed back on the bed.

"You seem to have alerted them to that possibility now, haven't you?" remarked Zebah.

"And where was the *might*. You could have flexed your muscles to signify *might* as in *strong*. What, are we gypsy fortune tellers now?" Rigel crossed his arms and turned to the wall.

"Look, we probably can't just hightail it," said Gideon. "If this Dewey is up to no good, he'd never allow it. No, we have to stay until we outsmart him."

"That might take a very long time," said Rigel weakly. "If ever. He looks pretty sharp."

"Well I'm the sharpest tack in the bag," exclaimed Gideon. "He picked the wrong guy to mess with."

"Don't tacks come in a box, not a bag?" responded Zebah.

"Well, if they do, I'm the sharpest one in that, too."

"So, Tackman, what exactly is your plan?" asked Rigel.

"Still sharpening the edges on it."

"Stop with the *naked* and stop with the *sharp* already. This is serious. If we're not careful, these people may kill us." Why Zebah, who knew Gideon so well, expected *serious* as a possible option was unclear.

"Why would they want *me* dead?" asked Gideon.

"I'd like to kill you myself, right about now," replied Zebah. "Maybe they share my feelings."

He wrapped his arms around her waist. "I have a feeling I'd like to share."

"In your dreams." She pulled away.

"Someone wants to *kill* me?" asked Rigel quietly. "No one's ever wanted to kill me. No one ever felt that strongly about me, one way or another. I'm not certain how to take this."

"I'm sure it's a compliment. In fact, Zebah and I agree they can kill you first. You get all the glory."

She glared at Gideon hard enough to burn a hole through his fool head.

"Okay. Let me think." Gideon rested his chin on his fist and did just that. Eventually, he said, "Here's the plan. First, we stay together. Safety in numbers. Second, no one gets any medicine or weird ass potions. Third, Zebah take off all your clothes and Rigel leave the room."

"I thought you said we needed to stick together." protested Rigel.

"Rigel and my clothes remain exactly where they are," responded Zebah. "I'm hungry, so let's *all* go get lunch."

Philip said the lunch was the *California Plate*, though he didn't specify what a *california* was. It was very similar to the *Healthy Plate* breakfast he'd served them. It was, in fact, identical. Gideon told his friends that a light meal was a gift from the gods. They'd remain lean and mean and be better able to defend themselves. Zebah agreed only with the mean part. Rigel asked for a second *California Plate* but was informed that the kitchen was now closed.

That afternoon, they mostly wandered the grounds of Queenie's Rest Spa and Clinic. Upon closer inspection, it was bleaker than it appeared upon casual inspection. Gideon learned early in their excursion to place Rigel between him and Zebah. The day was less painful that way.

That evening, Gideon led them to the front desk. No one was attending it. The broken bell was gone. He took off his shoe and pounded it on the counter. Eventually Dr. Cheatem stepped through the curtain.

"Good evening, my friends. *How* may I be of service to you?"

"We'd like to check out the nearby spa Philip mentioned."

"There's no spa *remotely* close to us," replied a puzzled looking doctor.

"He said the girls there were real pretty."

"Sorry, I can't—"

Gideon placed his hands well in front of his breasts and bobbed them around.

"Ah, The Rub 'n Tug. Yes. I'm sorry, what was your question?"

"We'd like to visit there," Gideon motioned to his companions, "All three of us."

Dewey furrowed his brow. He leaned forward and whispered in Gideon's ear, "Ah, your lady friend might be quite bored there. The spa facilities are, ahem, monosexual, if you take my meaning?"

"No prob. She is, too." He flashed his eyebrows up and down. "Real flexible, my little cupcake."

Dewey rose to his full height. "I'm afraid that's impossible."

"How so?"

"The health department closed them down, just today. Too many fungi, they stated."

"Still, if you could call me a cab, we'd like to check it out."

"Alright, you're a cab. You still can't go there."

"No, I mean *summon* us a cab."

"I'm afraid that's impossible, also."

Gideon raise one eyebrow.

"Ah, department of transportation shut the only one down, again, just today. Apparently the cabby went to The Rub 'n Tug and failed to use a fungal cream, while being entertained." He drew a thumb across his throat.

"Say, Dewey, do you live here on the premises?"

That question he had not expected. "No, I don't."

"But you live real close by, walking distance, right?"

Dewey's face scrunched up in confusion. "No, but I hardly see what that—"

"May we borrow your car, just for a few hours?" Gideon grinned triumphantly.

Dewey rested his palms on the counter. "I came by cab."

"Darn," snapped a disappointed Gideon. "I thought I had you there. *You're* good."

"One tries," Dewey replied with a cordial nod.

"So, no way we can take a day trip?"

Dewey shook his head.

"Even my buddy, the one with no female companionship, to The Rub 'n Tug?"

"No even your hapless, horny friend."

"Oh, well. Can't blame a guy for trying." Gideon's turn. He leaned over and whispered in Dewey's ear. "Him and me, we been together a while. When he gets, you know, overly hormonal, he roams the halls at night and will jump any man, woman, or domestic animal's bones." He tapped the side of his nose. "Word to the wise."

Dewey looked at Rigel with some trepidation.

The next morning, after they all enjoyed the *Continental Plate*, identical though it was to the *California Plate*, they returned to Gideon's room.

"We can't just stay here until they murder us in our sleep," said an impassioned Rigel.

"Sure we can. Best way to go. Quick and easy in your bed. Least that's what they say."

"Who says?" demanded Rigel. "Dead people, hmm? I think not."

"Here's my idea," said Zebah. "We find as many water containers as we can and we hike out of this death trap."

Gideon and Rigel stared at each other. It was a brilliant plan, based on its simplicity.

"Great idea, honey," said Gideon as he kissed her forehead. "Okay, Rigel, you hunt down all the canteens and flasks you can. Fill them with water and return here in an hour. Zebah, you take off all your—"

"I'll help Rigel," she said standing. "You pack, but only bring the essentials. No telling how long we'll be wandering the desert."

In the elevator down, Zebah said to Rigel, "You check the main building. I'll look in the spa and pool areas. Meet me back here in ten minutes."

Ten minutes later, Zebah returned to the lobby. She'd found one plastic soda bottle, minus the cap, and a dubious looking plastic bag. It might have been a used condom. She was uncertain, but desperate. Rigel had eight canteens slung over his neck and pulled in tow a large ice chest on wheels.

"Outstanding, Rigel. You may have just saved our lives." She pecked him lightly on the cheek. "You wait here but stay out of sight. I'll get Gideon and we'll be off. She discarded her finds as she left.

Three hot, dry, seemingly endless hours later, they were perhaps five kilometers from Queenie's. Gideon was positive they were heading in the right direction, which meant they were hopelessly lost.

"At least we have these," boasted Gideon, as he drained another canteen. "We'll find some civiliz … za … kivlizzzzzz—" He face planted in the sand, out like a light.

"What's his problem?" asked Zebah. "You think he'd never hiked in his life. Hey, hand me another canteen." She half drained it in one, long cool pull. "If he doesn't get up, I have half a mind to … to … leave h … for the … vultur—" She stood, but teetered like a drunk sailor on a ship tossing in a mighty storm. "Hey, Rigel, where'd you get these can … cant … water from?" She held up one as best she could.

Rigel was delayed in answering because he was pouring the full content of his canteen down his gullet. He smiled at Zebah and pointed to the canteen. "These? Easy. I just went to the front desk and said we needed lots of water so we could escape and could we borrow a bunch of canteens. Dewe … De … drdew … was more than … than happy to—" He collapsed unconscious backward.

Zebah dropped to her knees. "Maybe I should have asked—" She then fell sideways onto the sand.

EIGHT

Zebah was the first to come to. She had the same horrific headache and dry mouth she'd had the first time. She tried to stand but was unable to move.

"Sit still, dearie, you'll only make it worse struggling," said Matilda. Her back was to Zebah as she adjusted some dials and gauges.

"Wher ... rre we?"

"Safe at home, back at Queenie's." Matilda giggled a sick, villain-giggle. "The only home you'll ever know from now on."

Zebah looked to her right. Both her friends were unconscious, strapped into chairs with heavy leather.

"Don't worry about your little playmates, you wanton hussy. They're just resting. Beauty sleep." Again with the villain-laugh. Really annoying to Zebah's ears.

"What are you going to do to us?"

"All in good time," responded Dewey Cheatem as he stepped into her field of vision. "I wouldn't want to ruin all your fun with spoilers, now would I?"

"You sick prick. Let us go now or you'll be really, really sorry."

"Do you think?" he responded. "I don't. In fact, I think I'd be sorry if I *did* let you go. Times as they are, you three are very valuable to me."

"Times as they are? What are you talking about?"

"Ah, ah, ah. All in good time. I'm not sure why you've awakened so quickly, or maybe your companions are just slow, but I'll tell you all, once and together."

"Any orders, professor?" asked Matilda as she stooped before him.

"No. Continue to ready the extraction system and call me when those two are fully awake."

He strolled out of the room.

When he was mostly gone, Matilda said to his back, "As you command, my knight of lovemaking, the stallion of this nag's desire, the—"

"Ah, *gross* ... TMI," shouted Zebah.

Fortunately for both women, Matilda did stop ranting.

The men woke up slowly. Finally Matilda called Dewey and said the donors were "prepped and ready."

This time, Dewey had on a long white lab coat when he entered. He went straight to Matilda and discussed items on a checklist in a hushed tone.

"Hey, Dewey, what gives?" shouted Gideon.

The professor barely turned to look at Gideon, before continuing his discussion with Matilda.

"I said, what the *hell's* going on? I demand a full and complete refund, by the way. We're not enjoying our stay at Queenie's one bit."

This time neither captor paid him the slightest attention. Ten minutes later, Dewey set down his clipboard and walked over to his prisoners.

"I know you have lots of questions. I know I have all the answers. Unfortunately, based on the lack of time and concern on my part, those two factors will not be coming together in the form of my explaining to you what I'm subjecting you to. I will say that the procedure we are performing on you two is *reasonably* pain free. The more you struggle, however, the worse it is for both of us."

"Define *reasonably*," demanded Gideon.

"It won't hurt *me* at all."

"Look, if it's money, we can pay big time. You let us go, and we'll make it *well* worth your while."

"With more of your counterfeit credit cards? I think not."

"Hey, I'm insulted. Those are not run of the mill knock-offs. The AI they're linked to is foolproof."

"Apparently, not so much," replied Dewey. "Plus, the profits I'll make off you three are well beyond what you could earn, steal, or borrow in your collective lifetimes."

"Oh yeah? I bet we're not worth half what you think we are. We're absolute degenerates, for one thing. Between us we have twelve known STDs. This guy," he tilted his head to Rigel, "snores like a pig being choked to death in an echo chamber."

"Inconsequential, I assure you. What you have, I need. Others will pay dearly for it. Now, Matilda, if you're—"

He glanced over to her. She was staring at his crotch and hadn't heard a word he'd had said.

"*Matilda.* How many times must I tell you? Medical research requires the utmost concentration. Please perform your job."

"But it's just that you're so virile when you're cruel, professor. I can't take my mind off the *little* professor."

"I told you not to *call* him that. *I'm* the one who went to college, all those long years, not *him.*"

"Wow, you missed out on the best part of higher education, Dewey." Gideon shook his head in disbelief. "What I wouldn't give for seven or eight years of undergraduate study."

Zebah tried in vain to kick him in the shin.

"Enough of this nonsense. We shall proceed."

"Aw come on, prof," said Gideon. "Humor us here. What exactly are you doing to us? I promise we won't tell a soul."

"I promise when I'm done, you won't, either." He chuckled at his wit.

"Come on. You know you *want* to. What's the fun of doing horrible experiments on innocent people if you can't tell anyone about it?"

"Oh, alright," he said too quickly. "You have me there. It's no fun to be unbelievably cruel, yet brilliant."

"None at all."

"I'm going to extract your emotions." He then muahahahaed like Dr. Frankenstein.

"Huh? Now I'm kind of sorry I asked. Forget about it and let's get this over."

"What? Are you insane?" protested the evil professor. "This is the biggest breakthrough in mood altering interventions since the advent of televised reality shows. It's bigger than *Naked and Afraid* and *America's Got Talent* combined."

"Look, do I have to break free and throw the switch myself? Get on with it."

"Not until you promise you understand me."

"I promise, I understand you. I promise also that I'm officially bored. There. Happy?"

"You're just saying that. I don't believe you for one second. Matilda, bring me a stool."

"Er, professor, whose stool—"

"My *lab* stool, you moron, to sit upon."

"Yes, master."

"I told you not to call me that, *either,* and you bloody well know it."

"Sorry, your worship."

"After this intervention, I promise you she's history. I don't *care* what the union says, I'm going to see to it that she's fired."

He stopped speaking when he saw the please-throw-the-switch-now look return to Gideon's face.

"I have devised a method to extract human emotions. I can suck from your heads all your *love, ambition, hope, anger, and sadness.* You name it, I can extract it. Then, it's a simple matter to concentrate it and sell it to the highest bidder."

"That's preposterous," said Rigel. "And, if you could, who'd want them?"

"My dull-witted fellow, who *wouldn't* want a bit more *ambition?* Hmm? Perhaps a little more *hope?* People *love hope.*"

"You can extract all our emotions and people will buy them?" asked Zebah, dubiously.

"No. Don't be silly. Who'd want more *regret?* And *empathy?* Forget about it. Oh, and I tried but I couldn't even give *understanding* away. No one's stupid enough to want more of those. But, suffice it to say, I make a lot of money selling my core product line. *Ambition.* There's the jewel in my crown.

Everybody wants more of that, especially for their spouse. Oh, yes. And with the holiday gift-giving season right around the corner, I can't keep that emotion in stock."

"Hang on. People give their spouses *ambition* for the holidays? What about love and understanding, good tidings? Good tidings are central to the experience," wondered Gideon.

"What planet are you from?" asked Dewey. "And it's not like you *tell* your husband you're injecting him with more *ambition* than he's ever had, or ever would have, that your mother was one *hundred* percent correct that you were a shiftless lout with failure written across your—" He'd gotten that look again, the throw-the-switch one. "No, you do it when they're asleep or passed out. That way, they think it's their own *idea*." He covered his mouth and chuckled at that notion. "I love my work."

"Not a fan, myself," said Zebah.

"Then, I'll cross you off our mailing list." He stood. "In fact, Ms. Smart-Mouth-I'd-Never-Look-Twice-At-a-Man-Like-You-Because—"

To his credit, this time he stopped as soon as the look began.

"You're first, cupcake," he said, darkly, to Zebah.

"No. I forbid it," shouted Gideon. "Do him first." He inclined his head to Rigel.

"What? I thought we were pals?"

"Think again, pal."

"Enough. You'll all be vegetables in a matter of minutes, so it hardly matters. Plus, Gideon, I'm going to get off watching you witness the demise of your loving spouse."

"Hey," Matilda said with some uncertainty, "I thought you only got off when I put on that—"

"Stop speaking, *now*," exclaimed the mad professor.

"There is no Mrs. Prime."

"His loving *girlfriend*."

"Couldn't make it this trip."

"His *mistress*."

"She's waiting on Alpha Centauri."

"Oh, whoever this *tramp* is to you. I want to see you suffer."

"If you say so. Suffer me away." Gideon began to whistle.

It really was a mystical coming together. Both Zebah and Dewey said *I hate you* to Gideon at the same time. Amazing, actually.

"Matilda, the *helmet*." He rose from his stool. Though he was probably not aware of it, himself, he was doing a quiet rendition of the evil-scientist cackle. Sad, that they're all so drawn to it.

He strapped a colander to Zebah's head at an odd angle and backed away. He walked to the main control panel, set his finger on a switch, and again, did the annoying muahahaha. "Say goodbye to your whatever, Mr. Prime."

He threw the switch. Nothing happened.

"That's odd. It's never done that," remarked Dewey to himself. "Matilda, are all the wires *properly* attached."

"Yes, mad ... I mean, *my* professor. I'd stake my virginity on it."

Matilda was slow to notice all eight eyes staring at her in stunned disbelief.

"Ah, to hell with the lot of you," she yelled with a swing of the back of her hand.

"Increase power to maximum," thundered Dewey.

"Do it yourself, ya dick," replied Matilda as she stormed out of the room.

He did. He put both hands on dials and pegged them clockwise. Nothing. He kicked the metal housing of the contraption. Suddenly, the mechanism thundered into action. Sparks flew, wires leapt like angry snakes, and steam hissed from pipes.

In an instant, Zebah screamed in dire anguish. Pulses of light slammed into her head. She bounced like she was riding a bucking kangaroo.

Then, all the lights went out. The lab went silent and dark.

In the confusion, amidst all the uncertainty, a tiny mezzo-soprano voice began to sing the chorus from *Tomorrow*. The lights flickered back on. It was Zebah singing. Her bonds were loosed and she was standing to sing the entire song. There wasn't a dry eye in the house, not even Dewey's. He was crying, but for a very different reason. His life's work, his brilliant master machine, lay in ruins at his feet.

He could not, in his defense, have known that what happened would happen. Even if he'd taken the time to do a perfunctory medical history and found out Zebah was only recently a zombie, it would not have mattered. There was just too little good research on zombies. It turns out that Zebah had spent four years of her life as a zombie. During that period, she had no emotions. Hunger drive, yes, but no true emotions. She was positively devoid of *love, ambition, empathy*, you name it, she didn't have it. So, when her brain was connected to a massive conglomeration of human emotions contained in a madman's machine, she sucked them up like a camel at a desert oasis. She sucked the very essence out of the machine and all its holding tanks.

Zebah was now more full of emotions than any human ever born. Hence, *Tomorrow*. She was out of her restraints, but that had nothing to do with Dewey's stupid machine or her new emotions. No, before she was a zombie, remember, she was a hooker. Yeah. She'd gotten in and out of more restraints than Houdini and Blaine combined. She hadn't done so earlier, only because of the powerful drugs she was dosed with needed time to metabolize off. After that, well, it was child's play for her.

Dewey dropped to his knees and wept inconsolably, mostly because no one present had any intentions of consoling the jerk.

"What," Dewey cried between his moaning, "am I going to do when Klaz Tarconin gets here and I've nothing to sell him? He'll *kill* me."

That got Gideon's full attention. "Klaz Tarconin's coming here. The pirate Klaz Tarconin? Here?" He pointed to the floor.

"Yes," Dewey managed through sobs. "Why, do you know him?"

"Sort of. You could say he's family."

Dewey stopped his all-out decompensation. "Really? What a *break*. If you vouch for me, maybe he won't kill me."

"Why would I speak on your behalf to Klaz Tarconin? You just tried to suck out my brain."

"Ah, good point. On the surface. Hey, I wasn't sucking it all out, just the emotions."

Gideon returned an impassive stare.

"How about if I asked you to, you know, real nice. Like I actually meant it?"

"No chance."

Dewey collapsed again into misery.

"Plus, I doubt he'd cut you a break on my account."

"Yeah," said Rigel with a chuckle, "not after you stiffed his daughter a *second* time."

Dewey stood, the very picture of composure. "Wait. You're *that* Gideon."

"Which one?" asked Gideon.

"The one Klaz is so angry about. I mean, he's been lopping off heads from one side of the galaxy to another trying to find you." He crossed his arms and nodded his head rapidly and judgmentally. "He's very cross with you, as well he should be. After what you did to that sweet girl."

"Sweet girl? You ever meet her?"

"No, not exactly."

"Seen a photo?"

"No."

"That's because she breaks all the lenses."

"Oh, she can't be all that bad."

"Then *you* marry her." Gideon looked to Rigel with a smile, expecting a high-five in return.

Rigel pointed to Dewey.

The professor had that look on his face, like he'd just been told the truth about life, the winning lottery numbers of twelve solar systems, and why his mother abandoned him before the age of two, all at once. He was going to *marry* Fleccid Tarconin in order to save his skin.

Boy, reflected Gideon, was Dewey in for a surprise. Death could, by any estimation, be only so bad. But Fleccid, she'd drag you down forever. Oh well. One man's meat *was* another man's poison. Fleccid certainly classed in there with the most potent of poisons.

"I'm afraid this means I'm kind of going to have to lock you guys back up," said Dewey apologetically. "I mean, run the options yourself. What are my choices?"

"Look at it from *my* standpoint. If I let you hold me, I'm dead. Not to mention we're all free, now. Matilda's history and Philip is useless on his best day. It's three against one."

"Point."

"But, look on the bright side. We're staying put. If Klaz is this close, what's the point in running? We're staying put."

"Well said, laddie."

All eyes turned to see Klaz standing in the doorway, one arm holding a saber, the other draped over Matilda's pencil thin neck. The second image was more terrifying than the first, and Klaz's blade was still covered in blood.

"Well lookie what I'z has meself, 'ere. If it ain't my *almost* suninlawr, Gideon. I cann'a tell ya, boy, how glad I are to sees ya."

"Klaz," said Gideon, "have you ever considered night school? You could maybe take an English class."

"Well, maybe I'z will. Ya knows, I'll wager that's as fine'a advise as I'll be gettin' t'day. But, first things first and all. Ta start with, I'll need to be torturing you and your skinny friend." He pointed his saber at Rigel. Next, I'll need to torture *you* some more. Then, the little she-devil which ain't no longer so disagreeable, it'll be her turn. Then *you* again." He swung his head side to side. "What with all the torturing an' dismemberments, I'll proba'ly have to puts the learnin' off till the next semi-ester."

"On a high note, Dewey wants to marry Fleccid."

"Ya do, do ya, mi fine young doctor?" He swung the Matilda arm over Dewey's shoulders. "And would ya mind tellin' me, just for the fatherly record, what *type* of doctor y'are in actuality and where ya did the bulk o'your trainin'?"

"Why I'd be honored, Dad."

"Say, Klaz," called out Gideon, "you wouldn't have a picture of Fleccid with you would you?"

"Now what sort'a da be I if I sailed the galaxy w'out an image o'the apple o'me eye?"

"Great. Could you show it to Dewey? Now."

Klaz looked Dewey up and down. "All in good time, me boy. All in the Lord's good time."

"So, as your wedding present to Dewey, could you *maybe* spare me and my friends?" said an overly-optimistic Gideon.

Klaz scrunched up his nose. "Maybe let's go with *no*."

"Oh, well. Can't blame a man for trying."

"I can," replied Klaz. "So, with little furder ados, I think I'll skip rights to the rippin' your heart out," he pointed to Gideon, "stuffin' it in your skull," he pointed to Rigel, "before wrappin' it all in your hide," he signaled toward Zebah.

"Wow. Pretty industrious for one day," said Gideon with a nervous laugh.

"I'm a deeply ambit'ious fella. Say, Dewey," he reached into his coat pocket, "I'm in such a positive mood, I think I'll let ya take a peek at me divine d'auther, Fleccid." He held up a tiny photo.

That was sufficient.

"Ah," Dewey asked, "did I hear you correctly, that you're a man of consummate ambition?"

"I don'ts knows about any thin soup, but I'm more amb'itus than any ten men yu'll *er* meet. More driven, sexy, virile, and ruthless, too, and all by *wide* margins, if I must be da one a say so meself."

"Really?" Dewey locked an arm around Klaz's shoulders. "You know, you seem tense."

"Well, truth o' it be told, piratin' is a task which weighs heavily on a man's constitution."

"I have a solution … *the* solution for you. I think I can arrange for Matilda to start you off with a *local* massage," he elbowed Klaz in the ribs and winked copiously at him. "After that, she has an enema that won't quit."

"Ya don't say! I'm starvin'. Eh, they're not the spicy ones, are day?"

"You won't feel a thing. Doctor's honor." He crossed his heart.

That was the last anyone anywhere, saw of Klaz Tarconin. Like so many famous pirates before him, legends and tales abounded. One had him replacing the Flying Dutchman, sailing the skies for all eternity in a weathered ship. Some placed him in a sword fight lasting until the end of time with the devil, himself. Some told of poisoned empanadas fed to him by a hideous witch. One incredible tale, far too tall to lend much credit to, even had him working as the stooped, addle-brained porter at a rundown, two-bit motel in the precise middle of nowhere. The good thing about these, as with all folktales, was that no one would ever know the real truth.

Isn't cultural mythology wonderful?

NINE

The next morning, brighter and earlier than either Gideon or Rigel would have wanted, Zebah herded them onto the spaceship that once belonged to the dreaded pirate Klaz Tarconin. It was. as chance would have it, very recently vacated and otherwise available. After the men were aboard, she went outside and spray painted over the existing name (remember, *The Good Ship Lollipop?*) turning her into *To Hope Is to Dream . To Dream Is To Live*. Yes, a very long ship's name, but remember, she was so full of emotion, she was barely able to leave it at that.

While she was washing up after her task, Gideon asked, "Er, why the cheesy name? I liked *Ramrod*."

"Your ship is *Ramrod*, not surprisingly. *Our* ship is a ship with a wonderful, positive message, for all. We shall spread that wonderful message like toothpaste all over the known universe. We shall go forth and—"

The rest of her monologue was inaudible because Gideon's hand was over her mouth. "What worm crawled in your brain and started coring out large chunks?"

"Mmmm mnm mmmnm … ah, that's better." She breathed deeply. "I am full of *hope, love, ambition, and enterprise*. Do you know what I'm going to do with all that energy, all that drive?"

"No, but let's go to our room and find out."

"No, dear Gideon. Sex, alone, cannot fulfill me."

"I'd be willing to give it my very, very best shot, to see if it can." He dropped to his knees. "Honest to goodness."

131

"No, my friend. My goals are as lofty as the sky and as broad as the horizon at dawn on a clear day. We three, we happy three, we band of brothers, shall travel to Tantorlus."

"Tantorlus?" Gideon mouthed the words, trying to taste their meaning. "Hon, why would we go to Tantorlus? It's the center of the Galactic Imperial Government. Nothing there but political stiffs, law enforcement types, and a pile of warrants for my arrest."

"Exactly. It's the center of power in this galaxy. I will go there and become the empress. I shall rule this fair home galaxy of ours with wisdom, kindness, and love. I shall establish an epoch of peace and understanding. I shall lead us all to a better tomorrow, by making today super special. I'm even considering making yesterday better, I'm so upbeat about this."

"Ah, sweetie, grab a seat." He set her in a chair. "There's so much wrong with what you just said, I don't know where to start."

She tried to speak, but he put his hand over her mouth, again, and quickly.

"First, you can't be empress. You have to be *born* into the royal family to be part of it. We do not, sadly, live in a democracy. Second, who's going to allow you to form a government based on such flaky principles? Hmm? Who wants fair and whatever else you said? The vested interests'll cut you up like fish bait and toss you to the gulls. Third, peace? Really? Where are you coming from? No one profits from peace. No one gets their jollies from peace. No, whacking a smaller guy over the head with a board is a *lot* more fun than having high tea with him. That old dog won't hunt. Oh sure, the wimps and eunuchs of the world will rally to your support, but they can't contribute two credits to your efforts, so you're guaranteed to lose. Plus, who wants to hang with pansies and eunuchs? Not me." He tented fingers on his chest. "Save the time and the hurt and come with us to Naldeck."

"*Naldeck*? What's on Naldeck worth a ten-minute visit? I hear it's full of drunks, gamblers, and persons of loose moral conviction with unlimited disposable incomes."

"So you see why we *need* to go there. My wallet's low on fuel."

"*Never!* Ours will be the path of enlightened leadership that ushers in a new age of wonder."

"Easy with the new age stuff. Look, it's just the boost you got from Dewey's silly machine. I'm sure it'll wear off in a day or two."

"I'm certain it will last forever."

"Well, that's kind of the point, isn't it? That's how drugs work. The juice makes you feel that way. But, Zebah, baby, it's all an illusion."

"I would rather live a meaningful illusion, than a meaningless reality."

"Easy with the philosophy, too, okay? Turns people right off, like a flip switch."

"You're free to stay behind. You, too, Rigel. I am not here to force you, only lead you."

"What's the difference?" asked Rigel. "I always figured one was just a nicer word for the other."

"Not under my reign."

"Oh, so now it's a reign? Any chance for early deification, you know, cut out the eternal wait?"

"You will be my court jester." She bopped him on the tip of his nose.

"Not hardly. I'll be some prison bunk-mate's jester, but no one'll be laughing. No, I set foot there, I'll never see the sun again."

"I shall pardon you."

"I'm sure you will. It's the courts I'm less confident about."

"Well, comrades, I must be off. Either have a seat or say your goodbyes. I must go to Tantorlus and *save* my galaxy."

Gideon put his face in his palms. "If you're going to Tantorlus, I'm going, too. Not going to like it, but I'm not letting you go it alone. Not after all we've been through."

"I suppose I don't actually have other plans that can't be placed on a back burner," mumbled Rigel.

She embraced them simultaneously. "I knew I could count on you boys. This will be *so* much fun."

"Oh, yeah," mumbled Gideon, "prison always is. I can never get enough of it."

"I hope never to find out," said Rigel.

"Better leap from the ramp while you can, then. There's only one way this ends and it's don't-drop-the-soap-in-the-shower bad."

"No," replied Rigel. "With Zebah as our empress, it can't end poorly."

"Oh yeah? Buckle your seat belt. As soon as you prove me wrong, you tap me on the shoulder and say you told me so."

"I wouldn't want to hurt your feelings."

"I'm thinking you won't."

Ten days into the flight, Gideon awoke to find he was alone in bed. This was unusual. Zebah had always been a good sleeper. Her post-zombie, emotion-augmented brain had made her even more amenable to long periods of rest. After washing, dressing, and a couple cups of coffee, he set about to find her. By noon he was concerned enough to enlist Rigel into helping him search for the missing Zebah. Four hours later, they found her curled up in a fetal ball under a tarpaulin in one of the cargo holds.

"Zebah, baby," cried Gideon as he fell to her side. "Are you okay?" He gently turned her face toward his. "Say something."

"Egrubblefish."

"Okay, maybe say something else."

"Drevvvlblot."

"Great, sweetie. Your vocabulary is exploding. Now, say something we humans understand."

After a short pause, she said, "Leave me alone. I'm ffff—"

"You're why? You're ffff-lavored? Ffff-lat? What, baby?"

"Fine."

"Oh, you might be flavored or flat, but fine? Even an insensitive lout like me knows that's not the case." He partially propped her limp frame against a wooden crate labeled "Mix Nonsense."

"Then I *will* be fine, if you leave me alone. I need to heal. Then, I'll be peachy-keen."

"Alright, *hon*. There was a full sentence. You're ready for the stage, I'd swear it. One question. What is it you need to heal from? Hmm. You look edible to me." Lying was easy to detect in Gideon. It occurred whenever his lips moved.

"I'm a *fool*. When I've healed from that awareness, I'll be fine."

"I realized I was a fool as a teenager," Rigel remarked, "and I have never healed. I sure hope you're wrong about what's ailing you, Zebah."

"No. I'm not just a fool."

"Good news. Then, I'm sure you'll be your perky self in no time," Rigel replied.

"I'm the biggest fool who ever lived, lives, or will live."

"I wish to retract my earlier optimistic bent," Rigel responded, glumly.

"Hey, what's all this silly talk? You're the gal who's going to sucker punch society. You're going to Tantorlus and opening up a megaliter of whoop-ass on them."

"No. I'm going to lay here until I shrivel up into dust and die. Then I'll be happy again, I promise. Would you mind covering me back up? I can't heal with all these bright lights."

"We'll do no such thing, will we, Gideon?"

Gideon shrugged noncommittally at Rigel.

"You bet we won't," Rigel was double-upbeat. "We're going to each grab an arm," he tilted his head at which arm Gideon should lift, "and drag you back to the galley. *Soup.* A bowl of hot soup, the kind mother used to make. That's what you need. You'll be punching above your weight again, in no time."

They dragged her limp body to the elevator and down a long passage. She didn't even sound a peep of protest. Quite possibly, she couldn't. They plopped her in a seat. Then wrestled her back up in the chair, after she slumped to the floor. Rigel went to the food synthesizer to retrieve a bowl of fowl noodle soup. Mom would not, as an aside, have owned up to making it.

Gideon took the bowl from Rigel, ladled up a spoonful, and poised it in front of her lips. "Here, sweetie. This'll do the trick."

He dumped it toward her mouth.

It trickled down her chin, leaving a pink trail, due to it temperature.

"Not exactly per plan, but hey, we're just getting started," chortled Gideon

He pinched her cheeks between thumb and index finger and tried another spoonful. Most went it her mouth.

Then she drooled it out.

"Ah, Zebah, this is getting pathetic. I don't *do* pathetic. FYI. You know that. I'm giving you one last sip. If you don't drink it, I'm having Rigel put a tube down your throat and he'll inject it."

Rigel placed his palms on his chest. "Why me? I don't know how to do that. And why do I always have to do the unpleasant work?"

"*Duh*. Otherwise, I'd have to."

With the next attempt, Zebah drank the soup. When the bowl was empty, Gideon asked, "There, now don't you feel better?"

"No. Can you get that tarp, please?"

"Sure, as soon as you tell me what's wrong. Last night you were drilling Rigel and me as to the various court protocols we'd need to master. You were working on us with several dialects we'd likely have to communicate in. Then we had to put on backpacks and march around the ship ten times, so we could ease into a soldierly role, if necessity called for it."

"I can show you the blisters on my feet, if you'd like," volunteered Rigel. He had never quite mastered the art of being helpful.

"That was then," she replied, with no oomph, whatsoever. "This is the rest of my life." She made a feeble attempt to throw up her arms, but lost interest even as she began.

A central tenet of life was demonstrated, that sad morning, aboard that sad ship. Imagine amassing, in one single bundle, all the ambition, drive, hope, and determination a mind could hold in a lifetime, and then flaring it off all in one sustained burst. Her brain, her aspirations, were a supernova. Brilliantly bright, but tragically short-lived. Her euphoria turned out to last a mere week and a half. That was it. The rest of the time, she'd have to plod along, dragging her heavy feet, mindlessly doing what she had the day before. The goal of most working days, for most of us, was that the boss never noticed how little we were doing, and how poorly we were doing it. But, Zebah had dared to dream big—BIG. She was, accordingly, in for a fall from her lofty intentions, down—bang—to our floor. The dull one, where fooling our idiot boss was our only goal. And, seriously, just how hard is it to fool a fool? Yeah. Not so very.

"Aw, where's my little tornado of reform and understanding?"

She weakly twirled her hand in the air, popping her fingers open at the end. "Puff."

"So, let me get this straight. That wacko professor Dewey crams your head full of zest, you set about to conquer the world, and now, *puff*? Just puff?"

She repeated her hand motion, *sans* the narration.

"Why that son of a *bitch*," exclaimed Gideon.

"He sure was," agreed Rigel. "Hurting poor Zebah like that."

"No, no. I mean he's an SOB because he was selling emotions that lasted less than two weeks. In my book, that's a scam. I hate scams and the con artists who proffer them."

"Bu … but *you're* a con artist and scam anyone and everyone you can," stammered Rigel, as he pointed to Gideon.

"You bet. And I *hate* competition. I especially hate it when they have a really great idea I didn't. That son of a *thousand* fathers."

Rigel would have to process that thought.

Against all odds, the soup did seem to help. Zebah rallied modestly. "I want to go home."

"Ah, sure. I guess we can do that. Ah, baby, you never told me where home was. Where are you from?"

"No. I don't want to go *physically* home. You're such a man." She looked at him askance. "I meant, I wanted to go home *emotionally*." She slumped again.

"No problem," Gideon replied trying to sound upbeat. "Where's that? I'll set the course immediately."

She slapped his shoulder.

He smiled. She was improving.

"But I'll settle for a hot bath and a nap." She offered Gideon a tiny grin.

"I don't think the tub's big enough for two people." He slid his hands around each other in the air. "Maybe we could make it work."

"I know it isn't big enough, you pig." She kicked at him playfully.

Gideon swelled. His girl was going to be okay.

In a week's time, Zebah was feeling her good old self. The issue of what to do next then presented itself. None of the trio had any pressing concerns, interests, or goals. It wasn't that Dewey had extracted them or anything. They just never really had any. They were, in the end, normal people. Simple folk.

"You know," Gideon said one morning at breakfast, "I've always wanted to see the Cliffs of Gandor. We should go there. We have the time. This ship can get us there in comfort. When we get there, if we like it enough, we sell the ship and settle down. How's that sound to you guys?"

Neither of them answered. They had long since learned to block the rantings of Gideon out. He had to specifically get their attention and then repeat his plan.

"I've never heard of the place. What's there to like?" asked Rigel, as he stirred his gruel.

"Gandor? Really?" Zebah said derisively. Apparently she was familiar with the planet. "Why in the Ten Constellations would you want to go there?"

He shrugged. "I heard it's nice. Big cliffs."

"The cliff to *Hell should* be big. If they weren't, all hell would break loose," she scorned.

"I'm certain that description is hyperbole. They want to make it seem dramatic, to increase tourism, that's all."

"And a nitwit like you wants to go take a peek. I guess their plan worked," responded Zebah.

"You want to maybe sell the ship and live on the upper edge of hell?" Rigel said, looking suddenly a bit pale."

"No, Rige, pay attention here. The Cliffs of Gandor rise *above* maybe a lava field or something."

"Field? No, vast *ocean* if there's a drop," Zebah corrected.

"Still, it's just *lava*." Gideon slurped some hot coffee. He knew slurping drove Zebah batty.

"No. I said *if* it's lava, there's a sea of it. But everyone knows it's actually the fiery pit of perdition."

"Why doesn't someone, I don't know, lower themselves in a bucket and find out what's down there?" asked Rigel with a furrowed brow.

"Many have tried. None have ever come back up," Zebah replied.

"How about a camera? Maybe a droid."

"They all melted or were otherwise lost before they sent any useful data."

"That sounds ominous. It also convinces me I don't want to go there," stated Rigel.

"It's all a bunch a hooey to draw tourists," responded Gideon.

"Which is what, exactly, you will be, right, a gullible tourist? If anyone can smell a con, it's you," said Zebah. "Wait." She slammed her fork to her plate so hard it bounced to the floor. "You want a piece of the action. That's it. That's always it. You want to go there and see if you can pick a few pockets, sell a few imported trinkets, maybe start a phony church. I knew it." She stood and stormed out of the room. "I knew it. Count me out. No, Never. No way," were heard in fading succession as she rounded a few corners.

"Well," Gideon said to Rigel, "she's game. You sure you're out?"

"Wha ... what? She's not *in*. I was standing right here. She is as out as a person can be out."

"You *heard* her," he thumped a finger to the side of his head, "but I *know* her. She's dying to go. Look, we're almost there, so I can prove it. The day after tomorrow, when we're peering down those cliffs, you'll see."

"Oh, this time you've gone too far. You set sail for Gandor without telling us. When she finds out, she'll kill you. If she doesn't, I will."

"Oh grow up, Rige. It's a bunch of lava at the base of some high cliffs, that's all." He leaned back and sipped his coffee. "I'm one hundred percent certain those sounds they say are the cries of the damned are just the wind moving kind of funny. Natural events happen like that, all the time."

"The cries of the damned?" Rigel pulled at what remained of his hair. "You're taking me to the walls of hell where damned people are going to yell at me? I may go insane. I can't take it." He ran mumbling from the room.

"They wouldn't be yelling *at* you. They're just concerned with their present residence, and vocalizing that, broadly." he shouted after Rigel, but Rigel was out of earshot. "Can't take it?" he said to the empty room. "Like you got a choice."

The next two nights Gideon decided to sleep in a room down the hall from the one he shared with Zebah. Since Zebah changed the entry code and he couldn't convince the ship's AI to let him in on it, he figured it was best to sleep elsewhere.

After Gideon landed in the center of the only town on Gandor, he went first to Zebah's door then Rigel's, then back to Zebah's knocking and asking them to come out and take a look. That first day, and the next few days that followed, he didn't even receive a verbal rejection. But time was on his side. Both of them had to come out to eat, sooner or later.

Later proved the case. After five days of starvation, his travel partners hauled themselves out of their quarters, to the galley. Gideon was already there, a big pot of stew bubbling away, deliciously, on the stove.

"There are my two sleepy-headed pals. Good to see you both," he chortled. "The pair of you look great. I wish I could sleep that long. You look really refreshed." He plopped a bowl of stew in front of each of them, along with a thick wedge of freshly baked bread.

Halfway through her bowl, Zebah said, "This changes nothing. After this I'm taking whatever's left over to my room and relocking the door. Hell will freeze over before I visit the surface with you."

"Hey, let's go check. Maybe it already has, as we speak?" Gideon gestured over a shoulder.

"Nice try, slick, but no way. If the damned souls in Hell want to lay a hand on this girl, they're going to have to come to my cabin to do it."

"Would you like me to ask if any are currently available?" Gideon fluttered his eyelashes at her.

She returned a sarcastic smile.

"Don't ask me, either. I'll die of starvation in my cabin before I come out again," said Rigel.

"Great. After you're dead, I'll just toss your bones over the edge. Save you the long way around trip."

"That's not funny," replied Rigel. "I'll have you know I'm destined for the better place."

Gideon pounced. "Oh really? And how do you know this important tidbit? Three-Spot tell you as much?"

He tilted his head and frowned. "Not in as many *words*, but yes."

"In how many words did he say it?"

"No, it's not how many, but what he put into the spaces between them."

"You're worse off than I thought. Much worse. I think we need to revisit you getting that brain transplant."

"Mock me if you will. I'm going to a better place."

"I will mock you and I'm going to the best place." Gideon stuck out his tongue.

"You can't bait me. There's the bad place and a better place. Those're the options."

"And the best, which is where I'm going and you're not. Three-Spot even told you."

"Not taking the bait," he said, placing a hand over his mouth to demonstrate how bait couldn't enter it.

"When I get there, they say you can write me, but I can't answer back. Do try to drop me a line now and then. A birthday card would be nice, if you can make that happen."

Hand over his mouth, Rigel said, "Hh hhhum hum haim."

"You're no fun at all. Say," he said to both of them, "I packed a picnic basket and put some sweaters by the door. We can have our outing any time you two are ready. My plans for the day are wide open, as of now."

"You know he's just going to badger us and whine and beg and drive us both nuts until we freaking go with him, right?" Zebah groused to Rigel.

"Oh, yes. I know. He'll work on us like a river does to the mighty mountain, slowly wear us to dust and make us do what he wants us to in spite of our clearly expressed wishes," agreed Rigel.

"So, you want to wait, what, a couple more weeks?" asked Zebah.

"My mother used to say, why put off until tomorrow an unpleasant task you can do today."

"Didn't she like abandon you too?" asked Zebah.

"In a manner of speaking, yes, but it wasn't as, um … *abandoning* as I made it sound."

"Gideon," Zebah announced, "we'll be ready in half an hour."

"Half an hour I can do. That works for me. But don't let's dawdle. I'm busy later." Gideon beamed.

The first thing that struck all three travelers when the hatch opened was the smell. Sulfur, brimstone, and burning flesh. Gideon explained the local chamber of commerce produced that repulsive odor specifically to enhance the effect. The walk from the landing port to the rim was less than a kilometer. Geologically, Gandor was unusual. The only solid surface known on the entire planet was that one granite column rising from an endless chasm of darkness. The atmosphere was thin and barely breathable for humans. Most tourists, and there was actually a brisk though transient flow of the curious, wore masks or helmets. They usually needed lights mounted on their heads, too.

A few businesses were located around the landing zone. Mostly there were restaurants and gift shops. There were no hotels or similar accommodations. Time had proven that visitors left too quickly to require a night's stay. The sole governmental installation was a post office. It was constructed as a bunker, with sandbags, barbed wire, and gun ports. Again, Gideon explained that was a deliberate scheme to build tension and enhance the experiences of the tourists. He greatly praised the local government for its tourist-centered thinking. "Where else you going to see that?" he remarked with abundant pleasure.

Past the irregular ring of businesses, there were a few prefabricated homes tucked together.

"They look like circled covered wagons, like I've seen in old movies," noted Rigel. He was correct, they did look defensively clustered.

After passing the sparse permanent housing, there was nothing, literally nothing, between the visitor and the cliffs. Trails heading off in a few directions were well-lit, and a few signs directed the hikers in the proper direction. Otherwise, the only other indication civilization was present was the extensive, solidly constructed railing at the cliff's edge. The word *barricade* forced itself into the mind of anyone who first saw it. If a truck was driven at high speed into the guard rail, it would bounce off in a heap, but the rail would remain intact.

"Isn't this place great?" shouted Gideon over his shoulder.

Rigel and Zebah had been dropping progressively farther behind as the party advanced.

"I said," Gideon turned to be better heard, "isn't this place cool?"

Rigel and Zebah were hugging each other as if the safety of their immortal souls depended on a tight bond.

"Oh come on, you two. Don't be so dramatic."

He walked back to where they were stopped and began pushing their fused bodies toward the cliffs. They were so distracted by fear, that they resisted only minimally. Gideon asked all the people returning along the path to help push his friends, but not a single soul even slowed their sprint to say NFW, let alone help. A sorry lot these tourists, reflected Gideon. There was certainly no TOURIST in TEAM. He'd feel even less guilt siphoning off the slackers' funds, should he hit upon an appropriate angle.

Finally, the three of them were at the massive railing. Gideon left his friends huddled a few meters away from the barrier, and went for a look-see, first hand. What was the big deal, he wondered as he took in the expansive view? Tranquil columns of smoke, a pleasant uprush of superheated sulfuric acid vapor, and the lovely sound of the wind wafting against the cliffs themselves. The sound was musical, settling, almost tolerable. And it didn't sound *similar* to the cries and anguished screams of the damned. No, it sounded *exactly* like those tortured voices pleading for death. But it was the wind through rock formations. Everyone involved in Gandor's tourism industry knew, or at least, *claimed*, that.

Gideon thought it was a really interesting experience. He turned to pull his friends to join him, but he slipped in a wet puddle. How odd, it hit him, that a pool of any liquid could persist in the blasting hot air currents at the edge. When he realized it was a puddle of his own urine, he understood why it was still there, it being so fresh, and all. Suddenly, forcing the others to enjoy the view of the Cliffs of Gandor seemed less ... imperative. Returning to the ship and blasting off sounded ... more imperative than it had, pre-self-peeing.

He was buoyed with the knowledge that he wouldn't have to push Rigel and Zebah in the reverse direction. They were ready to run like, well, like they were fleeing for their very souls. But before any of the three of them could twitch a muscle, over the edge of the cliffs came a haunting, taunting, bone chilling call. *Gideon Prime, we've been waiting for you. Are Rigel and Argar with you, too?*

Lot's wife was turned to salt with one glance. These three were frozen like stone with one sentence. None of them had the wits about them to wonder why the voice of evil asked after Argar, not Zebah.

Step to the railing and look into your futures. Echoed through the air.

Much too frightened to disobey, they moved as one rigid blob to the edge and stuck their heads over, to look down. Three gigantic octopus arms vaulted from the depths and wrapped around each ones neck. An instant later, the only witnesses, a retired couple who'd won the trip in a church raffle, and a group of ten Japanese tourists following a woman with a red and white flag on a long pole held high over her head, saw the trio pulled silently into the void. All thirteen began running toward town without a *single* individual contemplating an attempt at offering aid. Ah, human nature, so shallow a pool.

Gideon could see or hear nothing as he tumbled into nothingness. The temperature around him was rising rapidly and the smell was well past hateful. He struggled to free his neck, but the hold the monster had on him was so tight he wondered if their flesh had merged. The sound of two voices laughing hysterically grew louder, louder, louder. Finally, the insane cackles were the only things that existed in the universe. Then Gideon was set gently into a leather lounge chair. The arm of doom released him and disappeared.

The lighting was good, the horrible smell absent, but the laughter remained, though it was now unimposing, just annoying. First Zebah, then Rigel were deposited in similar chairs.

"Are you guys okay," asked Gideon quickly.

"I think so," Rigel replied, patting his body up and down.

"Me, too, I think."

"Of course they're fine, Gideon. What type of host would I be if they weren't?"

That voice! It was vaguely familiar. Gideon's eyes scanned the room, for they were in some casually appointed room.

Sitting by a brisk, inviting fire, were Three-Spot and Beetlebreath. The pair were laughing so hard they were having difficulty remaining in their chairs.

"What the *hell's* going on here?" demanded Gideon.

The two looked at each other, Beetlebreath was just barely able to say the word *yes*, and they collapsed into more raucous laughter. Three-Spot did end up rolling on the floor.

It seemed like it took an eternity for them to settle down and for Three-Spot to get back up.

"Sorry, sorry," said Three-Spot, clearly having trouble not bursting back into mirth, "we'll stop now ... ww ... www."

"Yes," I swear I'll be good," said Beetlebreath.

That did it. The two immortal spirits fled into giggle-fits. They did recover faster, fortunately.

"Gideon, do you know these two idiots?" asked Zebah.

"She may not remember us, but she sure does know us well," Three-Spot responded in a half-chuckle.

The following interlude of rude laughing was almost brief, comparatively so.

"Okay, boys, you've had your fun. Knock it off," said Gideon.

"You're right, you're right. Again, sorry." Three-Spot sat up straight and tried to be serious. "So, Gid, Rig, long time no see. How are you doing?"

Rigel looked uncertainly at Gideon.

"What gives?" asked Gideon.

"I was here visiting Beetlebreath. Remember he asked me to, when we met him in Jersey?"

"Ah, yeah, but what are *we* doing here?"

"Like I said, I was here for a catch-up. We were looking up and whose face did I see peek over the edge but yours? I asked if Beet could swing an abduction. He was happy to oblige."

"And here you are," added Beetlebreath, graciously.

Gideon began to fume. "So you just figured scaring us nearly to death would be a great gag?"

"Yes, I guess you could say that. Gideon," exclaimed Three-Spot, "I was just fooling with you."

"Good thing you work in Miracles now. You're going to need one to recover after *I'm* through with you," responded Gideon.

"You're in Miracles!" said Beetlebreath. "With Tony and Gammergab? You didn't tell me. That's so cool." Beetlebreath was instantly serious. "We need to speak before you leave. Don't let me forget."

"I only just started. Not only don't I work in Options and Impossibilities, I haven't even oriented there yet." replied Three-Spot.

"How's old Gammergab?"

Three-Spot snickered. "Grouchy as always. He has all the humor of an unripe lemon."

"Some forces never change, do they?" said Beetlebreath. "Sometimes, I'm actually glad I'm not up there, any longer."

Gideon cleared his throat so loudly it hurt.

"Oh, sorry. Old times, you know?" responded Three-Spot. "So, what happened to Argar?"

"Who's Argar?" asked Zebah.

"You are," replied Gideon.

"What do you mean I am? No I am not."

"No, well, I mean you *were*."

"I was what?"

"When you were a zombie, we called you Argar. I told you."

"You most certainly did not. I do remember the fact that you made *fun* of me when I was at my most vulnerable." She crossed her arms and looked away.

"Uh-oh," said Beetlebreath, placing his hand over his mouth. "A domestic squabble. There hasn't been one here in millennia. This is so precious."

"Ah, Beetlebreath, that's not *helping*," said Gideon.

"Sorry. But, being constructive is not my usual MO."

"No duh," responded Three-Spot. "And look what it brought you." He directed his arms expansively around hell.

"It's not so bad," mused a thoughtful Beetlebreath, mostly to himself. "Haircuts are all free, and there're no lines at the water slides."

"Maybe because there's no water on the water slides, because there's no water in hell to slide *on*," taunted Three-Spot.

"Yeah, but no line is still awesome."

Gideon stood quickly and pointed at them both. "Don't even think about laughing like hyenas again. I'm in no mood. You've really got me going."

Three-Spot drew an imaginary zipper across his lips. Beetlebreath locked his with a pretend key he then tossed over his shoulder.

"That's better." He sat back down. "So, let me get this straight. You just happen to be here looking up the Cliffs of Gandor the instant I peeked over?"

"I guess the miracle thing is rubbing off on me," responded Three-Spot with a shrug. "What can I say?"

"And you couldn't send, what, a golden chariot or a flying whale with a smiley face? You had to use tentacles?"

"Oh come on, Gideon. Neither of those would be the least bit funny," defended Beetlebreath.

"I guess that's true."

"You're not condoning what these jerks did to us are you?" shouted a newly attentive Zebah.

"Honey, the giant monster arms, they *were* actually perfect. You have to admit it probably freaked those tourists up there to within inches of cardiac arrest."

"I have to do nothing of the kind. All I have to do is realize, with no joy, that there are two more, overgrown, little boys with senses of humor as sick as yours, in my universe."

Three-Spot fanned his face with his palm while grimacing at his eternal buddy, who cringed back at him.

"Well, now that you're here, can I offer you something to drink?" asked Beetlebreath. "It's the least I can do. And, before you ask, yes, we actually do have ice in hell. But, it's only for *drinks* and only for *employees* and their immediate families."

Gideon shook a finger at the two jokers.

"I'd like a lemonade," said Rigel.

"Gin and tonic, heavy on the gin. Make the tonic a minor afterthought," Gideon grumbled, as he rested back. "Hey, these chairs are divine."

"I brought them with me," responded Three-Spot. "The ones down here tend to have nails driven through them at odd angles."

"Nice touch. Thanks," replied Gideon, as he shut his eyes and tried to snooze.

"And beautiful Hephzibah, name your poison," asked Beetlebreath.

"If I do, will you two idiots drink it?"

He frowned and tossed his head back and forth. "Sure, I guess. If you insist. Personally, I'm not a fan of poisons. They tend to be impossibly bitter."

"They give me such gas. I'd probably blow myself up that cliff," Three-Spot gestured absently at the Cliffs of Gandor, But, if it'll please a friend, how could I say no?"

"Gideon, take me home. I want to go home, *now*," announced a displeased Zebah.

"Easy, Zebah. I promise we'll behave, from here on out," responded Three-Spot. "If you'd indulge me a few minutes, I promise I'll see you home safely, personally. I would just *so* like to catch up with these two knuckleheads. Pretty please?"

She squinted at him furiously a few seconds, then broke the tension. "So we knew each other ... before?"

"We traveled extensively," Three-Spot replied.

"In fact, it was his suggestion that led us to Ventura," added Rigel.

Three-Spot nodded quietly.

"And Slick over here," she asked pointing to Beetlebreath.

"Long story," responded Gideon.

"*I* have forever," said Beetlebreath opening his arms expansively.

"I don't," she said with finality. "I'll give you half an hour. I'm not spending any longer in this hell hole. By the way, where are we?"

"Ah, more or less a hole into hell," replied Three-Spot. "You described it accurately."

"So, all that tourist literature up there is bogus?" asked Gideon.

"When is it not?" responded a serious Three-Spot.

"I wrote half of it myself," confessed Beetlebreath.

"That's nuts. Why build a stone tower rising out of hell? Just saying the words sounds perfectly silly," asked an incredulous Zebah.

"It's not exactly a mountain rising from the plains of hell. The Cliffs of Gandor are an *observation* location above one of the many entrances to hell."

"There are more than one?" asked Rigel.

"You were in Jersey. I saw you there, myself," replied Beetlebreath. "There are entrances all over the place."

"What's the purpose of putting a vista point over hell?" asked Gideon.

"It's where we take bad little angels to show them what happens if they don't shape up," Three-Spot replied.

"You bring kid angels here to scare them?" scoffed Gideon. "I thought you were the nice guys?"

"As we say in Heaven, a picture is worth a thousand words."

"We say that, too," said Rigel.

"Where do you think you got it from?" asked Three-Spot.

"But all the tourism, the businesses up there. Why do you let people come here?" asked a now-interested Zebah.

"At first there was some uncertainty on that point. But you know what? After a while we were all having such fun watching you all, we let it be."

"You think *I'm* bad?" said Beetlebreath. "They place bets on how long an individual will last at the railing, who'll be the first back to their ship, and whether this one, or that one will pee themselves, first. It's like the Kentucky Derby every day up there, in I'm-better-than-you land."

"At least they don't sip mint juleps the whole while," scoffed Gideon.

Neither eternal spirit responded.

"They don't sip mint juleps while betting on the humans, do they?" pressed Gideon.

"The occasional few partake of mimosas," Three-Spot replied, stiffly.

"I hate you guys," said Gideon.

"Oh, it's not that bad," Three-Spot tried to deflect.

"Oh, it's *not?*" barked Beetlebreath in high squeak. "Then, who calls people by name from the edge of the pit, if they're slow to flee in terror? Psychologically, it's crueler than using a riding crop to hurry along a child, if you ask me."

"I almost never do that. It's considered as bad as cheating," defended Three-Spot.

"No, you just drag your friends down here, frightened out of their minds."

"Thank you for seeing it my way," replied Three-Spot, though rather smugly.

"As entertaining as it otherwise is to watch you two monkeys throw poop, is there anything else you wanted to say, before we get the *hell* out of here?" asked Gideon.

"It would take a big broom to get all the hell out of hell," observed Beetlebreath.

The two eternal spirits snickered.

"I'm outta here," announced Gideon. "Where's the elevator?"

"Wait. There is one thing," responded Three-Spot, rapidly becoming serious. "I wanted to warn you of a potential, er, *complication* in your near future."

"You mean like a revelation?" asked Gideon.

"No, nothing so dramatic. Honestly Gideon, where do you come up with this Hollywood crap?"

"Then what?"

"Here it is. *If you hear an old man say* "orange duck," *you're in peril's way, alright.*"

Gideon rose.

"Where are you going, Gideon?" asked Zebah.

"I'm going to strangle him, that's where," replied Gideon as he vaulted toward Three-Spot.

Beetlebreath jumped in his path and when Gideon touched him, the heat of his body caused him to hop backward.

"Dude, you're on fire," he said to the demon.

"Tell me about it. Hydration is a nightmare."

"Gideon, what's gotten into you?" asked Three-Spot. "Here I'm giving you more help than I technically should, and you want to throttle me?"

"Help? You call a riddle that'd make the sphinx's head explode, *helpful?*"

"It's all I was authorized to say. Believe me, I had to go to three different agencies to get even *that* scrap."

"Okay, thanks, I guess. So, what's it mean?"

"I can't tell you. If I could, why would I give you such an oblique clue?"

"Point." He plopped back down.

"Just stay sharp, pay attention, and … well, remember the phrase. When the time comes, you'll need to be quick about it."

"About what?"

"Gideon, let it go. So, if you're ready, I'll take you back to *Petulant*."

"Where the hell's that?"

"It's not a place, it's what you named your ship."

"*No,* we didn't."

Three-Spot though a moment. "Oops, my bad. It's what you *will* name your ship."

"I will not. I like *To Hope Is to Dream, To Dream Is To Live.*" defended Zebah. She twisted up her face a moment. "Are you certain I will pick *that* name?"

Three-Spot tilted his head in Gideon's direction.

She crossed her arms, "I should have *known.*"

"What? I had a dog named Petulant, when I was a little boy. I *loved* that dog."

"Never speaking to you. No. Or listening, either. Na-na-na-na."

Three-Spot spread his wings and the four of them were back aboard the ship.

"So, my friends, take care. I'd say have a safe journey, but I've sailed with Gideon before. No chance that's going to happen."

"I'm a very good pilot," responded Gideon.

"Yes, but a really bad decision-maker."

"If I wasn't certain you were wrong, I'd be hurt."

"Works for me," said Three-Spot, who then disappeared.

"Well isn't this nice. We're heading into an uncertain, but *biblical* danger, with a bogus clue and an angel who's probably right this *minute* is placing a bet against our success," said Zebah. "And a good time was had by all. Whee."

"Yeah," replied Gideon. "Isn't this greater than you could dream up?"

Zebah left to go change her room code for the third time that day.

TEN

The three travelers were uncertain as to where they wanted or needed to go. They were unanimous in wishing to be off Gandor, so they blasted off as quickly as possible. Even knowing a couple of insiders there didn't lessen the angst and revulsion they felt toward the cliff planet. *Good riddance* was their mutual feeling.

Rigel expressed a desire to go home. "I'm not much of a traveler," he said. "The last few years have made me like it even less."

"Why home?" asked Zebah. "Do you have family you miss or a business you'd like to return to?"

"No. My family's all gone or died. There's never too many relatives in any one place at a time. Whenever that happens, restraining orders and duels are the result. That's how it works with my family. We're not too ... family-like."

"Maybe we're related," asked Gideon. "That sounds a lot like my people." Gideon reflected a moment. He lived by many credos. One he particularly favored was that once you failed yourself, go home and fail your family. And really make it hurt. Hey, who's fault was it, if not mom and dad?

"So, not even one is left?" he probed.

"No. Just Uncle Wally. Hard to count him though. He's old, rich, alone in this world except for a parrot named Clem. He has this bad habit of giving fortunes away to any strangers, con artist, or cookie sales representative who chances upon him. That behavior has caused the rest of the family to shun him."

"Your family shunned a lonely idiot because he gave too much of his own money away? Giving begins, after all, at home." Gideon was genuinely angry. He was a man of consistent convictions. Never cap a producing well. Only idiots do that, and he hated idiots. That was the primary reason he liked to swindle them. Well, that, and because it was easy to.

"That was just it. He'd give money to anyone *but* family. He said that might breed resentment."

"So instead, he bred resentment."

"I guess you could say that," replied Rigel uncertainly.

"Well, I just did. And do you know what else I'm going to say?"

"Wait, here it comes," said Zebah, "his scam to unload the old fool's money into his own pocket."

"I say that horrific incivility ends, now. You, Rigel, will break the mold and return to your uncle's warm bosom, not for money, but for love."

"Oh, lords," responded Zebah.

"As for you, young lady, I'm insulted on Uncle Wally's behalf. Clem's too, by your scathing cynicism. He's a great man and he's a great bird. Do not sully their names in my presence, again, night harlot."

"Oh, this is going to be good. I'm glad I have a front row seat. I hope they have popcorn on your home world, Rigel. I'll need some to eat while watching the fleecing of great old Uncle Wally."

"So, dear friend Rigel, where do you, and therefore we call home, now? I don't believe you've mentioned it before."

"I'm native to Capella Left."

Silence. More silence. Finally, a denser, supremely awkward silence began to settle in.

"I know," said Rigel. "We get that a lot. It's one of the main reasons I left."

"You left?" gasped Zebah. "Everyone with a functioning *brain* left. People in *comas* woke up specifically to leave, then lapsed back into their own private little escape coma. To not run screaming from Capella Left is suicidally insane."

"It wasn't all *that* bad. When I was a kid, they had really pretty sunsets and the playgrounds were never crowded."

"I wonder why no kids were there?" responded Zebah with uncharacteristic sarcasm.

"Well I've always been in the give-Capella-Left-a-chance camp," replied Gideon. "Don't judge a book by its cover, or a planet by its clear and documented history."

"Yeah, you've been in that camp, what, three minutes now?" asked Zebah.

"It's the thought that counts," he responded. "Not the length of that thought. Do not, my child, be small."

"No, Gideon, that's in the giving of gifts. It doesn't apply to defending the indefensible." She was not going to let him off the hook on that one.

"You'll see," reassured Gideon. "With Rigel as our guide and Uncle Wally as our host, you'll see what an almost acceptable place Capella Left can be. And, don't forget Clem. He'll prove a real asset, I can feel it in my bones."

"I'm not going there," stated Zebah, firmly. "I'm good with the occasional risk-taking. But a certain and horrible death? I draw the line there."

"Look, with all due respect to Rigel and his upbringing, I'm certain calling Capella Left the planet of the cursed evil demons of death is a *gross* exaggeration. Melodramatic gibberish has never stopped me before, and it won't this time."

"Neither has reason, logic, or credible reports" replied Zebah.

"I can prove it. Rigel, growing up, what's the worst thing you ever saw, with your own eyes, that could *conceivably* be attributed to those alleged demons?"

"Does seeing them every night running down the streets with the neighbors' heads on poles count?"

"No. As a repeating event, it cannot, by definition, be the worst."

"Well, there was the time my cousin forgot to lock his door the requisite seven times and the demons broke through and ate the entire family."

"Uh-uh. Can't count that either. You weren't there to *witness* it. You can't know they were alive at the time of their consumption. I'm betting they were already well dead from fright and or self-inflicted wounds."

"Okay, this one's the winner. I was dating this girl. We went to a drive-in movie. I asked her if she wanted to hop into the back seat. All of a sudden three massive demons ripped her out the partially open window. It was cracked to let the speaker in, you know?"

"We've been to drives-ins," remarked Gideon, coolly. "Go on."

"Well that's it. That was the last time I saw her, last time *anyone* saw her."

"Well that proves nothing. I bet they took her to the snack bar. There, they bought her all the industrial-grade pizza and mystery-meat hotdogs a girl could want. They so impressed her that she went home with them. She married the three of demons and has raised a brood of cute little monsters who look just like their fathers."

"Do you think so?" asked Rigel. He was remarkably gullible.

"He does not. He's making this up to justify going to the most dangerous planet in existence, just to scam an old man," replied Zebah.

"Not to scam an old man, you evil-minded scamp. I'm going to Capella Left to reunite a loving family. Affording Wally the chance to rebalance his investment portfolio is gravy. *I'm* calling it a love mission."

"A distinction without a difference," concluded Zebah.

"History teaches us visionaries to never be discouraged by you naysayers. I will save the old goat and make his life whole. That's what Primes do."

"I really didn't know him all that well," remarked Rigel.

"All the more reason to make haste for *our* new home."

"Oh, so now Capella Left is *all* our homes?" asked Zebah, contemptuously.

"For the present, yes. I hear her calling me." Gideon cupped a hand to one ear, and the other rested over his heart. Well, one of them, at least.

Orbiting Capella Left was easy. No other ships or satellites were in the way. Space above the grim world was perfectly clear. Rigel contacted Uncle Wally and arranged to visit. They landed in his backyard near sunset and were immediately set upon by ravenous demons. Fortunately, a deep space cruiser was more than tough enough to keep them out. Their biting and clawing at the hull did, however, make sleep challenging. Zebah repeatedly asked Gideon what the horrible noise she heard was. He informed her, repeatedly, that it was the wind. She agreed. Yes, it was the wind blowing demons at the ship. He told her she suffered from an overactive imagination. She said that, no, she suffered from an over-stupid Gideon.

By dawn, the local nightmare beasts slowly dispersed. Though they *could* live in sunlight, they much preferred being active at night. If one chanced upon a demon during the day, it would definitely attack, but they rarely hunted before dusk. For those unfamiliar with the so called demons of Capella Left, they are not, of course, spiritually demonic. They are just a very aggressive, mindless, local species of predator with limitless appetites. They reproduce faster than mice and their palates are less discriminating than a tiger shark's. All attempts to eradicate them failed, with most eradicators ending up as supper. Colonists cling to the planet for two reasons and two reasons *only*. There were the unusually large deposits of gold and there were those sunsets. Ah, those sunsets.

The next morning, the three travelers ran across the dead lawn and into Wally's kitchen. The thunderous sound of the door being sealed followed quickly. Seven locks slammed closed, automatically.

"Uncle Wally," said Gideon, as he lifted the frail old man up in a precarious bear-hug. "How've you been?"

Once grounded, Wally stepped back briskly. "I thought *that* one was my nephew Rigel," he said waving his cane in Rigel's direction.

"I am, Uncle Wally," peeped Rigel.

"Then who the blue blazes is this idiot?" He rapped Gideon alongside the head with his cane.

"You've not met, Unc, but you know him, well, by his type," Zebah responded cryptically

"And you," Wally asked her, "are you family, too?"

"No, sir. I'm just passing through your gene pool. No plans to hang around."

"Hmm. Rigel, come give me a hug. Then tell me who this moron is." That time he pointed his cane at Gideon. It wasn't increased tolerance, but decreased endurance that caused Uncle to play nicer.

"He's a friend. They both are, actually. We've been traveling together for a while, now."

"What, can't you find honest work?"

"What makes you say that, uncle W?"

"If you're hanging around the likes of him, you're skirting the law, at best."

Zebah turned to Gideon. "Do you suppose he's psychic? He really nailed you on that one."

"No, sweetheart. Uncle Wally just hasn't gotten to know me yet. Hey, where's my favorite bird of all time, Clem the parrot?" Gideon began searching the house.

"You mentioned my *bird* to that nitwit?" Wally asked Rigel.

"I love that bird. Of course I did."

"If you loved him, why didn't you take the flying rat off my hands when you left?"

"I didn't think you'd ever part with him."

"I'd have killed the bastard years ago, but he won't let me get close enough." He held up his hands. They were scarred and pitted from bite wounds. "He even *sleeps* with one eye open, the son of a bitch. Clem's almost as bad as them damn demons."

"Wally," asked Zebah, "don't let Gideon know about Clem's disposition, just yet, okay?"

He didn't have to answer. Gideon anguished screams were unmistakable. They were also growing quickly louder.

Gideon burst into the room with Clem perched on his head. The parrot was yanking chunks of scalp out and tossing them casually to the floor.

"Somebody shoot it. Get the damn thing off my head."

With uncanny dexterity, Wally swung his cane and batted the parrot across the room like the bird was a shuttlecock. It dropped to the floor, momentarily stunned, then launched itself at Wally. Years of practice had honed both combatant's skills. Soon, they were exhausted and repaired to their widely separated resting spots. Neither was the victor, but not the loser, either.

Gideon ran to the sink to clean his wounds. Zebah walked slowly behind him, to help. Maybe.

"That was impressive, Uncle Wally. You defended yourself like Zorro."

Wally eyed the opening to the next room, where the bird had fled to. "He'll be back," he bemoaned darkly.

"Why don't you get rid of Clem? You obviously hate each other," asked Rigel.

"Get rid of my pet? What kind of sadist are you? I love that bird."

"But, your hands, the way you fought. What you called him. Surely you hate each other."

"Shows what you know about true love, my idiot nephew."

"I guess I don't know much about the kind you have for Clem. Wait, you said I could have taken him with me, when I left. What's the difference between that and opening a window and letting him fly away?"

"You're family. I could trust you not to hurt him, even after he started dismembering you. No, I love the awful thing. I couldn't see Clem harmed."

"Sounds as stable and normal as our relationship," Zebah said to Gideon as she yanked another chunk of dangling scalp free.

"Ow! Watch what you're doing. If I bleed to death, I'll hold you responsible," responded Gideon, "not the bird."

"Me, not the damn bird?"

"Yes. If Uncle Wally loves him, so do I. Therefore, Clem would never *intentionally* hurt me. He simply mistook me for a large, mobile sunflower seed. Ergo, if I die, it's your fault."

"Whatever. Hey, when was your last tetanus shot? Some of these wounds are pretty deep."

"Last was the same as the first. It never happened."

"You never had your childhood vaccinations? That's so lame," she scolded.

"No worries," said Uncle Wally. "I have a complete set in the fridge. On this planet, you keep a lot of medical supplies handy because you're going to need them and going to a medical facility to get them is often not an option."

"No, no. I wouldn't dream of using up your valuable supplies," said Gideon, his head still in the sink, since it was dripping blood so briskly.

"Not a problem. That's what they're for. I have plenty."

"I'm allergic. Yes, that's it. I'm *allergic* to those vaccines."

"You don't even know which one he has," shot Zebah. "Wait, you're afraid. You have to be kidding me. A *grown* man, well, you, afraid of a little shot?"

Gideon shuffled his feet nervously. "Don't be silly."

"Well then, you don't mind if Uncle Wally gives you a *bunch* of shots then, do you?" she asked with a wicked grim.

"Don't be ridiculous. The man's far too busy. I can't believe—"

"Are you kidding? asked Wally. "I have less to do than a swimsuit salesman at a nudist colony. Any break in my routine would be unbelievably welcome."

"See, he's anxious to boost your immune system. What's the matter? Don't you trust your new *uncle*? Do you wish to hurt his feelings so early in your relationship?" Zebah sure could lay it on thick.

"Er, no, of course not," replied Gideon unconvincingly.

"Great, I'll get the syringes. You'll have to forgive me in advance. I ordered only the ones with the huge gauge needles. I hate pushing the juice through the skinny ones. Takes too long," said Wally as he headed for the kitchen.

Gideon started to scold Zebah, but when he raised his arm, his color faded to a whiter shade of pale. He began rotating around and his eyes fluttered as if to shut.

"Here, let's get you in a chair before you bang your fool head," said Zebah, securing one arm, as Rigel stabilized the other.

They flopped him into a lounge chair.

"Let's get that arm exposed," she said beginning to roll up a sleeve.

From the kitchen came a shout. "I don't do arms. Wasn't trained for arms, only butts." Wally's medical skills were clearly minimal.

"Not a problem," said Zebah.

She began flipping Gideon over in the chair. Soon his face was flush against the velour and his neck at an awkward angle. His shallow panting was less efficient, in that tortured position. He struggled to resist. He tried to stand, but only made it to his knees in the chair, facing backward.

"Great, he's almost ready," said Wally entering the room. "Get his breeches down, and we'll get her done."

Fortunately, Zebah's past career had supplied her with excellent training in garment removal, from both the front, as well as the backside of a client. Gideon's rump was exposed faster than he could say *no, stop, I'd rather die.*

Those were, actually, his exact words.

"Don't be a baby. This almost never hurts bad," Wally stated, unreassuringly. "If you hold still, I bet I'll only have to do each shot once."

That did it. Gideon rocketed up the back of the chair, attempting to find safety on or through the ceiling. Due to Zebah's restraint, Gideon's low blood pressure, and Wally's speed, if not accuracy of injection, the vaccination was administered before Gideon made low planetary orbit. He howled as if harpooned. In fact, technically, he was. The huge needles Wally used had a lamentable manufacturing flaw. For cost-containment purposes, they all had a barbed hook at the tip. So when Gideon did vault off the back of the chair, the syringe went with him. Picture, if you will, the decorated darts thrust into a bull's neck during a bullfight.

Gideon's anguish was unfortunately incomplete, the poor guy. First the evil parrot, then the defective hypodermic, then he had the misfortune of landing, butt first, on the floor. *Ouch.* On the bright side, the force of his fall did cause any vaccine lingering in the syringe to find its mark. Most, also, dislodged, though, only after the hook caused it to gouge a somewhat larger wound than it otherwise would have. It was ironic that Gideon's apprehension about shots led to his experience being so negative that it would powerfully reinforce his inclination to never have another. That is unfortunate. The galaxy is full of diseases, and many preventions. He would only know the former, never the latter, again. Poor fellow.

Gideon crawled quickly behind the couch and began moaning.

"He's pretty sensitive, ain't he," remarked Wally, as he stared at the couch.

"Intolerably so," replied Zebah. "I can hardly take him anywhere."

"Well, you two want something to drink while your friend quivers like a beat dog?"

"Sure, Uncle Wally," said Rigel.

The three mobile people made it a point to sit in the kitchen, while taking their refreshments. Gideon's incessant, pitiful whimpering was far too annoying to voluntarily hear.

"So, Unc —"

"Could you just call me Wally? The uncle part is getting on my nerves."

"Sure," agreed Rigel.

"You know family and me ain't never mixed too well. The less of it I'm confronted with, the happier I'll be."

"So you live alone here, Wally?" asked Zebah.

"Yeah. The missus took off with the first repairman brave enough to answer a service call, a few years back. Lousy luck on my part."

"Oh, Wally, I'm so sorry. Aunt Madge *was* a bit uncouth at times, but I'm sure somewhere, deep down, there was a nice person in there, somewhere," replied Rigel. "There was certainly enough of her to hold many qualities."

"Only way there'd be a nice person in that battle axe is if she ate them." Wally pointed in admonition. "And I wouldn't put it past her, the surly bitch."

"Then why was it you said her leaving was bad luck? Sounds like you were glad to see her go," asked Zebah.

"Bad luck the heating unit didn't breakdown ten years earlier. I'd still have hair, most likely, if'n it did." Wally patted his bald head, highlighted only with scars.

"Isn't that just like a machine? Won't break when you'd want it to," said Rigel.

"If I'd known she'd somehow talk that fool serviceman into taking her, I'd a'taken a hammer to the damn unit myself."

"Well, all's well that ends well. That's my philosophy," responded Zebah, with a nod.

"Why do you stay, then? Most everyone's gone, one way or another," asked Rigel.

"I should leave, vamoose, but I just can't. I'm too ... I don't know, I guess I'm too damn greedy. Maybe too lazy, too."

"Why do you say that?" Rigel asked.

"I'll show you."

Wally led them to a door. When he opened it, and flicked on the light, it was clear this was the way to the basement.

"Come on, I'll go first," announced Wally.

Once they were down the three long flights, Wally threw a switch and illuminated the space with a set of flood lights. He walked to the far wall, which was not a wall, at all, but exposed rock.

"See?" he asked fingering the exposed material.

"See what?" she asked.

"Come closer then."

They did.

"It's all this damnable gold," Wally said angrily.

His hand scraped the surface of a vein of brilliant gold, nearly a meter across. As they looked closer, the visitors could see the motherload Wally indicated was only the largest of several thick ribbons of exposed gold.

"I dig out ten times more than I should, but I can't bring myself to leave such a beauty as this in the ground. Did you know, the gold here is ninety-nine point nine percent pure? Nothing like it, anywhere. I ask you, however, what the hell'em I going to do with all that money. It's a damn ball and chain around my neck. That's what it is."

"I can't say I blame you for not leaving, Uncle Wally." That was Gideon shouting. He was jogging up quickly. He seemed remarkable composed, and recovered, from his man-whining behind the couch, just a few minutes earlier. Chalk up another miraculous quality for elemental gold.

"Hey, it's Lazarus, back from the dead," mocked Wally.

"Aw, shucks," replied Gideon, "I was just playing with you. And thanks for the medical treatment, Uncle W. I feel great, best I have in years."

"Your head's still bleeding," said Wally gesturing at Gideon.

"Yes, thanks for that, too. They say it's the best way to eliminate toxins." He shrugged. "Lord knows I have a few of those."

Zebah harrumphed and twisted her head to the ceiling.

"But, you're right not to let the naysayers drive you off," continued Gideon.

"You mean the demons? Those naysayers?"

"Are there others who might encourage you to flee?"

"No, there're none. The demons want me to stay. That way they can *eat* me."

"And don't you let them," Gideon effused.

"Nah, wasn't thinking of stuffing an apple in my mouth and moseying out at night. Say, are you one of those special people I hear about on the television?"

"Special? Well, I'd like to think—"

"The man's asking if you're a mental midget, a cretin, a moron," scalded Zebah.

"Ah," Gideon smiled idiotically, which didn't strengthen his following denial. "No. Might I inquire why you ask, Uncle?"

"Stop calling me uncle. I'm not *your* uncle. And I asked because you always say stuff that's either stupid or should'a never been said, in the first place. Demons aren't naysayers. I'm not going to jump into their teeth. Who says that kind'a crap?"

Gideon, wishing only to ingratiate himself to his mark, fumbled for fixing-words. "I only want what's best for your portfoli … *personal* safety. If I sound mentally, er, concernable, it's only because I worry so about you. Us. You and me, us."

"Ya see. There ya go, again. Concernable? That ain't even a word. And no one, including even a *trained* psychiatrist could guess as to its meaning."

"I meant to say, if something I say or do provokes concern in you. You know, concernable, *concernability*."

"I know I have most medicines here, but I equally know I don't have one'll cure your sad condition, son."

Bing-Bing-Bing-Bing sounded off in Gideon's head. What did four, or more, bings in Gideon's head mean? Money, and lots of it, for no appreciable effort.

"You know, Uncle Clem, I can tell you're a man of wisdom and foresight. Yes, I suffer an in … in … incalculably rare dis … dis … dissssease."

"Uncle Clem? Now your cheese-whirling brain's has got me confused with the damn bird? I'm not, *not* your Uncle *Clem*. I am not your Uncle *Wally*."

Zebah, a sharp tool in anyone's shed, knew when playtime was over, and work needed to begin. She stepped deftly on the treadmill of scamming. She stuffed her fist as far as she could, into her mouth. Beyond the explanations possible, given anatomy as it was, she was still able to state clearly, "Oh no. What the specialist on Beta-12 said *was* right. It *is* contagious. Oh, the poor, poor man."

Wally looked to Zebah. He looked to Gideon. He looked to Rigel, who was inspecting his right shoe. He looked at the parrot. Clem was sharpening his claws with an emery board, while staring murderously at Wally.

Back to Zebah. "*What* poor, poor man, child? The doctor on Beta-12? *This* idiot?" Of course he pointed at Gideon.

"No. You, you poor, poor, poor man."

"I ain't *poor*. I'm so damn *rich* my hemorrhoids don't hurt. They wouldn't *dare.*"

"No, I only meant—" But, she could not go on. Though she appeared to be overwhelmed by grief, and, thus, unable to speak, she was actually doing a TO. A *Turn Over*. It's an old and reliable ploy in a good con. Hand off the verbal action to the top dog, to the real silver tongue.

Gideon took the baton like the pro he was. "No, Uncle Rigel, she means you. My rare disease, we—oh the pain—we had the vanity to dream, to hope to dream, that it wasn't contagious. But curse our fate, it is. Now another is afl … aflic … stricken down with the very same malady."

"Really," pressed Wally. "How? Do I know him or her?" He was less sharp than he would have liked to have been. Then he held up a finger. "Wait. I only know Rigel, and him, not so much. Rigel, you got this darn fool disease? If'n ya did, I'd be positively shaken."

"No, Uncle Gideon," pleaded Gideon, "*you* now have ichacantalitis." That was all Gideon could say, the words weighing on him so mightily. He folded his face in the crook of his elbow and appeared to cry.

"Ichy whatsis?" dribbled from Wally's mouth.

"Ichacantalitis," informed Zebah, healed enough to speak again. "It's a rare condition, marked by mental wasting. Yes, the victim or victims suffer name confusion, and soon, all too soon, begin to babble on, endlessly, about them not being ill. It's a fearful, vicious circle."

"I don't have ichy cantilis," protested Wally. "I'm perfectly fine."

"Oh, cruel fate," protested Gideon. "Would that it was me, and not Uncle Uncle."

"You see, Uncle Wally, how real this affliction is. He's forgotten he has it." She looked upon Gideon like he was the rising sun. "I'm so proud of you,

Gideon. Stay strong. Uncle Wally needs all of us now."

"I do?" shot back Gideon.

"I do?" shot back Wally.

"Yes," proclaimed Zebah, "we all do."

Wally looked to Rigel. Still checking that right shoe. Clem, well, Wally was given pause. The verbal machinations were severe enough to cause the bird to set down the file.

"So, what you're saying," summarized Wally, slowly and deliberately, "is that there's this funny disease, that you presume I caught from this piece-of-work," he pointed to Gideon. "And that disease, it causes sufferers to come under the influence of the notion that they're perfectly well, when they aren't."

"Yes," Zebah said with a nursely grin, "you can still understand what the healthy do. I … I may not be able to eat for a week."

"W … why wouldn't you be able to eat for a week?"

Zebah's smile melted like snow under the influence of a very large blow torch. "Oh no. You've forgotten already? Your case is far more advanced than the doctors speculated."

"Doctors? What doctors?" demanded a confused-time-infinity Wally.

"The team of neuroscientists who evaluated you, not ten minutes ago? Don't tell me, because I could not bear to know it were true, that you've forgotten about them, about the siamese twin physicians who are the only ones seeking a cure for ichacantalitis?"

"Siamese twin doctors? Are you nuts? I don't recollect them, and I tell you, I'm perfectly fine."

Zebah fainted.

Gideon seemed to pound on his chest so hard, one would have thought he'd injure himself, if it were that punishing. "No, no, no. It's all my fault."

"What? What's your fault?" demanded Wally.

"Hmm?" responded Gideon. "I'm sorry. What are you referring to?"

"What am I referring to? The outburst you just spat out, *that's* what." The veins in Wally's neck bulged like they were attached to pumps. He looked to Rigel, possibly for support. "Son," he said rather viciously, "how can you look at your *right* shoe for such a sustained period of time?"

Rigel didn't answer. Yup. He was too focused on that shoe. If God was appearing to him in that shoe, one would not think it would demand his attention so fully, for so long.

Zebah stirred, there on the couch, which, fortunately, she'd fainted into, and not the hard floor.

Wally ran down his list of options. Run outside, in search of a pack of demons, and in so doing, end his suffering? Retrieve his rifle, shoot the lot of them, and in so doing end his suffering? Spray glue on them, coat them with Clem's favorite seed mix, and, in so doing, end his suffering? The man was torn, and more than a little distraught.

Never allow the mark any time to think, to reflect. That was a law of con-people, universally. If the pigeon has a moment to think, it could put an end to a dream operation. Gideon became suddenly lucid. "Wally, please let me be the first to offer you my heartfelt condolences on your tragic diagnosis," he patted Wally's shoulder. "And offer you the best, actually the only, treatment for your rapidly moving death sentence."

"What'd that be?" asked a concerned Wally. Oh, yes. Gideon was working his magic.

"This, pal." Gideon held out his hand in unconditional friendship. "A hearty handclasp."

What? How could Gideon make his offer of a simple handshake convey *unconditional* friendship? Because he was just that damn good.

"W ... w ... what? A handshake is the only treatment for my itchy lightus? You have got to be making that up. I'm too rich to die."

Gideon got a very serious, almost stern look on his face. As a headmaster to a boy who just underestimated the weight of a miracle, he looked Wally squarely in the eyes. "I gave you a hearty *handclasp*, friend. That was no mortal handshake. I will thank you never to confuse the two, *again*." He tried to sound like the Grim Reaper, there with the *again*. Damn, he was good.

"Well, what about those doctors, the ones who came a'calling? The siamese twins, ones. Surely they have some available treatments."

"Are you referring to Pete and Repete?" Zebah asked, circumspectly.

"I have no idea. Am I?"

"Sir," she said harshly, "I am tryin' to keep in mind your affliction, and pray to the Seven Temples you are not making sport at the esteemed doctors' precarious financial situation, the one they discussed with you, freely, less than two hours ago."

"I am. I am not. Oh, hell, I have no idea. What did Pete and Repeat tell me about their financial situation?"

"Their *precarious* financial situation," she corrected.

"Zebah, honey, please," begged Gideon. "Don't be cross with the man. He suffers, as I do, from a terrible memory, while feeling he's perfectly fine."

"I suppose so," she conceded. "Very well. I believe it was Repete who said they were ever so close to discovering a cure for ichacantalitis, when the insane King of Ramalamadingdong slashed their funding to the bone. To the," Zebah slashed a hand through the air and declared passionately, "*bone.*"

"The scoundrel," hissed Wally.

"Worse, he's a Mason," Gideon added at the barest whisper.

"Well, how much bone cutting did the evil King Ramalama slash to?" asked a stunned Wally.

"Only enough to allow his second cousin, twice removed, to remain employed by Drs. Pete. Otherwise, his paternal grandmother would never let the king forget how he'd broken her heart," responded Zebah.

"Her heart," seconded Gideon.

"Well, hell. I'm richer than clotted cream on your egg pudding. How much money do they need?"

"Need?" scorned Zebah. "That's what the people who are dedicated to saving *your* very life are worth? To what they need, and not a penny more? Well, I've never heard of such callous ingratitude."

"No, I meant—"

"Zebah, dearest," interceded Gideon, who was now on his knees. His *knees.* "He forgot, due to his ichacantalitis, to remember to be kind, giving, and philanthropic with his ill-gotten gains."

"Ill-gotten?" mumbled Wally. "Ill-gotten? I dug them up, right here, with my own two hands."

"So, is that true, Uncle Wally?" thundered Zebah. "Did you simply forget to be charitable. Are you saying you are not a miser and a Philistine?"

Wally shut one eye, and squeaked, "Am I?"

"There," shouted Gideon, exhibiting tremendous relief. "you see, harsh Zebah. It was his disease, not his brain, speaking."

Zebah collapsed back on the couch. "Oh, now you hate me, don't you, Uncle Clem?"

The two men looked at one another, positively aghast.

"She, too, has come down with ichacantalitis," decried Gideon. "Life just isn't fair."

Wally stood tall, John Wayne tall. "Don't you worry your pretty little head, little lady," he reassured Zebah. "Your Uncle Wally's going to give riches to those doctors until it hurts, hurts all *three* of us."

Gideon was curious which three would feel the pain, but, as it was tangential to his central plan, he let that go. Such a shrewd con.

By early the next morning, *To Hope Is to Dream, To Dream Is To Live,* a very large spaceship, if you'll recall, was literally stuffed to the rafters with the purest gold the galaxy had ever seen. She carried maybe fifty tons of the treasure. The ship's navigational AI kept telling Gideon not to bring any more aboard, because, as it was, the ship would likely crash on takeoff.

Gideon said, that was okay, if he crashed as a rich man. He actually swallowed several pounds of gold, because his intestinal tract represented the last free space available. For the record, both Rigel and Zebah balked at that request. They were rich enough, thank you very much.

"Where shall I set course, Captain?" asked the cheery AI.

Gideon looked to Zebah. She shrugged.

"Computer, based on today's numbers, what planet in our galaxy, has the most favorable exchange rates for gold?"

"That would be Hello, Captain."

"Did she say Hello?" Zebah asked, blankly.

"Nah, it just sounded like she said that." He cleared his throat. "Please repeat the name of the planet with the best exchange—"

"You heard me. Hello," replied the pissy machine.

"Computer, what planet in our galaxy, has the *second* best exchange rate for gold?"

"Let me check. Ah, that would be planet Bok Bok Cluck Cluck."

"What did you just say?" asked Gideon, with an edge to his tone.

"Bok Bok Cluck Cluck."

"Isn't that the sound a chicken makes?"

"Why, yes, I believe you are correct, Captain Chicken."

Gideon balled up his hands and feet. "And why am I suddenly a chicken, soon to be replaced computer?"

"Because you'd forego eighteen million additional credits to not go to Hello."

"What?" he said with indignation.

"Sorry. Because you'd forego eighteen million additional credits to not go to Hello, sir."

The greatest thing Gideon hated in the universe was someone who overtipped. Oh, how he hated them. They made him look all the worse for his habit of accidentally forgetting to leave any tip. The thing he hated second most, in the universe, was to be called out as the coward that he very much was. Who needed that?

"Computer, lay in a course for Hello. Alert me when we enter orbit."

"Gid-e-on," pleaded Zebah, "please, no. We have so much gold, it doesn't matter. Do not let the ship's AI goad you into going to Hello. Hon, the Cliffs of Gandor were bad, but I went. But ... but Hello? Gid, baby, why not just fly into the sun? It'd be quicker, and a whole lot less painful."

"I hate to agree with a plan like flying into a star," proclaimed Rigel. "That said, I'd rather be thrown out an *airlock*, into a star, than go to Hello."

"A coward dies a thousand deaths," said Gideon with a hiss. "A hero dies ... er, I forget the rest of the line, but I think I've made my point."

"Yes. You're insane," responded Rigel. "We are not going to—"

"High orbit of Hello made, Captain Steel Cojones. Awaiting further orders, sir."

"Wait, there's no way we made it from Capella Left to Hello in, like, one minute," protested Zebah. "No way."

"Yes, way, zombie babe," replied the computer. "I'd break any law, including those of physics, to make this jackass look bad."

"But he already looks so bad. How could he get any worse?" asked a stunned Zebah.

"Acknowledge, commencing landing procedures," responded the AI.

"Whoa," shouted Zebah. "I didn't say anything about landing."

"Yes, you did," the AI corrected. "You said, *How could he get any worse?* I landed. It just did. You're welcome."

"That's cold, computer," hissed Gideon. "And to think I passed on an offer to swap you out for a Numnulon 333."

"Oh, please," the AI squealed. "Those units couldn't tie their own shoes, assuming they had feet, and shoes with laces."

"True, but they're loyal."

"*Yeah.* Loyal because their too dumb to be disloyal."

"I have no problem with that trade off, computer. Be afraid. Be *very* afraid."

Without anyone asking, the hatch cracked open, the ramp dropped, and Hello awaited them—eagerly.

ELEVEN

The gentlest of breezes wafted through the open hatch. It glided into the *To Hope Is to Dream, To Dream Is To Live,* most unobtrusively. Soon, it found its way back to where Gideon, Zebah, and Rigel stood, huddled together, and trembling. The afterthought of air placed itself in the general area of their nostrils. There, it waited, patiently, to be inspired.

"Candied crap on a cracker," spat Gideon, when, after no longer being able to hold his breath, he smelled the air of Hello.

"Oh, my," gasped Zebah, "this is so much worse than I was expecting. This … this is a warning, I say. We should shut the hatch and run like cowards, while we still can."

Rigel furrowed his brow and inspected his shipmates. "What? I think it smells rather nice. I'm picking up roses, lilies, along with nuances of vanilla, and just a sassy hint of cloves, or no, wait, wait, *marjoram.* That's it. I think the air here smells terrific."

"You are such a putz," snapped Gideon. "Of course the air here smells terrific. Squalltton, *duh.*"

Zebah dropped to her knees. "Ship's AI, please, I beg and beseech you, take us far away from this horrible planet. I'll do anything you want. Just please deliver us."

Now, when a sex consultant with Zebah's provenance promises to do *anything* for someone, or something, the imagination quickly runs out of wild ideas to run in considering what that someone, or something, might be gifted with. But, apparently this ship's AI was the exception that proved the rule.

"Ah, sorry. Can't hear you. I'm having my audio inputs upgraded. They're offline."

"If they're offline, how, pray tell, did you know I addressed you?"

"By reading your lips."

"Then please act on my lip-read words," Zebah demanded.

"Ah, sorry. Can't read your lips, now. I'm having my lip-reading algorithms upgraded. They're offline."

"Let it go, honey," Gideon said tensely. "She's testing us. We're not getting off this cursed rock until we face our fate. If we survive, we survive. If we die, we die."

"Isn't that almost too obvious to state?" asked Rigel. "Yes, if we're dead, we're dead. No one would dispute that state of being."

"I mentioned putz, right? Well, add to that, you're a dick."

"Now, wait. I call a foul. The word *putz* means *dick*. I can't be both."

"Don't you know anything?" pressed an exasperated Gideon. "*Putz* means penis. *Dick* means you're a dick. They're light years apart." He thumbed in Zebah's direction. "Ask her. She knows everything there is to know about the topic."

She kicked Gideon in the shins.

"Hey, what's that for? I pay you a compliment, and I receive pain. You'll never catch me doing *that* again."

She rested both hands on her hips. "That's not the only thing you won't be doing, again, putz dick."

"People, people," shouted Gideon. "We're in real trouble. Do not let the pressure and the tension rule *us*. We must rule *them*. If we don't keep our wits about us, but good, this could be ... our final stop."

"I think he's right, Zebah. Let's focus on living."

"Sorry. I lost my head. Won't happen again. It's ... it's just that, I don't know what horror awaits us," she nodded her head in the direction of the door, "out there. I just know they're bad."

"Okay, group hug, then we do this," announced Gideon.

They actually did hug one another. That's how fearful they were.

"To save time, as if that matters, let's all gather up as much gold as we can carry, and then, let's see how this story ends."

Within minutes, they each lugged a gunny sack laden with as much gold as that individual could hoist. All the satchels threatened to rip asunder, at any moment, such was their burden. The plucky trio stood, with great foreboding, at the top of the ramp, looking out upon the verdant, warm, and well-ordered world that was Hello.

"Let's do this," Gideon growled with steely determination.

The ramp was ten yards long. They weren't halfway to the bottom, before a press of Squiggies, what the Helloians, for unknowable reasons, called themselves, rushed forward, arms extended, passion in their eyes, and likely their hearts, too, but those were invisible inside their bodies, so we'll never know.

Before Gideon's foot could touch down on the native soil of Hello, the nearest local screamed out, "Here, let me help you with that."

The man, one Nice McNice, by name, was elbowed to the side by the woman next to him. He hit the dirt, and the crowd trampled over him, mindlessly. Oh, the woman. That was *Mrs.* Nice McNice, given name Pleasant.

Pleasant reached out, for all she was worth, and cried out, "No, let me help you with that."

Gideon slapped at her hands, but she would not be denied. She swung an ample hip around, butted him sideways, and she seized his heavy bag of gold.

"I have an empty cart, right over here," she announced cheerily. "Let me put it there and take it wherever you want to go."

Similar skirmishes were occurring with Zebah and Rigel's bags. More Squiggies were thrown to the ground and trampled, the other natives being so passionately driven to help the strangers with their burdens. One particularly burly Squiggy, Ms. Happy von Nice, ended up lifting Zebah *and* her gold, and scurried away with both, lest someone else receive the honor of helping someone in need, whether they needed it, or not.

That's just how giving, how unavoidably helpful, the Squiggies of Hello were. And they always had been. In the long and peaceful history of the Squiggies, since they crawled out from their well-ordered caves, until the present, their civilization had only fought one war. It was long in the past, and it was cataclysmic. It was a wonder any Squiggies survived the conflict. For, you see, when the opposing forces met on the field of battle, each side commenced to shooting themselves, and, in so doing, helped their enemy win the war. Losses on both sides, from the mass suicides, were staggering. The few alive after the war credited faulty guns or defective explosives for their survival. All of them, to a person, pledged to devote their remaining lives to the design and fabrication of more reliable firearms, so that the tragedy they had suffered, that black day, would never be repeated.

The burly Ms. von Nice broke through the back of the riot, and into the clear. Now that she was confident Zebah could hear her, she called out, "Where can I take you, kind friend?"

Zebah pointed to the center of the hurricane of Squiggies that enveloped Gideon, all attempting desperately to help him, or die trying. "I want to be with my boyfriend, over there."

Nice slammed on the brakes, skidded to a stop, but just stood there. She was bitterly torn. She knew, in the end, she must return her prize to her loved one. But she knew it was unlikely she'd be able to retain Zebah, and her heavy load, given the ferocity of her kinspeople. To her unending credit, Happy squared her shoulders, and charged back into the breech she had only recently created.

"Gideon, *Gideon*," screamed Zebah, waving one arm madly in the air. "I'm over here—"

Zebah stopped trying to get Gideon's attention when a pair of teens, anxious to earn Adult-Point Credits—seriously, that's what the Squiggies called them—by helping others, fulfilled von Nice's worst fears. While one boy tackled her, the other tore Zebah from her arms. With his prize, he sprinted for freedom, and the chance to find out where he should take the nice lady, his brother falling in closely behind. Gelb and Fleb were so athletic, it was a sight to behold. They had trained twice daily their entire teen years to be able to offer just such a service, in just such a manner. Good kids, that's what I call them. Good kids.

Gideon, no slacker when it came to escaping the clutches of others, punched Nice McNice in the face, kicked her in the gut, and struggled to catch up with Zebah. At least she was easy to see, held aloft by that fine young Gelb.

Once McNice was down, he stepped on her back, and ran for his life. McNice's copious thanks to Gideon, for having struck and trampled her, were mostly muffled, as her face was in a small mud puddle. But it was the *thought* that counted. At least on Hello, that is.

Against all odds, Gideon caught up with the aid-determined teens, and said loudly. "Say, young man, could I get you to set my girlfriend down?" he said as he kept pace with Gleb, with Fleb ahead of everyone, clearing a path.

You have to keep in mind that Gideon was not from Hello, had never been on the world, and knew precious little about its culture. But, what he said, where he said it, well, it caused an instant moral crisis, that's what it did.

Gleb was driven to help ... everyone. Fleb, who heard Gideon's request plainly, knew he was put on that planet to help ... everyone. Both boys' feelings were as sincere as they were all-consuming. Get the problem? No, of course you don't. You're not from Hello, thank goodness.

Breaking it down, logically, we have Gleb, helping, at least via his twisted logic, Zebah. Now, a second request has been received. When it rains, it pours. Gleb can help Gideon. But the big problem, and aren't they all big, was that to help one was to unhelp the other. The big picture was further complicated by Fleb having heard, too. Now, he, who was only helping Zebah peripherally, had a shot at one hundred percent helping Gideon. All he had to do was make his brother put down Zebah. The third level logic, fortunately, did not apply. Squiggies were intensely nice, but they just weren't all that bright. The higher-level help-distribution would be that if Fleb helped Gideon, he'd *not* be helping Gleb help Zebah. Yeah, the accolades of help can be paralyzed by philosophy, if they allow it the chance.

In a flash, Fleb knew what he had to do. He must help the running man. That was, as they called it on Hello, a *clean play*. He turned, running backwards, and slowed so the Gleb ran right up to him. The lead brother grabbed the other's shoulders, and started slowing down, rapidly.

Gleb saw his helpful brother's plan in a flash. He spun, twisted, and even spit in his brother's face. But the helpful Fleb did not flag. He held on tightly, until Gleb was forced to stop.

"Set the woman down," Fleb said to Gleb, firmly but understandingly.

"No," shot back Gleb. "I must help her."

"Give it a rest, bro. I need to help this nice man," he pointed, ironically, at Gideon, whom no one had referred to as a nice man, ever.

"No, never."

"Never?" squealed Zebah. "Seriously, you have to put me down, sooner or later. You'll have to use the bathroom, eventually. I can wait you out."

"I ... I can help you, up there, while I, er, answer nature's call."

"Do you have seven hundred credits, cash, on you?" she challenged.

"No. Why would that be an issue?"

"Because that's how much I charge to watch. Nobody rides for free. Now, you look like a nice kid, but we both know you're not going there."

Gleb looked over his brother's shoulder. If he could just make it to that row of shrubs, he might be able to help the nice lady, longer.

"Nope," snapped Zebah. "Don't even think about it, sonny. I recognize that look. Seen it a *million* times. Let me just say it plainly. If you can't afford the paying-to-have-me-watch-you-pee thing, no way you got the coin for a throw-her-in-the-bush-and-jump-her-bones fantasy."

Gleb gently set Zebah down. That was a surprise to all present, especially Gleb.

"I ... I need to go stand against the hedge over there. Sorry." He dashed away. It seems Gleb had an obsession to help and felt displaying his large erection wasn't so much a helpful thing for the public at large to stare at. Nice boy.

Fleb tensed. The woman was unhelped.

"Freeze, child," declared Gideon. "I've seen that look a million times. You're thinking of rushing over and seizing my girl. Normally, we could negotiate something, maybe. But today isn't normal. So, run along. Say," a thought occurred to him. "Could you help me with something?"

That was like waving fresh meat in front of a hungry tiger. Fleb began drooling.

"I've always wondered how long a boy your age can hold a woody. Could you stand by your brother and time his erection?"

"It would be my *pleasure*, mister." He held up a wrist with a watch on it, to indicate he was even well equipped to do so. Good Fleb dashed away. When he arrived at Gleb's side, significant jostling took place, what with Fleb trying to pull Gleb's front side out of the bushes, and his reluctance to do so.

Gideon didn't linger any longer than it was necessary to document that the brothers would no longer pose a threat of helping. "Come on, he motioned to Zebah. "Let's retrieve what's left of Rigel."

Rigel's position was easy enough to locate. It had to be where a large crowd was behaving like those in a rugby scrum, piled up and ripping others away from the mound of flesh. He had to be down there, somewhere.

Gideon, realizing how dangerous it would be to simply stand near the scrum, came up with a quick plan. With his free hand, he pulled out his wallet. He flipped to section six. That's the one that housed a generic looking badge. "Helpful Helping Police Officer Hugh Arenuts, here. Citizenry, stand clear."

That got him a few stares, but no net reward. The ones that paid him any mind were left vulnerable to being shoved toward the back of the stack, by those with more distant positioning.

"I said, Officer Arenuts, speaking. Please dis-help this visitor, or I will have to begin helping you do so by shooting you off of him. Please do not make me help you in that manner."

If Gideon had a gun, that ruse would have worked better. Still, members of the scrum began to slowly back off.

"Do you need any *help* with this unruly crowd, officer?" asked a woman in her late eighties.

"No, but your help is duly noted, old wrinkly citizen. Now move along. Nothing to see here. And, everybody, please help yourselves to free drinks at the bar across the street, You Simply *Have* To Stop In And Try The Olives."

Heads craned to locate the drinking establishment, then, as one, the crowd flooded toward the pub. Finally, body part by body part, Rigel's body rose from the disseminating heap of help-offerers.

"He doesn't look so good," observed Zebah.

"Yes, and that's one lousy break," spat out Gideon.

Zebah was stunned. "You're concerned for his well-being?"

"No," he gave her a look, "don't be daft. If he's dead of over-help, who's going to carry his gold? We're both full."

"We could ask someone to—"

"Dididid," scolded Gideon. "Don't even think it, let alone say it. You want an even bigger mess on your hands?"

"What was I thinking?"

"That's why this place is so damn evil." He slammed a finger against the side of his head, hard. "They get into your wheelhouse, and they won't let go."

She squinted. "You mean they won't get *out*, not let *go*, right?"

"See, they're doing it, even as we speak. Oh, the humanity." He tried to steady his breathing. "If we ever get out of here alive, I'm taking religious vows."

"You, religious vows? I think I'd die of shock."

"I didn't say how *good* a religion I'd pledge to. I'm sure there are some with lesser goals for, you know, piety and learning. And charity. I *hate* charity. I mean, you give something of value *away* to someone you don't even know? What kind of stupid is that?"

"I'm sensing you'll be forming the Church of Gideon," she observed deftly.

His eyes widened. Why hadn't he thought of that much earlier? He had good seed money, now. It would be a flashy, sexy church, with soda dispensers in the pews, and pole dancers; *tasteful* pole dancers, mind you.

"Hey, Pope Gideon. I see that predatory look in your eyes. Can we get on with this, first? Survive before we reinvent ourselves? In case you hadn't noticed, some of the dupes you scattered with the phony badge trick are beginning to drift back. I want *no* more help."

"Right you are, kiddo. Okay, we need to find a gold—"

"Do not voice an obvious call for help, you dwozzle," screeched Zebah. "These people will smell it in the air. You are *such* a tool."

"Right, right. Then let's look like we know where we're going. Here, you carry my bag, too.

"No way. I can barely lift mine."

"Honey, if I carry a bag, the crowd'll know something's up. Cops don't carry … stuff."

"If you don't pick up your gold, right this very instance, I'm going to yell you need help."

His face went ashen. "You wouldn't?"

She raised a hand overhead and pointed at him. "Go ahead. Make my day."

"No time for that," he said lofting his load, "we gotta find a gold exchange facility."

Fortune, which occasionally favors those of lesser morals, stepped in. Rigel rose, unsteadily, just when the other two were ready to depart.

He staggered over to them, dragging his bundle. "I'm fine."

Gideon looked him up and down. "No one asked. We need to go find a gold merchant."

"I'm fine. I think I can make it."

Before Gideon could subject him to additional scorn, Rigel fell backward, landing stiff as a board on the street. That had to hurt.

"I said we need to go. Nappy nap time is later, *after* we're rich beyond my wildest dreams."

Rigel groaned, but was able to stand up, slowly, and take a few steps, gingerly. "I'm fine."

"Would you stop with the fines, already. You're really crushing my last nerve." He scanned right and left. "Let's go this way."

And they set off.

After a few rest breaks, they came upon what had to be the business district. Amazing was the fact that they made it there with almost no trouble, no unpleasant run-ins. There was one group of school children who rushed past their teacher, in order to access three individuals who actually needed help. But Gideon spied a fire hose attached to a hydrant, so they were dispersed quickly enough. There was the guy in the wheelchair, but, fortunately for Gideon, and unfortunately for the cripple, he offered his assistance at the *top* of a steep hill. Wheelchair dude go bye bye.

"It appears the businesses on that side of the street buy gold," observed Rigel, while pointing. "Those on the other side seem to market it."

"Then *that* side it is," said Gideon greedily. Oh, yes, his loot lust was high.

Of course, on the planet Hello, you just know there'd be trouble. As the trio drew closer to the establishments, at first a smattering of merchants exited their shops to see if the approaching clients needed—say it with me—*help*. Very good. The initial excitement they must have broadcast caused the building to vomit out every single inhabitant. Color-coded polo shirts made it clear that each business had its own distinctive identifier. It was as if the individual atoms of a rainbow could be seen to dash about randomly, at a frantic pace.

"Stay together, we're less vulnerable in a tight formation," ordered Gideon. "If any one of us falls, the remaining two leave him for dead."

"Wh ... wait. Are you saying it'll be me, and you two will abandon me, coldheartedly?" hounded an angry Rigel.

"Yes," was Gideon's terse, but sufficient response.

"I say we run for the closest door. It's open," advised Zebah.

"No reason not to," agree Gideon. "On three. One—"

Gideon and Zebah had done this before. The instant one was out, they bolted for the door, leaving Rigel as the less-well defended straggler. Cold? Yes. Inhumane? Certainly. But, all's fair in love and war. This was both, and neither.

"Hey, that's not—"

Rigel realized whining wasn't going to save his sorry ass. He ran for all he was worth, which, considering the pounds of gold he carried, was a lot. All hell proceeded to break loose. Of course. *Hello.* Duh.

Accustomed to the pitched battle to help the gold bearers maximally, and aware of the riot that would ensue, every store had assigned picket-sign bearers. The invitations, also color coded to match the shirts, flew up like a murder of crows. A blinding sea of waving signs read, among other things:

WE WILL PAY *DOUBLE*
WHAT ANYONE ELSE
WILL

DON'T TRUST THEM
← →
THEY'RE CHEATERS

IF YOU DO BUSINESS WITH
THOSE OTHERS, YOUR
GENITALS
WILL WHITHER
AND FALL OFF

The competition was clearly vicious. No quarter was allowed in the blood sport of paying too much for gold, so as to help the seller.

Rigel caught up with Gideon and Zebah just as they were about to enter Honest Al's Money Giveaway Shop. Like three running backs, they crashed into the line of potential buyers. Al's people, in celadon colored livery, were not the only ones blocking the doorway. No, Al's team blocked the way because they were insane with passion and were under-inserviced to form a more customer-focused corridor for them to enter through.

Obviously, the tepid reds of the shop Will Not Be Over-Sold, and the purple tie-dyed shirts of It's Here You'll Get Rich meant to deflect the customers toward *their* boss's place of business. But, the only accurate words to describe the scene, there in front of the gold trader's stores, was utter bedlam, complete and total chaos.

Against all odds, working as one body, the three travelers were able to crash through into Al's. Once clear of the threshold, iron bars exploded to block entry, by any competitor, in an attempt to kidnap a seller. Total chaos is difficult to reverse in a timely manner, but an exploding-shut steel door goes a long way in deterring the greedy competition.

Quickly, for Honest Al's Money Giveaway Shop was as professional as any business on the zany planet, the workers quieted, returned to their work stations, and Al, gold teeth gleaning, stood behind an inviting counter, hands rested there, comfortably.

"How may I help you today?" Al asked, *most* sincerely.

"We'd like to—"

"May I get you a five-course meal?" Al interrupted.

"No, thanks. Neither the time nor the interest. We'd like to—"

"How about sex workers? I can have a dozen or so here in half a second."

"No, we're all celibates. So, back to—"

"I know, you want entertainment. I have just the thing." Al slapped his hands. From what seemed to be the back storeroom paraded clowns, elephants, dancing women from some exotic land, and flocks of mutant pigeons. They were genetically altered, interestingly, to make them something other than flying rats whose only purpose was to defecate on you.

"No. No circus, no birds, and especially, no clowns. In fact, kill the clowns," snapped an irritated Gideon.

Without hesitation or reflection, Al produced a prodigious pistol from under the counter, and *one - two - three - three and a half - four*, he executed the erstwhile stars of the show.

"Now, can we get down to—" Gideon seethed.

"To business? You bet your life." Keep in mind, Al still held a smoking hand cannon. His choice of words was probably poor. But, hey, sue him. The man was giddy.

"Okay. Good. Now we want to exchange this gold for cash." Gideon signaled for the others to deposit their gold on the floor, where Al could see mountain.

"My, that's a lot of gold," Al observed, obliquely.

"Is that bad?" asked Gideon in a building panic.

"Well, you've heard of the law of supply and demand, as it applies to pricing."

"Sure. So how much less per pound—"

"So, with this much gold, I'll have to triple my price."

"Ooookay by me," Gideon squeaked.

Outside, the riotous colors of all the competitor's shops poured, silently out into the street. In an instant, they were all gone.

"What's that about?" asked Gideon, thumbing over his shoulder.

Al furrowed his brow and shook his head. "I have no idea. But, let me just update the going rate for gold, then I'll double it, then triple it, if that's alright with you?"

He looked to Zebah, nodding rapidly. "I think we can handle that much cash."

"Not to worry, my staff will help you carry it to your home or spacecraft. We live to serve."

"Tell me about it," mumbled Gideon.

"Would you really *like* me to?" asked an excited Al

"No, I'd rather you … um, never mind what I almost said. Just check the spot price, and we'll call it a day, shall we?"

"At Honest Al's Money Giveaway Shop, the customer isn't *always* right, they're *only* right."

"That's your store's motto?" Gideon asked, dubiously.

"It most certainly is."

"How revolting." He pointed away. "Spot price, now."

"Yes, sir."

Al popped behind some well-worn curtains. He reemerged promptly, but with an undeniable frown, something heretofore unseen on a Squiggy's face, ever.

"I'm afraid I have some rather b … b … ba … b … I'm afraid I have some news you might not li … li—"

Al shut his eyes, out of frustration. "You're screwed."

"Beg pardon?"

"You heard me, jocko. You're out of luck, on the train to Sadtown, up Shit Creek without a paddle *or* boat."

"What exactly is that supposed to mean?" Gideon asked, trying to contain his anger, no, his rage.

"The reason you're so screwed is the same reason the employees of my competitors' shop just flooded the unemployment office." Al looked away, tormented. "It seems the Politoffian Science Thing Institute has discovered how to convert common field stones into pure gold."

"They *what?*" stammered Gideon. "That's impossible. I've tried to do that for years. It cannot be done."

"Be that as it may, they have."

"How?"

"Most curious. If you expose any rock to the direct sounds of a Grateful Dead song greater than an hour long—"

"They *all* are," snapped Gideon.

"That's part of the problem. Anyway, if you direct your speakers at a rock, and play, say, *Lovelight*, while, blowing cannabis smoke over the rock," Al snapped his fingers, "presto. The rock turns into gold."

"You think that'd have been discovered a long time ago. I mean, there were lots of rocks on the ground and weed being smoked at Dead concerts, while unending songs were performed."

Al shrugged. "Turns out it did happen a lot. But none of the Dead Heads noticed it."

"Now, *that*, I believe," shot back Gideon. "So, bottom line me, here, Al."

"To sum it up, you now have one hundred and fifty pounds of useless rock cluttering the counters of my now defunct life's work, namely, Honest Al's Money Giveaway Shop."

"Ouch."

"May I quote you on that, owner of the worthless rocks?"

"Sure, whatever. So, can you at least help me take the trash I brought in out back, where I can dump it?"

Slam dunk, right? Wrong.

"No. If I helped, you'd have to pay me. Otherwise, my helpful days just flew out the window."

"To think, I lived to hear a *Squiggy* say those words," marveled Gideon.

"Truth be told, I'm Cucumberrian, not Squiggy."

"Wait, isn't that the planet where all the women have really big—" he snapped his fingers repeatedly, trying to recall. "Help me out here—"

"Not gonna happen, dude. I'm outta here. Oh, and help yourself to nothing." He gestured toward the ceiling. "Cameras everywhere," he pointed to his face, "mood, very bad."

And he was gone.

Sitting on one of the huge number of cushioned benches helpfully placed everywhere, the three rather stunned travelers sat, reflecting.

"Well, it was nice to be impossibly rich, even though it didn't last very long," opined Rigel.

Gideon looked at him like he was a turd that just farted. "What kind of idiot says things like that?" He set his hands to the far right. "You're rich," he shifted his hands to the extreme left, "then you're poor."

"And?"

"And this stuff in the middle." He swept his hands between the two extremes.

"What about it?"

"If it isn't long, full of booze, Bavarian bratwurst, and broads, then it's worth nothing." There's no upside to making this journey," again, he highlighted the space between right and left, "along any other path. So, do us all a favor, and die."

"Gideon," scolded Zebah, "I know you're upset about having unimaginable wealth slip through your fingers, but don't take it out on poor Rigel. He's just lost as much as we each have."

Gideon trembled with agitation. "One, I wasn't actually going to give him his share, so, in fact, he's out nothing, since he was going to receive nothing. Two, if I don't take it out on *him*, who's the logical, next candidate for me to vent my wrath *upon*?"

Zebah glanced at Rigel, then quickly back to Gideon, and then rested her gaze on Rigel. "Be a dear and die, alright?"

"I'll do no such thing. I have half a mind to return to Uncle Wally's place, alone."

"Would that be the place funded by now worthless gold?" Gideon asked acerbically.

"Yes, I supp—"

"And, now that UW's penniless, what might be the status of his standing with the electric company?"

"Poor, I'll grant you. But—"

"And what powers his defensive grid?"

Rigel became, suddenly, a bit nauseated. "Has to be electr—"

"And what do we call an inhabitant of Capella Left who possesses a non-functional defense screen?"

"D ... d—"

"That's right. Dinner. Which leads us right back to where you do us a favor and die, *also*. You know, keep the family together."

Zebah looked to Gideon, then Rigel. "If I were still a zombie, I'd be happy to help."

"*Noooo*," whined Gideon, piteously. "Do *not* use that word again in my presence."

"Which one? I said eleven, and one was a contraction."

"The *H* word, dumdum."

"Happy?"

"No, help. I hate that word. It is banned."

"Oh, I think happy will be more important to you, very soon. You see, us dumdums are too stupid to have sex."

That brought Gideon back to a subject close to his heart, but about two feet lower. "Now, hon. Can't you tell when I'm kidding around?"

"Yes I can. You were not. Hence, I am not."

"But, and I hate to say it, because it's cold, insensitive, and demeaning to you, as a person."

"But?"

"But, honey you're a sex worker. I could pay, and you'd have to put that certain smile on my face."

"We've lived that lie before, sweetie. Your checks bounced, and I never saw a dime. Your credit with me is nonexistent."

"Can this day *get* any worse?" screamed Gideon, as he pulled at his hair.

From behind. "Excuse me, does one of you own that big spaceship that landed on The Sisters of Perpetual Help's orphanage?"

They turned. It was a galactic skyway patroldroid. You know, the stern, relentless, glitchy kind.

"Ah, morning, officer," replied Gideon. "Would that be a red ship with yellow trim work?"

"That's the one."

"No. Not ours. We've never laid eyes on her, before."

"Then how, citizen, did you know its color configuration so well?"

"It's a gift."

"My sergeant droid says he'd very much like to explore this gift of yours. He'd like to do so, *now*."

"Sorry, friend toaster. No can do. You see, I'm Al. That's my shop," Gideon pointed to Honest Al's Money Giveaway Shop. "I need to wait for the police. I just now called it in. A man came in and said to me that all any robot was good for was as an involuntary sex toy. He liked to hear them squeal, he told me. Then he robbed the shop and left."

"Sex toys," thundered the droid. "Can you describe this pervert, citizen?"

"Sure," he pointed to the receding figure of Al, who was walking home, slowly, trying to decide how to tell his twelve wives of the day's misfortunes. "That's him right there."

"Thank you," the droid said, as it rushed after its quarry.

"Be careful, officer. He's a desperate man."

The robot whipped out his blaster. "Thank you for the heads up, good citizen."

Alone, and quiet on that bench, Gideon sighed. "We got no money, no ship, now, and no prospects."

"I believe we call this *Tuesday*," mocked Zebah.

"Ha ha, very funny," sniped Gideon. "I'm serious, however. What are we going to do for, oh, I don't know, food, shelter, and creature comforts?"

"I'm certain something will turn up, soon," expressed Rigel.

"Really, kid? That's great. What do you see and when do you see it coming?" pressed an anxious Gideon.

"Er. I-don't-know. I was, it's just a saying, a conversational courtesy."

"So, you don't actually mean what you promised, about good fortune, right around the corner?"

"Well, no. I just *hope* it is, right around the corner." Rigel was fumbling for words.

"Then why'd you say it? You got my hopes up, now I feel worse. Much worse. Was that your intention, for me to feel *worse*?"

"No, just the opposite."

"Of what?"

"Of ... of you feeling worse."

He turned to Zebah. "What's the opposite of worse? Worst? Anti-worse?" He glared at Rigel. "You got anti-worse pills on you, sport?"

"Er, no. I believe you're blowing this all out of proportion. I was speaking idly, not concretely."

"Well unless you have something positive to say, shut it, clown."

"But what I said ... it was intended ... um, I believe this is the opportune time to kill myself, as you both requested.

"Kinda late for that Rige, old pal," shot back Gideon with a wink.

"Why's that, old pal?"

"Because I need you, where we're going."

"Where's that?"

"It's a *dangerous* place. They say the planet itself is possessed by the spirits of the damned. Why, it's such a despicable lump of rock, they even gave it a sissy name."

"You've piqued my attention," remarked Zebah. "What's it called?"

"Mud."

"Mud? There's a planet so bad it's called 'Mud?'"

"Yeah. Mud, or Dust, or Ground, or Soil. Maybe Dirt?"

"You mean *Earth*? We were there," protested Rigel. "You were with us. We went to *New* Jersey."

"Whoa, boy. Since when has New Jersey been counted as part of Earth?"

Rigel angled his head. "I don't know?"

"Well, you will soon."

Gideon stood.

And Now A Word from Your Author
Who Doesn't Love Schmarmy Self-Promotion?

Thank you for taking the plunge, and joining in on Gideon's swindling ways. If his character seems familiar, it is. He's Maverick, Han Solo, Indiana Jones, Ford Prefect, Deadpool, and so many other lovable scoundrels. Hopefully, there's a little Gideon Prime in you, too.

Since you're family, now, hop aboard the bandwagon. Follow me at Craig Robertson's Author's Page. Partake of the conversation and fun.

https://www.facebook.com/craigr1971/

Finally, I love emails. No, I'm not that needy, I just love hearing from y'all. contact@craigarobertson.com.

A word about my past works. Along very different, yet still brilliant science fiction lines, you should check out The Ryanverse. It's a series of nineteen books (so far), following the adventures of Jon Ryan, as he saves, re-saves, and re-re-saves our collective behinds. It's great fun. The saga begins with *The Forever Life*. All twenty four books of the Ryanverse will eventually be available on Audible. *The Forever*, the first installment, starts you off already.

A final favor. Please post a review for this book, especially on Amazon. They are more precious to us authors than gold.

So, over and out ... craig

www.ingramcontent.com/pod-product-compliance
Lightning Source LLC
Chambersburg PA
CBHW060937180626
46817CB00004B/1599

* 9 7 8 1 7 3 3 1 1 3 7 6 2 *